DEATH IN THE HARBOUR

DEATH IN THE HARBOUR

An Inspector Alun Ryga Mystery

Pauline Rowson

Fathom

Death in the Harbour

First published in 2020 by Fathom

ISBN: (paperback) 978-1-9160915-8-0

ISBN: (ebook) 978-1-9160915-7-3

Copyright © Pauline Rowson 2020

Fathom is an imprint of Rowmark, Hampshire, England PO11 0PL

Acknowledgement and Author's Note

With grateful thanks to the people of Newhaven, East Sussex who helped me with my research for this novel. In particular my thanks to Andrew Gilbert for his amazing knowledge of Newhaven history; Stewart Nash for his historical information on Plumpton Racecourse; Martin McKay of the British Transport Police History Group; Kevin Gordon, former British Transport Police Officer at Newhaven; Newhaven Museum; and the information gleaned and photographs displayed on the excellent website http://ournewhaven.org.uk/index.aspx including the cover picture supplied by Ben Franks of Lantern Slides taken by photographer Ellis Kelsey.

Sharp-eyed Newhaven residents may note that some of the places and street names have been changed. I hope they will forgive me for using poetic licence. Except where actual historical events and characters are being described for the storyline of this novel, all situations and characters in this publication are fictitious and any resemblance to living persons is purely coincidental.

Pauline Rowson

Adventure, mystery and heroes have always fascinated and thrilled Pauline. That and her love of the sea have led her to create her critically acclaimed gripping range of crime novels set against the backdrop of the sea on the south coast of England.

The Inspector Andy Horton Series

Tide of Death
Deadly Waters
The Suffocating Sea
Dead Man's Wharf
Blood on the Sand
Footsteps on the Shore
A Killing Coast
Death Lies Beneath
Undercurrent
Death Surge
Shroud of Evil
Fatal Catch
Lethal Waves
Deadly Passage
A Deadly Wake

Art Marvik Mystery/Thrillers

Silent Running
Dangerous Cargo
Lost Voyage

Inspector Ryga 1950 set mysteries

Death in the Cove
Death in the Harbour

Mystery/Thrillers

In Cold Daylight
In For the Kill

For more information on Pauline Rowson and her books visit www.rowmark.co.uk

One

Ryga stepped into the shelter of the London shop doorway out of the pelting rain, and, with a quickening heartbeat, read the short paragraph at the bottom right-hand corner of the newspaper:

War photographer, Eva Paisley, among injured servicemen

US Marines and 7th Division infantrymen have been surrounded by Communist Korean and Chinese forces south of the Chosin reservoir and are under fire in sub-zero temperatures. Allied aircraft are supplying the trapped troops with ammunition and food. Wounded men have been evacuated to hospitals on the coast, with some being flown home to Britain, among them eminent war photographer, Miss Eva Paisley.

That couldn't be all there was? he thought desperately, flicking through the rest of the newspaper. There must be more. But there wasn't, just a lot of tosh on the latest movie star to arrive in London, a married politician who was said to be having an affair with an unnamed woman, and the weather, which hardly ever changed these days unless it was from rain to fog and back to rain. Surely the war in Korea deserved more than this, he thought with disgust, tucking the paper under his arm and hurrying to the newspaper vendor on the corner of the street. Perhaps there was more in one of the other newspapers. He bought three. Then, in the shelter of another doorway, out of the invidious December rain, he scoured them. Nothing. Not a single line on the Korean War. No one wanted to read about war. They'd all had enough of it with the last one for six years – memories

1

were still sharp. People were terrified of another world war, so they did what they always do, he thought, a little despondently – they closed their ears and shut their eyes to it.

He threw three of the newspapers into the first litter bin he came to and hurried back to work along Victoria Embankment toward his office at New Scotland Yard. Was she critically injured? he wondered. Blinded, even? Pray God, no, not that for such a talented photographer. Perhaps it was only a slight wound. But they wouldn't fly her back to Britain for that, not unless she had decided to return, he thought hopefully. Or perhaps it was so serious that they had no option but to airlift her home to a specialist hospital. He felt cold inside.

He made his way to the first floor, where in the office which adjoined his he greeted Sergeant Jacobs with, 'Read that.' He quickly entered his office, picked up the telephone and asked to be connected to the War Office. Jacobs came in with a worried frown on his round, malleable face.

'The RAF might be able to tell us where she was flown into,' he suggested. 'It could be Northolt given that she lives in London.'

As Ryga was about to reply his call came through. 'This is Detective Inspector Ryga, Scotland Yard,' he announced into the receiver, gesturing Jacobs into the seat opposite his desk. 'I understand from the newspaper reports that Miss Eva Paisley's been injured in Korea. I want to know how seriously and where she's been taken. Yes, it is urgent. No, I'll hold on. All right. Call me back as soon as you can.'

'Maybe she's OK and is at home. I could telephone her, leaving your line free in case the War Office get back pronto, although I wouldn't hold your breath on that, sir. If she answers I'll put it through to you.'

It was a good idea. Ryga retrieved his wallet from his inside suit jacket pocket. Extracting a business card, he handed it over to Jacobs, who returned to his small, smoke-filled office where Ryga watched him through the glass panel as he lifted the receiver and asked to be put through to Eva's number.

Hanging up his Macintosh and hat, he told himself that she was probably all right and he was worrying for nothing, but he also examined his reaction to the disturbing news. He had naturally been concerned about her going to Korea, but there had been nothing he could do to stop her. He had no call to prevent her. She was an independent woman – there were no ties between them. She was also an experienced, talented photographer and had been involved in many theatres of war, including D-Day. They weren't involved romantically, or even professionally. He'd only known her for a week while on an investigation on the Isle of Portland in Dorset in September, but that didn't stop him worrying about her.

She'd sent him a telegram at the end of September saying, *Au revoir*. He had known that meant she was on her way to Korea. *I'm a war photographer, Ryga, it's what I do.* He'd rejoined, *aren't there things you can chronicle here in the UK?* There was after all plenty of hardship, austerity and homelessness. Victory had created as many problems as war.

He rose and crossed to Jacobs, who shook his head as he replaced the receiver. Eva wasn't in her apartment. There was nothing for it but to wait for the War Office to call.

Ryga's telephone rang. He swivelled back and snatched it up but it was his chief, Detective Chief Superintendent Street, summoning him to his office. Curbing his disappointment, Ryga asked Jacobs to listen out for his phone and to get as much detail as he could if the War Office called while he was with the chief.

Walking the short distance along the corridor to the adjoining room, Ryga knocked and entered Street's office. For once it wasn't filled with his pipe smoke. The reason seemed to be the visitor sitting across the desk from the well set-up fair man in his mid-forties. She glanced up at Ryga with an anxious expression. She was late forties, smartly but not expensively dressed in a black coat with a small black hat perched on her dark curly hair, black gloves folded neatly in her lap on top of a black handbag – a smallish square one with a leather and suede trim – and by her side was a black umbrella. Her lined face was strained and her eyes looked tired.

'This is Mrs Myra Swinley,' Street introduced her. 'Inspector Alun Ryga.'

Ryga took her hand, noting the fatigue in her face and a sadness in the depths of her toffee-coloured eyes, but also the set of her chin and the firmness of her mouth. There was a cup of tea on Street's desk in front of the woman, but it hadn't been touched and she hadn't removed her coat. Not because Street's office was cold – on the contrary, the gas fire hissed on low and it felt stuffy. Through the closed windows came the noise of the traffic on the Embankment punctuated by an impatient vehicle horn and the toot of the barges on the Thames.

Street gestured Ryga into the chair next to the woman. 'Mrs Swinley's husband was Police Constable George Swinley.'

Ryga noted the use of the past tense. That would account for the woman's sombre appearance and her sorrowful expression.

'George and I joined the force together,' Street continued. 'He served with me, here in London, until he met and married Myra in 1921 and moved to her hometown of Newhaven on the south coast. He transferred to the police there.' Street addressed the woman directly. Gently he said, 'Tell Inspector Ryga in your own words, Myra, and in your own time, what has brought you here.'

She nodded and turned her gaze on Ryga. 'My husband was a conscientious and clever policeman, Inspector. He could have become a sergeant, an inspector even, but he was never ambitious and he enjoyed meeting and helping people on his beat, as well as catching criminals. He had his police service interrupted by the war. He registered immediately on the outbreak when, as you know, men between eighteen and forty-one were obliged to. He was thirty-nine. It was before they decided to make the police a reserved occupation. But there you are, these things happen. He was in the Royal Artillery, in one of the anti-aircraft divisions moving around to different places: Dundee, Belfast, the Midlands, London and anywhere else they wanted him. He was part of the invasion force of Sicily and Italy in 1943 and saw action at Cassino. He suffered a head injury and was sent home for treatment at Graylingwell Hospital in Chichester. They specialized in that kind of thing for wounded servicemen.'

Ryga's thoughts flashed to Eva. Had Jacobs heard from the War Office yet? He pushed the thought aside and concentrated on Mrs Swinley's story wondering where it was leading and why the chief was interested, aside from the fact that PC Swinley had been an old friend.

'He made a good recovery, and was discharged, but it left him with bad headaches, which have become less frequent over time. George returned to his job with Newhaven Police in 1945 just after VE Day. Do you know the town?'

'I do. I sailed into the harbour while in the merchant navy before the war,' Ryga answered, omitting to say that he had continued to serve in the merchant navy during the war until his ship had been captured by a German raiding party in 1941. He'd then spent the rest of the war in a German prisoner-of-war camp. It wasn't relevant.

'Then you'll know, Inspector, that it's a busy working harbour and the only river harbour in the country. We live in Fort Road, which runs parallel to the harbour on the west side. It was my parents' house. My father – who was a master in the merchant navy – died in 1922 and my mother four years before that. I was their only child, although there had been a boy, but he died of diphtheria when he was two years old.'

Ryga could see from her expression, and the prolonged pause, that she was coming to the difficult and distressing part of her story. He caught the sound of a ringing phone as a door down the corridor opened, then it was silenced as the door closed, or perhaps someone had answered it.

She took a breath. 'Thirty days ago, on Tuesday the seventh of November, George was on the two p.m. to ten p.m. shift. He returned to the station at six o'clock for his half an hour meal break – a flask of soup and some sandwiches I'd made him. He seemed fine, his usual self, and resumed his beat at six thirty. He should have returned to the station to sign off at ten o'clock but he didn't. Sergeant Williams waited for an hour believing that George might be busy talking to someone, but when he still didn't return he got worried and sent out constables to look for him. No one could find George. Sergeant Williams reported to Inspector Holden at his home and they both came to see me. By then it was eleven thirty and I was beginning to get concerned. You see, at first I thought George was late because he'd got caught up on an arrest. Inspector Holden told me what had happened and asked me if there had been anything troubling George, or if he had been feeling unwell, but he seemed fine when he left home.' Again, she paused. Street nodded encouragingly at her.

She continued, 'Over the next few days enquiries were made around the town. The last person to see George was the vicar outside the church in South Road just on nine o'clock. George and the Reverend Isaacs talked briefly about the weather. It was very foggy. George continued on his beat. No one saw him again. On Saturday the eighteenth of November his body was found in the harbour by two boys who had been larking around on a handmade raft.'

'I'm sorry, Mrs Swinley,' Ryga said gently, and felt genuinely sorry for her loss.

She pushed her hands together and kept her eyes fixed on him, as though by sheer willpower she could prevent herself from feeling, and therefore from breaking down. Ryga sensed an inner strength about her. Something was holding her together and she'd cling to whatever it was for as long as possible. He knew that feeling. He'd experienced it in the prison camp in Germany, to hold on at all costs, to keep believing, even when you didn't, because to admit defeat meant collapse. She cleared her throat and looked down. Ryga flashed Street a glance. Street shook his head slightly.

After a moment, she continued, 'I asked to see him but they wouldn't let me. They said it would be too distressing.'

Ryga recalled the state of the bodies he'd fished out of the sea and of the Thames. The state of decomposition depended on how long they had been immersed. George Swinley's body would have automatically sank. His heavy uniform would have kept him submerged for some time until the putrefactive gas in the body had caused it to rise to the surface and float. In the Thames, at this time of year, it usually took between ten to fourteen days, a similar period of time it seemed with Newhaven Harbour.

She picked up the cup of what must by now be cold tea, her hand steady. Street asked her if she'd like a fresh cup but she shook her head. 'I nearly always drink it cold by the time I get round to it,' she said with a small smile. 'They knew it was George because of his uniform and his police number. He was a good man.'

There was short silence before Ryga said, 'How did he die?'

'The coroner brought in a verdict of accidental death. He said that because of the dark and thick fog, George could have become disorientated and couldn't see the harbour in front of him. He took one wrong step and that was it. Once in the water he found it difficult to get out, being weighed down by his uniform and his cape. He panicked, thrashed about, then swallowed too much water and drowned. There was no one to hear his cries, *if* he'd had time to cry out, because the coroner said he might have blacked out through one of his headaches.'

But there was a defiant gleam in her eyes that told Ryga she didn't believe that for one moment. It was that belief which was giving her inner strength.

'George would never have slipped. It's not right, Inspector Ryga. It doesn't feel right, and before you say it, it's not grief talking. Yes, my world has ended with George's passing but I *know* someone killed him. Perhaps not deliberately but it wasn't any accident,' she finished determinedly, eyeing them both, her pale cheeks now flushed.

'Why are you so certain?' Ryga asked.

She looked at Street, who said, 'Tell the inspector what you just told me. I'd like to see what he makes of it.'

'For a start, George was absolutely sure-footed, even in the fog.'

Ryga said, 'Here, in London, we have smog so dense that you haven't any idea where you are, and the horns from the barges on the river could come from anywhere.'

'George knew every inch of the harbour, both sides of it too, and the streets around them. He could walk them blindfolded,' she confidently asserted.

'Did the post-mortem determine whether he was alive or dead when he entered the water?'

She winced but answered steadily. 'The doctor said he was alive.'

Ryga nodded. 'You said "for a start". That means there are other reasons why you believe George was killed, aside from those you've already mentioned.'

'If he did slip, or he lost his way, or became dizzy, then where's his notebook? It wasn't found on him.'

'Maybe it fell out of his uniform,' Ryga said, though he couldn't see how it could have done unless it was in his trouser pocket. He suggested this but Myra Swinley was shaking her head.

'He never kept it in his trouser pocket, always in his tunic pocket, like all police officers do, and that was buttoned up when his body was found. George never buttoned it up without returning the notebook and pencil to it.'

'Did you mention this to the coroner at the inquest?'

'Yes, and to Inspector Holden. He said that no one had touched the tunic save the doctor to remove George's clothes before the post-mortem. And the doctor said he hadn't unbuttoned the tunic chest pockets. Inspector Holden said that George must have taken out the notebook to write in it, buttoned up the pocket, then lost his footing. The notebook went into the water with him, along with his pencil, but that's not right. And there's another thing,' she added, her eyes shining. 'How could he see to write in his notebook in the dark and fog?'

They were valid points. Ryga admired her reasoning. 'Wouldn't he have had a torch with him?'

'Yes, and he could have propped it up on a post, or the harbour wall, while he wrote some notes, but it was still in his pocket along with his whistle, gloves, truncheon, handcuffs and his wallet.'

Street reached for his pipe and addressed Ryga. 'After Myra telephoned me yesterday, asking if she could see me to talk about George's death, I called Inspector Holden. He said although they would never know exactly what happened there were no suspicious circumstances. It was a tragic accident.'

She sniffed. 'He would say that.'

Ryga could see by Myra Swinley's set expression she would never believe her husband's death was an accident. Many searched for reasons as to why their loved ones had died and clung desperately to false beliefs.

'Perhaps it's the case,' Ryga said. Then quickly added on seeing her expression, 'There's something else, isn't there?'

She hesitated and looked at each of them in turn. 'I've come this far so I might as well go on. I haven't mentioned it to anyone because I know what they'll say. You might say it too and tell me it's another reason why George was found dead and there is nothing suspicious about his death. If you do then . . .' She again took a breath and drew herself up. 'He seemed preoccupied of late. He never said anything to me about what was at the back of his mind and I didn't ask. I thought it might be to do with work.' Her eyes dropped to her hands. When she looked back up the pain reflected in them stabbed at Ryga's heart.

'Did your husband have any friends he might have confided in, outside of work, that is?'

'Not really. He wasn't one for clubs and pubs. He occasionally had a drink in The Hope Inn down on West Pier, but there isn't anyone I know of that he was close to. He was skilled with his hands. He built a small boat. It was his pride and joy. He liked to go out of the harbour in it. He keeps it in Sleeper's Hole, not far from where we live. He never got me in it. A landlubber is what I am and what I'll stay.' And suddenly the import of what she had said struck her. She quickly reached inside her handbag for a handkerchief. The tears rolled down her face but her crying was silent. Hastily, and with an effort, she composed herself. 'I'm sorry,' she said, rising. 'I've taken up too much of your time.'

'Not at all,' Street answered, hastily getting to his feet. Ryga followed suit.

Street said, 'I'll discuss it with the commander. It'll be his decision if we investigate, Myra. I'm sorry I can't do any more than that. I'll have an answer for you later today. Are you on the telephone at home?'

'Yes.' She gave Street her number. Street offered a police car to take her back to Victoria Station but she said she would walk. She needed the air. 'I've said my bit,' she declared, pausing at the door. 'I promised myself I would, and now it's out of my hands. I'll accept your decision, whatever that is.'

Two

'Well?' asked Street after she had been shown out.

'It could fit with suicide. He was preoccupied. He suffered debilitating headaches.'

'Which had lessened.'

'Maybe they had returned and he had managed to keep it from his wife. Perhaps he had become overwhelmed by his war experiences. People can be highly adept at disguising their real emotions. You knew him, sir, what do you think?'

Street took a while to get his pipe going before speaking. 'From what I can remember of George, he was thorough rather than intellectual. He paid great attention to detail. Serious but not morose. I can't see him killing himself but then I haven't seen him for over twenty years. A lot has happened in that time; he could be a very different man to the one I joined up with. We've all changed because of the war.'

Ryga silently agreed. If it hadn't been for those long years spent debating, analysing, reflecting and meeting his fellow prisoner, Simmonds, in the prisoner-of-war camp, he'd never have considered a career in the police. He'd have returned to sea. But Simmonds had got him his discharge from the merchant navy and recommended him for a job in the River Police. His involvement in two successful drug smuggling cases in the Port of London had brought him to the attention of the Criminal Investigation Department of New Scotland Yard, and since then rapid promotion to inspector.

Street continued, 'Inspector Holden said Swinley was a reliable constable, meticulous and trusted. He worked well with his colleagues, both young and old. He was adamant there was no mystery about Swinley's death. He hadn't been working on any criminal investigation and no one had it in for him. There was absolutely no reason why anyone would want to push him into the harbour.'

'But?'

Street smiled. 'I don't like loose ends.' He drew on his pipe before adding, 'Although this might always be one. We've had no official request from Newhaven to take up the case, and we're not likely to get it from Holden, judging by his defensive tone, but then that's to be expected – no one likes to be told they're wrong, especially by an "outsider", and he might very well not be wrong. As far as Holden is concerned the proper channels have been followed, a verdict given and that's the end of it.'

'He didn't mention the missing notebook and buttoned-up tunic?'

'No, and I didn't ask him about it because today was the first I'd heard of it.' Street drew on his pipe sending a blue haze up into the room. 'I'll see what the commander says, but I think he'll tell me we've got enough crime on our patch to investigate without sending a man down to Newhaven, especially when the coroner has already brought in a verdict of accidental death. And he's right, but a promise is a promise. You'd better brief me on what we've got outstanding, in case the commander asks, which he is bound to. Anything new on these furrier thefts?'

'We were hoping the latest one at the Alaska factory in Bermondsey on Monday night would give us something to go on, but we've drawn a blank. The only difference with Alaska's from the other five robberies is that they were all retailers and Alaska's aren't. They dye and recondition furs. Nevertheless, the thieves got away with some valuable mink and sable coats. None of the stolen furs have surfaced for sale in the markets or back streets, but then they're hardly the sort of thing the average person will buy. Only the rich can afford them.'

'And there's not so many of them about these days.'

'I beg to differ, sir – there seem to be plenty of people who made money out of the war and have managed to hold on to it,' Ryga replied with resignation, not bitterness. He'd learned not to waste time and energy trying to right wrongs he couldn't, with one exception, which he now voiced. 'And there are still the spivs making money on the black market.' He would put that right if he caught them.

'And they seem to be getting better at it and more prolific. Plenty to keep us busy, Inspector.'

Ryga agreed. He returned to his office where he anxiously addressed Sergeant Jacobs. 'Any news on Miss Paisley?'

'The War Office say that she's been wounded in the leg. She was flown back to RAF Lyneham in Wiltshire four days ago. She's not hospitalized and they have no idea where she is now. She's not in the armed forces so is free to go wherever she pleases.'

Ryga felt some relief and consoled himself with the fact that it couldn't be too serious or she would be in hospital. Perhaps she had gone to her late aunt's cottage on the Isle of Portland in Dorset where he had met her.

In his office he asked the switchboard to get the number. It rang. There was no answer. Perhaps she was recuperating with friends or relatives. At least she was safe. A leg wound would prevent her from dashing off to some other war-torn area or returning to Korea.

He applied himself to his work. As Street had said, there were plenty of crimes to keep them busy. It was dark when he decided to call it a day. Jacobs had already left for his home in Battersea where he lived with his widowed mother, wife and three children. Ryga rose and turned to the window but he couldn't see a thing. The air was thick with fog and with the sound of the barges on the river – one loud blast, another answering further upriver. Soon the fog would become the thick odorous, choking smog. This weather might keep the fur thieves at bay but equally it could present them, and other criminals, with increased opportunities to steal.

His telephone rang. It was Superintendent Street with the news Ryga had been expecting. Commander Harris had said they had no authority to investigate Swinley's death. Street said he would ring through and relay the news to Mrs Swinley. Ryga wondered how she would take it. He recalled how she had risen from her chair across Street's desk. Her voice had been even in tone when she had said that she would accept the commander's decision but her eyes had said something else. Maybe Street had seen it too, perhaps not. It wasn't sorrow or resignation, not even hope, but what? He couldn't put his finger on it.

He thought of PC George Swinley. Had he disturbed thieves who had pushed him into the harbour and left him to drown? There hadn't been reports of any crimes in the harbour, according to Inspector Holden. But what if a crime had been committed and hadn't been reported or discovered? Had George Swinley chanced upon smugglers, taking advantage of the foul weather, who had made their getaway by boat?

How experienced was the pathologist who had conducted the autopsy on Swinley? Had he looked hard enough for any signs that Swinley had been murdered, such as bruises and contusions? Maybe both were in evidence on the corpse but were explained by the body being knocked about in the harbour. From what Myra had said it sounded as though a GP pathologist had conducted the post-mortem, which was to be expected – forensic pathologists were only called in when it was a clear case of murder and not always then depending on their availability and the case.

Ryga again tried Eva's numbers, both her London flat and the house in Portland, without success. He ate in the canteen then headed for his small flat in Pimlico. He could barely see a foot in front of him. And even though he knew the way blindfolded it still took him four times longer than usual. As he'd silently predicted, the fog had become smog. The air was clawing, foul and sulphurous. It made him long for the crisp, salty air of the ocean off Portland in Dorset. As he let himself in, he also longed for company, and female at that. Two women had entered his life in September, Eva Paisley and Sonia Shepherd, the latter the landlady of The Quarryman's Arms on Portland where he'd been staying while investigating the murder of a man found in the cove nearby.

He'd thought of Sonia many times since his return to London, recalling her deep-set, dark, smudgy eyes, dark hair and shapely figure. He'd visited her twice since then. Once to tell her that he had managed to persuade the War Office not to pursue reclaiming the war widow's pension they had paid to her since her husband had been officially declared dead after Dunkirk, because she had genuinely not known that he had, in fact, been alive and a deserter. And the second time had been to make sure she was all right. He knew she might be struggling financially with the termination of her pension, but she had told him crisply that she and her young son, Steven, were managing, thank you. Maybe they were. They had friends in the community, but he could see that she was desperately worried, and understandably so. Sam Shepherd was a fraudster, a bully and a conman, and Ryga wanted nothing more than to see him get what he deserved. But the price would hurt Sonia, and he hated the thought of that. To date no one had been able to find Shepherd. Perhaps he had absconded to

America, as he had told Sonia he would. There was an all ports alert out for him and Ryga had asked to be notified if Sam Shepherd was located.

He tried to read but couldn't concentrate so he popped into the pub on the corner where he sat with a beer, watching the handful of customers come and go while thinking of The Quarryman's Arms and Sonia behind the bar with her quarrymen and elders supping ale. He felt a fondness for the Isle of Portland with its rugged stony landscape, its secluded bays, windswept hills and strong sea breeze. And he felt a fondness for Sonia. Eva had said that Sonia was in love with him, but she had shown no signs of that – quite the opposite in fact at their last encounter. Ryga understood her feelings of antipathy. After all, how could Sonia be fond of the man she believed would finally apprehend her husband and have him convicted? Not because she still loved her husband – she didn't by her own admittance – but for the shame it would bring on her. Everyone on Portland would know, and her son would be bullied because his father was liar, a coward and a crook.

Ryga spent a restless night with dreams of the war, Eva and PC George Swinley, which merged into becoming a crazy mixed-up nightmare with himself being chased. He was glad to wake. The smog was denser than ever and the stinking yellow air clung to everything, terrifyingly suffocating. He took the bus to work. It crawled at a snail's pace. He could have walked quicker but he had hoped that being inside he might at least avoid some of the choking smog. He didn't. It seemed to curl and weave its way through the open platform into the crowded vehicle with its coughing occupants.

Alighting long before his stop, he walked along the Embankment unable to see barely an inch in front of him, or where the pavement ended and the road began, let alone see the Thames. He heard it though. The swish of the water and the almost constant hooting of the barges. Maybe this was what it had been like for George Swinley.

Ryga took a handkerchief from his Macintosh and, before placing it to his mouth, wiped his running, stinging eyes. Had George Swinley done the same? No, the Newhaven sea fog wouldn't be sulphurous like this devil that enveloped him. Mrs Swinley hadn't mentioned her husband's handkerchief having been found on his body.

Thankful to be in his office with the windows firmly shut, Ryga applied himself to his work, hoping that a stiff breeze would spring up and blow the damn smog away. He made two telephone calls to two newspaper editors he knew, one at the *Daily Telegraph* and the other at the *Daily Express*. Both had published Eva's war photographs. He'd seen them in the newspapers in all their horror. They were though, he suspected, the tamer ones that wouldn't offend the readers too much but would, however, alert them to the conditions the British soldiers and others were experiencing in Korea. He updated each editor on the thefts from furriers, and a couple of other cases, then raised the subject of Eva Paisley, but neither editor knew where he could contact Miss Paisley aside from her London apartment, and both were curious to know what the Scotland Yard detective wanted with her. He fobbed them off with a story that having worked with her once on the murder case in Portland, he wondered now she was back in Britain if she might be available to assist the police again if needed. He hoped they fell for it because he didn't fancy them looking for news and creating it where there was none.

The smog stayed all day, making it dark, heavy and depressing. The deep blasts of horns from the barges, along with long, panicking ones, sounded almost constantly and were punctuated by the sharp, irritable horns of the buses and cars. It was late afternoon when Street telephoned him to say that he had called Myra Swinley last night and four times throughout the day but had received no answer. He said he'd try again later that night.

Ryga thought it unusual that she hadn't answered when she must have been impatiently awaiting Street's decision, or rather the commander's passed on by Street. Perhaps when Street had telephoned she'd been shopping, or had been in the garden and hadn't heard the telephone. And last night she might not have reached home when he had called.

Ryga was on the point of heading for home when there was a knock on his door and a constable entered. 'Telegram for you, sir.'

'Thank you.' Ryga took it and dismissed the constable. Telegrams always conjured up apprehension because they were often the harbinger of bad news, and he wondered if it came with announcement of a relative's death. Not that he had many, but there were still some aunts and uncles scattered about Britain. The telegram was not from one of them though and it didn't bring bad news. On the contrary, it brought the best possible news he could have received. It was from Eva. It simply said: *J'ai revien.* Her parting telegram had also been in French and simple, just like this one, no words wasted.

He smiled and called Jacobs in to relay the news to him. Of course, Ryga had known she was back, but now he not only had an address in Godalming, Surrey but more importantly a telephone number, which, reaching for his phone, he asked the switchboard to get for him.

A woman answered. Not Eva. He asked if he could speak to Miss Paisley and announced himself. He was invited to hold the line. He did so with a slightly quickening pulse, and a few moments later he was listening, with relief, to Eva's voice.

'I read the article in the newspaper, saw that the idiots had mentioned me and I wondered if you'd be worried.'

'I was. Am. Are you all right?'

'Of course. It's nothing. Just a bullet graze in the right thigh, luckily the fleshy part. Not that there is much flesh on my legs, which you'll have to take my word for because you've only seen them clothed in trousers. It was hardly enough to send me home, but I couldn't argue with the commanding officer and the doctor. It's all right, Ryga, it didn't do any serious damage. It just means I won't be doing the hundred-yard sprint for a while. But I am mobile and being looked after by my father and his wife.'

Not her mother then. 'When do you expect to be back in town?'

'Now if I could manage it,' she said, dropping her voice.

Ryga smiled. Knowing her even as briefly as he did, he suspected she was feeling like a caged tiger. His thoughts flicked to Myra Swinley.

'Are you still there?' Eva said.

'Yes.'

'What's the matter? Working on a difficult murder?'

'No, just some annoying robberies of furs.'

'And?'

'Are you psychic?' he joked.

'No, just desperate.'

'I'd have thought you'd have had enough excitement in Korea.'

'If that's the right word for it. Conditions are hell and not getting any better, but we'll save the political discussion for another time. What's bothering you?'

'If you were desperately waiting for a telephone call which would tell you if your husband's death might or might not be investigated by Scotland Yard, what would you do?'

'Nail myself to the chair next to the blasted instrument and urge it to ring with all my might. I'd be scared that if I moved even a foot away I might not hear it.'

'But she isn't sticking to the phone. The chief's been trying to get her all day without any answer.'

'Who?'

Ryga swiftly told her. He saw no reason not to, and he trusted her implicitly. He welcomed a fresh perspective on things. When he'd finished giving her the details there was a pause before she spoke.

'I think someone ought to knock on her door and check she's OK.'

Ryga's feelings exactly, unless Street had finally managed to speak to her. He said as much.

She said, 'Call me to let me know what happens. I hope to be back in my apartment on Monday, although my father might have other ideas.'

Ryga rang off, wondering what her father thought of her occupation. Maybe he'd given up trying to persuade her not to go to war-torn countries years ago seeing as it wouldn't make the slightest difference what he said.

He rose and crossed to Jacob's office, where he told the sergeant the good news about Eva. He'd just finished when Street entered, pipe in his hand and a deep frown on his forehead. This looked ominous.

'Pack your bag, Ryga. I want you to go to Newhaven.'

'The commander has changed his mind about investigating George Swinley's death?' Ryga asked, surprised.

'Yes, because I telephoned Newhaven and asked an officer to go round to see if Myra Swinley was all right. I've been worried that she isn't answering her phone.'

So Street had come to the same conclusion as he and Eva had done.

'There was no answer to the constable's knock on her door and the neighbours haven't seen her. He found a key under a flowerpot by the front door and let himself in. There's no sign of Myra. Her bed hasn't been slept in and there are remains of tea on the kitchen table. A neighbour, on questioning, says there aren't any relatives she would have gone to stay with. Besides, why should she when she was waiting to hear if we were going to look into her husband's death? I've discussed it with Commander Harris who's been in touch with the Sussex chief constable and it's been agreed that someone from the Yard should go down to Newhaven and look into this new development. If Myra shows up when you're there then fine, you return. Inspector Holden at Newhaven will book you into the Bridge Hotel. You're to catch the seven forty-five train from Victoria.'

Ryga looked at the clock. That gave him just under two hours for a police car to drive him to his flat and pack a holdall. It also gave him time to telephone Eva.

Three

There was only one person in the carriage, an elderly lady, reading an Agatha Christie, *The Thirteen Problems*. He hoped he wouldn't have as many on this case.

He smiled a greeting at her. She returned it and resumed her reading as the train began to slowly pull out of Victoria Station in several wheezing huffs and a plume of smoke which seemed to wend its way down the platform and into the carriage, even though the window was shut. He placed his holdall and murder briefcase on the luggage rack above him, sincerely hoping he wouldn't have to use the latter's contents – evidence bags, tubes, small bottles, rubber gloves, a magnifying glass and other sundry items. When he had spoken to Eva on the telephone and relayed where he was going, she had insisted that he keep her updated and he had promised he would do so, adding that he hoped her leg would soon heal. He'd no sooner sat when the carriage door slid open and a tall, slender woman with shoulder-length fair hair, wearing slacks and a well-worn and slightly disreputable dark-navy donkey jacket, stood in the doorway.

Ryga looked up, startled. 'My God! What are you doing here?'

'Gatecrashing your investigation,' Eva replied brightly.

The Agatha Christie fan peered at them curiously over the rim of her spectacles and then quickly put her eyes back on her novel. Ryga knew she was no longer reading it but eavesdropping into their conversation.

He quickly rose and, taking Eva's holdall, placed it on the rack above the seat as she eased herself down on to the seat opposite him and shifted her leg, the wounded one obviously. She looked more drawn that he remembered. She'd lost weight too. There were shadows under her blue eyes which danced at him mischievously. He

19

swivelled his gaze towards the elderly woman and back to Eva. Interpreting it, Eva said, 'It's all right, Ryga, I'm not stupid.'

'Sorry. I know.'

She smiled. 'I fancied a change of air and my stepmother was driving me mad. I think the feeling was mutual judging by the enormous sigh of relief she gave and the way her face lit up when I asked my father to drive me to Victoria. I just missed you on the platform – the timing was pretty tight. If it wasn't for this leg I'd have driven down to Newhaven myself. I thought you might need my third eye, and if you don't, then fine, there will be plenty for me to photograph. I haven't forgotten what you said in Portland in September about there being enough hardship and poverty in Britain to photograph without going off to war. I'm sure Newhaven is no different from the rest of the UK.'

'Where are you staying?'

'Same place as you, the Bridge Hotel.'

Ryga could see that their conversation was proving much more exciting than Agatha Christie. To Eva, he said, 'Would you like a cup of tea?'

'Coffee. And something to eat.'

'Let's go to the Pullman car.'

He rose and, placing his hat and coat on his seat, took down the brown briefcase from the luggage rack. His holdall could stay. The murder briefcase he would not leave behind. Eva pulled herself up with a slight wince and reached for her holdall. She had it down before he could help her and she extracted her camera case. Not because she was going to use it but because, like his murder case, it was too valuable and precious to leave behind. And he recalled what she had once said to him: a photographer without a camera is like a policeman without a whistle. The elderly lady looked as though she'd very much like to join them.

Sliding shut the carriage door they swayed their way to the Pullman car in single file. It was busy but they found two vacant seats. Ryga ordered coffee for two, kippers and toast for Eva and cottage pie and peas for himself.

'You're looking a little tired,' she said.

'I was thinking the same about you.'

'What's been keeping you awake? Work or Sonia Shepherd?'

'The former. Why do you suggest the latter?'

'Have you seen her?'

'Not recently. You?'

'Not since September. Not caught that rotter of a husband of hers then?'

'No.'

'Sonia can't move on until he's found. I hope he is. It would be awful for her to have months, maybe years, of wondering and waiting, half expecting him to show up again on her doorstep and threaten her into helping him. At least if you found him she could apply for a divorce and put him behind her for good. Can you get a divorce if your spouse has been legally declared dead?'

'I don't know.'

'I'll ask a lawyer friend of mine.'

'I seem to recall you didn't think we should search for him.'

'I've changed my mind. Wondering what will happen is worse than knowing.'

Ryga silently agreed. He'd had four years of wondering in the camp.

Their coffee arrived. When the steward left, Ryga said, 'Don't you have to return to the hospital for your leg wound?'

'Not until next Friday. Until then I can get under your feet or not depending on what you find. Myra might be home by now.'

'But you don't think so.'

'Do you?'

'No.'

'Then she's either taken off in despair and killed herself – unlikely given that she was waiting for your chief's call – or her husband's death is suspicious and whoever is behind it has abducted her and possibly killed her.'

'She could have had an accident.'

Eva scoffed to show what she thought of that idea. 'Her body might be found and it might *look* like an accident, but two accidents in the same family might be two too many. Was PC Swinley insured?'

'I don't know, but if he was there should be some paperwork in the Swinley's house. I can't see anyone killing him though, or Myra, for the insurance.'

'Why not? The insurance money goes to Myra – her will leaves it to a relative. Does she own the house?'

'Yes. It was left to Myra by her parents.'

'Then it could be a sizeable amount. Any children?'

'No. And no brothers or sisters on Myra's side anyway.' He didn't know about George.

'Might be a distant cousin.'

Ryga sipped his coffee. He thought of the tea things left on Myra's table. She had by all accounts reached home after her visit to London. But he quickly reconsidered this. How did he know the table had been laid by Myra? Someone else could have done that in order to make them believe she had returned, when in reality she could have been waylaid on her way home or pushed off the train even.

'You've thought of something?' Eva broke through his thoughts.

He expressed what had occurred to him.

'How do we know they *are* tea things?' she said. 'Myra might have left them there from breakfast on Thursday because she was in a hurry to catch the train to London.'

Ryga hadn't considered that.

Eva continued, 'Swinley could have been mixed up in something crooked and was killed as a result.'

'Not according to my chief who knew him, although that was some years ago and people can change, especially if under pressure. If Mrs Swinley has been abducted and killed to stop her going to the police then chummy's slipped up. He left it too late.'

'Perhaps he doesn't know she's been to see you.'

Ryga considered this as their meals arrived. They said nothing more until the steward had left, then Ryga continued, 'It's all speculation anyway. It's facts I need, and I'll start getting them tomorrow.'

'I'll talk to the locals about the Swinleys as I take photographs. They might open up to me, and I'll pass on anything I learn.'

'Are you fit enough? I mean your leg.'

'I don't take pictures with my leg,' she quipped, but smiled to soften the jibe. 'Besides, I've been told exercise is good for it, and there's no need to look at me like that, it's the truth.'

He knew he wouldn't be able to dissuade her and he didn't want to. He was glad to have her along, knowing that she wouldn't intrude. He wondered if he ought to tell his chief. Maybe later. Judging by his experience and knowledge of Street, Ryga didn't think he would mind. Street, like him, used whatever resources he needed, including human ones if it helped them to resolve a case.

Ryga prodded a fork into the cottage pie, which looked like brown sludge. He wished he'd had the kippers, which appeared much more appetizing. They started to talk about other matters; both evaded discussing the war. Ryga could tell that Eva didn't want to talk about her experiences in Korea and he certainly didn't want to discuss his time in Germany. He asked about her family and discovered that her mother had died when she was eighteen and her father had remarried three years after that. 'Fortunately I was of age and there was a war on.'

'You don't get on with your stepmother?'

'Two women in the house is one too many. I was unmarried, twenty-one and was about to be conscripted when my father had a better idea. He's a civil servant and at that time was on the Committee for Imperial Defence, which, you might know, was responsible for forming the Ministry of Information and had secretly been in operation since 1935, although it didn't officially exist until September 1939. My father thought I'd be safer working for the Ministry of Information in London than in the ATS, Wrens or the WAAF, and he couldn't see me in a munitions factory or as a Land Girl, more in a secretarial role. I saw other opportunities.'

'Photography.'

'Yes.'

A whistle sounded and the train was on the move again. Ryga hadn't even noticed it had stopped, he'd been so engrossed in his conversation with Eva. A portly man swayed past them, staggering against their table as the train swayed. He muttered an apology and lurched on his way.

'You were a keen photographer even then?' Ryga asked.

'Since the age of eight. I told you before that I can't paint, but Aunt Pru spotted that I had a natural flair for composition. She encouraged me with the camera, much to my father's horror, but my mother thought it was fun. I showed my boss at the Ministry of Information what I could do with a camera and suggested that I take a tour around the country and a series of photographs of women at war which could be used in various propaganda literature and posters. He took some persuading but I managed it and, of course, as time went on more women were needed for the war effort, so there was a greater need for photographs to show how rewarding and worthwhile all the various options were, helping to persuade women they were required to do their bit.

'From that came an assignment to photograph how people were coping with the bombing, which took me around London and to Cardiff, Liverpool, Portsmouth and Coventry, among other places. The sanitized pictures of smiling cockneys and others gritting their teeth and getting on with it the Ministry used while others I took showed the hard truth, the devastation, the anger and heartbreak, the dead, the injured. The country isn't ready for those yet, but it will be one day, and of others I took after the liberation of France, in Germany and of D-Day.'

'And Korea,' he said quietly.

'I'm not sure if the public will ever be ready for those,' she said solemnly, pushing away her empty plate. Then brightly added, 'But that's enough about me. How about you? You don't have to give me your life story, Ryga, not unless you're itching to do so, which I can tell you're not. Just the edited highlights will do.'

'It's simple – orphaned at fifteen, merchant navy until 1941, ship raided by the Germans, taken prisoner, released in 1945, followed by discharge from the merchant navy, Thames River Police, then the Met and Scotland Yard Criminal Investigation Department.'

'Finished? Your meal, I mean?'

'Yes.' He put down his knife and fork neatly on the plate, knowing she had sensed correctly that he had nothing more to say about his personal life. 'Would you like anything else to eat or drink?'

'No.'

'Then let's get back to Agatha Christie and her thirteen problems.'

'Couldn't have been very riveting, she's fallen asleep,' Eva said quietly as she opened the carriage door.

Their carriage filled up and emptied intermittently as the train made its faltering, lumbering way towards the south coast. Ryga read an evening paper left by one of the transient occupants while Eva studied them as though she wished to photograph them. She closed her eyes, and at one point he thought she might be asleep, but perhaps she was just avoiding conversation. She should have been recuperating in the sun and warmth, not travelling on a chilly, wet December night to a working harbour town. He felt guilty at her being with him, not that he had invited her, and even if he insisted she return to London, which he had no right to do, he knew she wouldn't.

It was raining in Newhaven when they finally arrived much later than he had expected. They'd had to change trains at Lewes and wait a considerable amount of time for the connection to Newhaven. Ryga had told his chief before leaving London that there was no need for anyone from the local police to meet him at Newhaven and that he would make his own way to the Bridge Hotel, which was just a short distance across the harbour from the railway station. Nevertheless, it was a wet walk and he was glad to step into the stuffy warmth of the small hotel, where he shook the drops of rain from his hat, wishing he'd had the foresight to bring an umbrella. Eva looked unperturbed, even though her wet hair was plastered to her head. The weather hadn't seemed to bother her at all, but then compared to what she had been through in Korea he guessed this must be balmy.

They signed the register, handed over their ration books and were told that breakfast was served between eight and nine in the small dining room on their right. Ryga asked if there were any telephone messages for him. There weren't. That meant Myra hadn't returned home, because Street had said he would instruct an officer to try her number periodically throughout the evening and a local constable was also to knock on her door. If she had returned a message would be left with him at the hotel.

They said goodnight on the landing of the first floor after agreeing to meet for breakfast at eight. Ryga's room was across the hall from Eva's. It was plainly but adequately furnished, comfortable and chilly. He switched on the electric fire. The bathroom was at the end of the corridor on his right. He unpacked, which didn't take him long, and stared out of the window through the slanting rain to the bridge spanning the River Ouse to his left and the faint glimmer of lights on the small island of Denton which bordered the river. Across from Denton Island was North Quay, which, from his brief visit here on board ship, he remembered as being incredibly busy. He could see the lights of a ship moored there now. He was itching to get started. He hoped that tomorrow would bring some answers as to where Myra was and what had happened to her. Above all, though, he hoped he would find she had returned home and was apologetic about all the fuss. But as he climbed into bed and tried to settle to sleep, he knew that was not going to be the case.

Four

He woke more tired than he had felt before retiring for bed. The mattress had sagged alarmingly and the springs had creaked so loudly that every time he turned over he was jerked from sleep. He was amazed he hadn't roused the occupants of the entire hotel. Although, judging by the registration book last night, there were only two other guests besides him and Eva.

After a quick shave and wash in the nippy bathroom down the hall, he returned to his bedroom and dressed rapidly. Clearing the condensation from inside the window, he stopped briefly to stare down into the street. The rain had ceased in the early hours and the temperature had dropped a few Fahrenheit. It was still dark but in the glow of the streetlight a cat wandered aimlessly across the road not even bothering to scuttle out of the way of a lorry, which stopped to let it pass. He smiled.

Eva was already in the dining room when he entered. Dressed in her usual garb of trousers – this time teamed with a polo-neck jumper – she was eating toast and marmite. He was glad to hear that her bed hadn't proved as uncomfortable as his, but then she said she had been sleeping rough for so long that any bed was better than none.

They had the small dining room to themselves. Ryga ordered tea, toast and scrambled egg from the waitress who eyed him with suspicion. After she had left to get his order, he said, 'Does she know I'm a police officer?' He hadn't given his occupation in the register – he'd left that column blank.

'Not unless you told her. I haven't. She's probably wondering why you took a seat at my table when every other table is empty. Her name is Ivy and I told her I was a photographer here to take pictures of the harbour and town. She couldn't see why because the place was as dull as dish water and nothing ever happened here – oh, unless you count that police constable who killed himself by falling in the harbour. From there it was easy to get her talking. I suspect it will be the same with others. She said the two boys who found the policeman's body are Tom Gileson and Colin Pleasant who live on Denton Island. I'll go over there this morning. It being Saturday the boys will be out playing. I'll see what I can pick up from them and anyone else.'

Ivy returned with a pot of tea and another containing hot water, along with a small jug of milk. Ryga smiled his thanks but got a toss of her dark head in return.

Eva laughed. 'She probably thinks you're a travelling salesman trying to pick me up and that you have a wife and four children in Barrow-in-Furnace. Are you going to make it public knowledge who you are and why you're here?'

'Not until I've spoken to Inspector Holden. Some local police officers get a bit defensive when Scotland Yard appear on the scene. And I don't want to get his back up and start off on the wrong foot by making him think I've come charging in and that the whole town know I'm here before he does, although he is expecting me.'

'Exceedingly diplomatic of you. I'll say nothing about you, of course. What will be your first move?'

But Ryga was prevented from answering by the return of Ivy with his toast and scrambled egg.

'Is there anything else, miss?' she said pointedly to Eva.

'No, thank you, Ivy. I'm just leaving.'

Ivy looked as though she would like to wait until Eva had left and ensure he didn't follow her. But a couple of men entered the dining room and she had to attend to them.

Ryga said that after speaking to Inspector Holden he'd visit Myra's house.

Rising, Eva said, 'Well, if you need any photographs you know where to find me.'

'Where?'

'Somewhere around the harbour. I'll leave you to enjoy your scrambled egg.'

He didn't. It was lukewarm and soggy. He was convinced it had been made from powdered egg.

He collected his murder case from his bedroom – he didn't like to leave it lying about for any nosy chambermaid to peer into – and walked the short distance to the police station, wondering what kind of reception he would get from Holden. They were of the same rank but Scotland Yard took precedence when on an investigation, which sometimes induced antipathy. He was, after all, trespassing on another police forces' territory and as such questioning the ability of its officers. He wondered how Holden would feel about this.

Cool and suspicious was the answer but not openly hostile. After shaking hands Holden waved Ryga into a seat across his untidy paper-strewn desk in a stuffy, cramped office at the back of the station overlooking a brick wall. He was a well-built man of about fifty with grizzled reddish hair, a pale, lined face and soft grey-blue eyes which studied Ryga warily. Ryga had expected someone younger.

'I'm not sure there is anything I can tell you, or add to what the coroner found at the inquest,' Holden announced a little defensively as Ryga placed his hat on his lap and his murder case on the floor beside him. He was hot in his raincoat with the gas fire hissing and seemingly on full blast, but he didn't like to remove his coat without being invited to.

Ryga said, 'It's worrying that Mrs Swinley is missing.'

'Only since Thursday evening,' Holden replied, intimating that Scotland Yard were overreacting. 'She could have decided to visit relatives or friends.'

'Leaving her tea things on the table?' Always assuming, Ryga added to himself, they were from tea and not breakfast as Eva had suggested.

'Perhaps Mrs Swinley acted on impulse. She is obviously deeply upset over her husband's death and not thinking straight. She could be unwell, mentally.'

'Which means there is even greater urgency to locate her. I'd like a constable to accompany me to her house.'

'PC Jenkins is on the station. He was the constable who entered Mrs Swinley's house yesterday and I asked him to wait as I anticipated you would want to question him.'

'Thank you. You have the key?'

'Yes.'

'There might be an address book, or details of relatives in the house, who we can contact and ask if they have spoken to Mrs Swinley.' But if she had gone to one of them that didn't explain why she hadn't telephoned Street to tell him where he could contact her.

Ryga shifted and resisted the temptation to remove a handkerchief and mop his brow. Holden seemed oblivious to the heat, which for a big man Ryga thought unusual.

'Did you, or any of your officers, attend PC Swinley's funeral?' he asked. 'I wondered if you met any relatives of the Swinleys or perhaps PC Swinley spoke of relatives to his work colleagues.'

'He didn't to me, but he might have done to some of the constables. As to the funeral, Superintendent Waltham at headquarters attended it along with myself. There were quite a few people there because PC Swinley was well known on his beat, and in the town generally, but we didn't go back to the house.'

Ryga thought the neighbours might know of relatives or close friends. 'What was PC Swinley like?' he asked.

'Thorough, methodical, reliable,' came the quick reply. 'A competent officer.'

'And as a man?' probed Ryga, wanting to get under the skin of the dead man and not just see him as a husband and officer.

Holden looked as though he wanted to say *I don't know what good this will do* but he held his tongue on that score and, after a moment, said, 'He was pleasant and friendly but not overly chummy. Kept himself to himself, didn't mix socially, but he wasn't standoffish.'

It was more or less how Myra had described her husband. 'I'd like a list of the contents found in his pockets.'

'I suppose Mrs Swinley has told you his notebook and pencil were missing.'

'She did. And that neither had been found.'

'On account of them being at the bottom of the harbour.'

'You don't know that for certain.'

'No one's handed them in.'

'Maybe they wouldn't if something in those notes was worth pushing PC Swinley into the water for. Was he involved in investigating any crimes before he died?'

'Nothing that would warrant such violent action, only the usual petty thefts, some vandalism.'

Ryga nodded as if to say I understand. 'Where exactly was his body found?'

'Lodged up against the gridiron at Railway Quay. It's the other side of the harbour, which wasn't part of his beat but then the tide and currents could have taken the body from anywhere in the harbour, as you probably know from your experience of the Thames.'

Ryga said he did. Holden didn't know he also had a nautical background and he didn't enlighten him. Maybe he would in due course, if it was relevant.

Holden said, 'The boys who made the gruesome discovery, Tom Gileson and Colin Pleasant, reported it to an officer of the British Transport Commission Police who fetched Sergeant Keaton. He's the officer-in-charge. His office is close to the harbour railway station and the Customs House but you won't find him there today – it being Saturday he'll be off duty.'

'I'd like copies of the boys' statements, the coroner's report and the post-mortem report. If you could have them, and that list of the pocket contents, ready for me when I return, I'd be grateful,' Ryga said, rising. Even if by some chance Myra was at home and answered the door to him, it wouldn't hurt to read through the reports.

'I'll make sure they're left with Sergeant Williams. He'll be on duty at two p.m. It's not his regular shift but my station sergeant has gone down with this influenza, so Sergeant Williams will be taking over for now. Will you be wanting a desk?'

'Please, and I'll also need the use of a telephone.'

'I'll organize it.'

Ryga wondered where Holden would put him; by his look and manner it could be in a cupboard as far away from him as possible.

Leaving his murder case in Holden's office, Ryga accompanied the inspector back to the front desk where a tall, lanky constable in his mid-twenties – whom Holden introduced as PC Jenkins – fished out a street map for Ryga on his request. Ryga was no slouch at six foot but Jenkins towered above him by at least six inches. He seemed an amiable young man and Ryga hoped he was intelligent, observant and articulate. As they set off towards Fort Road, Ryga asked how long Jenkins had worked with George Swinley.

'Just over a year, sir. Since I joined the police. He was very decent to me.'

'In what way?'

'He was patient when I made mistakes and gave me advice when I didn't know what to do. He wasn't one to talk down to you. Treated people with respect. Bit of a stickler for the rules, though, and for writing things down, but then that's not a bad thing.'

'No, it isn't, and police officers have to make sure they record things accurately.'

'Yes, sir.'

'Did you go out with him on his beat?'

'No. But I took it over after he went missing.'

'And has anyone said anything to you about how PC Swinley ended up in the harbour?'

'Nothing, sir, except what a tragic accident it was.'

They stepped around a small group of children playing with marbles and a little girl of about four wearing her mother's high heels. Their eyes followed them with curiosity. Jenkins smiled at them but their expressions didn't alter.

'They're good kids,' he said as they walked on. He nodded at a man and a woman talking in a doorway, who returned the gesture while studying Ryga inquisitively. At the end of the street they turned left and then almost immediately right, heading down towards the fort which the road was named after, built in the nineteenth century on the cliffs overlooking Seaford Bay to defend the harbour from the French and utilized again for defence against the Germans during the war. The army were still present but in the form of a Ukrainian Battle Area Clearance Unit, tasked with the removal of mines and unexploded ordnance from the beaches and the surrounding areas.

To Ryga's left was the railway track, running adjacent to the harbour, with a variety of craft moored alongside, including fishing boats and attracting, as usual, the shrieking seagulls swooping and diving overhead. The smell of fish and the mud of low tide mingled with the gritty metallic scent of the working town. Across the narrow stretch of harbour he could see, and hear, the whirr of the cranes as they towered and swayed over the cargo ships.

'That's Railway Quay where PC Swinley was found,' Jenkins said, noting Ryga's glance. 'Mrs Swinley lives just down here, sir, opposite the allotments,' which they were now passing.

A couple of men were tending their patches; another sat on a wooden crate before a smouldering furnace, smoking a pipe looking contented and reflective. Jenkins halted before a well-cared-for terraced house on their right. 'This is it,' he announced.

The small front garden boasted some bedraggled-looking winter pansies but the patterned tiled path to the varnished front door was weed-free. There were crisp white lace curtains in the downstairs front window between which, in the middle of the bay window, was a healthy-looking aspidistra. The upstairs curtains were pulled back in both of the windows. The milk bottle on the doorstep told Ryga that Myra hadn't returned, yet he knocked just in case. There was no answer.

Extracting the key Inspector Holden had given him, he addressed PC Jenkins. 'Give that bottle of milk to one of the neighbours and talk to both sides, ask them when they last saw Mrs Swinley and if they know of any relatives.' That should keep Jenkins occupied. Ryga wanted to see inside the house alone and soak up its atmosphere.

The immediate thing that struck him as he entered was the cold. He shuddered involuntarily. It was as though he sensed evil, which was ridiculous. He was a police officer who dealt in facts. He was letting his imagination get the better of him. But as he gazed around the pristine hall, he felt a sadness, or perhaps it was an emptiness. He was curious to know what Eva might feel on viewing the place.

Trying to shake off the feeling and not quite managing it, he took in the surroundings: the gleaming brass stair rods and shining mahogany bannister; the spotless green and brown patterned carpet with pale green linoleum between the edge of the carpet and the cream-painted skirting boards. The smell of beeswax and wood. The sound of a solemnly ticking clock, which suddenly struck the half hour, making him start. It was ten thirty.

He turned his attention to the coat stand on his left. It was so highly polished that he felt he might actually see his reflection in the wood rather than in the small central mirror. There was a man's trilby hat on the left-hand peg and under it a tweed overcoat, while on the right was a woman's raincoat. He assumed the overcoat, like the hat, had belonged to George Swinley.

He lifted off the trilby hat and tested it against his own for size. George Swinley had boasted a much larger head than him. Ryga placed it on the small shelf below the mirror and took down the coat. Both pockets were empty, as was the inner breast pocket. Holding the coat up against him, he saw that the owner had been bulkier but about the same height. There was no name sewn in it. The collar was a little worn, but all the buttons present. He wondered if the former constable's other clothes were still in the house or whether Myra had dispensed with them either by giving them to someone or putting them in the jumble sale. Somehow he couldn't see her taking them to a pawn shop. He'd get to the bedrooms in due course.

Lifting Myra's raincoat, he found a handkerchief in the right-hand pocket, nothing more. The coat held the faint smell of perfume. It wasn't the same coat she'd worn to London. That wasn't here, neither was her hat, gloves or handbag, but they could be in her bedroom. He hadn't noticed if Myra had been wearing any perfume in Street's office but then the smell of the gas fire, and Street's pipe tobacco smoke, could have disguised it. The umbrella, which Myra had been carrying, was in its allotted slot, so unless someone had taken it from her and placed it there, or she had two identical ones, she had returned home.

A telephone was on a small, gleaming oak table to the right of a door which was the understairs cupboard. He made a mental note to ask the exchange about the last call made and received from the number. The notepad beside the telephone had nothing written in it and from what he could see no indentation on the top page from any writing which might have been on a sheet of paper torn out. Surprisingly there was no address or telephone book in the tiny drawer. In fact, the drawer was empty. Myra must have kept a note of the numbers elsewhere, perhaps in a small book in her handbag.

He opened the understairs cupboard, thinking this must have been where Myra – and her husband when home on leave from the army – had taken refuge from the German bombs during the war, unless there was an Anderson shelter in the garden. The cupboard was fairly deep; it contained two empty shopping bags, a Bissell carpet sweeper, a wooden ironing board and a few other household bits and pieces. Nothing of interest.

Ryga made for the front parlour and found what he fully expected – a gleaming ice-cold room. The ticking clock was sharing place on the sturdy mantelpiece with a couple of ornaments and shining brass candlesticks, while there was a photograph of Myra and George on their wedding day on the sideboard. Also one of George in police uniform. Ryga compared the younger Myra with the one he had met. There was the same angular face, slightly slanting eyes and broad mouth. Her dark hair had that same wild, untamed appearance. The uniformed PC Swinley was exactly how he had imagined him – solid, upright, well-built, with a hint of a smile on his round face. In his wedding pictures he was dark haired but Ryga couldn't see the colour of his hair, or how much of it he had, in the police picture because of the helmet. The helmet. What had happened to that? Had it still been on the body when found? Myra hadn't mentioned it and neither had Inspector Holden. Maybe they had both assumed it had become dislodged when he fell in the harbour, but Ryga frowned at that thought as he continued his study of the room.

There was one further picture, that of a man who needed no introduction because he was wearing the uniform of a master in the merchant navy. This was Myra's father. He cut a commanding figure: square, solid, dark-haired and dark-eyed. And in another photograph Ryga could see him with, he assumed, his wife, Myra's mother – a petite, fair woman with solemn eyes that held a hint of fear, or was he seeing something that wasn't there? Perhaps she was mistrustful of the camera.

In the sideboard he found a box of cutlery, a floral-patterned tea set, a few crystal glasses and a bottle of brandy and sherry, which looked to have been there for some years. There was also a folder covered with wallpaper sporting tiny blue flowers and tied together with blue ribbon. In it, Ryga found the deeds to the house, the house insurance policy, the Swinleys' birth certificates along with those of Myra's parents and the latter's death certificates, George and Myra's marriage certificate and, sadly, George's death certificate. There were a few more photographs of the Swinleys' wedding and a couple of Myra as a child but no life insurance policy and no will. He put them back.

Against the wall to the right of the door was an upright piano. It was unlocked. Ryga tinkled a few keys and smiled at the sound. It was well tuned. He'd learned to play in the prison camp, which, surprisingly, had acquired the instrument, brought in, he had subsequently learned, by one of the more kindly German officers, for which they were grateful. They had nearly had to resort to burning it for fuel towards the end of their imprisonment but miraculously hadn't. Ryga wondered what had happened to it.

He'd discovered he had a gift for playing and a musical ear. He couldn't read music but he could quickly pick up a tune. He'd even ventured into classical music, which he found both soothing and stimulating. He attended a few lunchtime concerts in London when his workload permitted but hadn't touched a piano since returning home. There wasn't any room for one in his tiny flat.

The middle parlour was more homely and was obviously where the Swinleys lived. The fire had been made up but had long gone out. The brass fire instruments in their brass container – tongs, brush and poker

– were so shiny that they looked as though they had never been used but lifting the tongs and poker the blackened ends told him they had been. The mantelshelf in this room boasted two ornamental jugs of an oriental colour and style. There was nothing in them. Either side of the ornaments were more brass candlesticks with white candles, only slightly used, put there in case of emergency because the house had electricity. In front of the fire were two easy armchairs, not of such a sturdy a nature as those in the front room. These were made of fabric instead of leather as in the front parlour, and were clean with crisp cream antimacassars on the arms and the head rests.

Beside one of the chairs was a pair of slippers – Myra's – and beside the other chair, straddling the hearth, was a capacious tapestry knitting bag with wooden handles, inside of which he could see a skein of grey wool, a ball of navy-blue wool and some knitting needles. The scarlet patterned rug between the chairs was old and worn but was clean and of excellent quality. Unless he was mistaken it was Persian, perhaps another family heirloom of the late master's.

Finally he turned his attention to the table, the contents of which were of great interest to him and which he had saved studying until last, wanting to form a general impression of Myra first before doing so. There was a ruby-red cloth and on it was a floral-patterned tea pot, milk jug and sugar bowl with only a small amount of sugar in it. There was a tea plate with a knife beside it with the remains of some congealed butter on it, and a small dab of the same on the plate along with some breadcrumbs. Half a small loaf of bread sat on a round orange and yellow flower-patterned bread plate with the breadknife beside it. Ryga opened the tea pot. It was half full of black cold liquid. There were some sludgy dregs of tea in the bottom of the cup.

He committed the scene to memory and continued his tour of the rest of the house, which reinforced the fact that Myra was exceptionally house-proud. All was neat and tidy and in its place. It also revealed that she hadn't removed, and put away in her bedroom, her hat and coat because he couldn't find them, or the little black handbag with the suede trim anywhere. From the bedroom window he could see the allotments, the railway track and landing stages. Also the boats lined up along them both this side of the harbour and across it to the cranes and large ships of Railway Quay and further to the south, East Quay.

There was only one place left to check, in case Myra's body was inside it – the garden shed. Here he found only gardening tools, a work bench with tools, some wood, paint and a bicycle. There was no Anderson shelter and nowhere else in the small neatly tended back garden with its vegetable patch where her body could have been concealed.

As he returned to the pristine kitchen there was a knock on the front door. Before going to open it, Ryga diverted to the front parlour and picked up the photograph of Swinley in police uniform. From the window he could see the lanky PC Jenkins gazing around. Ryga opened the door and, without inviting him in, said, 'Is this a good likeness of PC Swinley?'

'Why yes, sir,' Jenkins replied.

Ryga removed the photograph from the frame, put the picture in the inside pocket of his Macintosh and returned the frame to the parlour. From what he had seen it didn't bode well for Myra Swinley. There were some things that had struck him during his tour of the house but he'd consider them later.

He listened to Jenkins' report as they made their way back up Fort Road.

'Mrs Farrah, the neighbour on the right, saw Mrs Swinley go out on Wednesday and Mrs Duncan on the other side saw her on Tuesday,' Jenkins relayed. 'Neither saw or heard her leave on Thursday or come home that evening. Both neighbours attended the funeral and the wake along with some of Mrs Swinley's friends from the church, St Margaret's in South Road.'

'None of PC Swinley's friends or colleagues attended?'

'No. It was a small gathering, although there was a crowd at the funeral – plenty of us went to that. I couldn't, I was on duty. The neighbours say that Mrs Swinley is a nice party, not overly friendly like, but always pleasant and well-respected, especially for her fundraising and war work.'

'Which was?'

'The Women's Royal Voluntary Service, which she still continues with, and charitable work through the church.'

'Any relatives?'

'None that either women know of and they've never heard her speak of any.'

'Myra said that her husband had a small boat at Sleeper's Hole. Where exactly is that?'

'We call it Mud Hole – it's over there, sir.' He halted and turned back. 'It's further down Fort Road, opposite the recreation ground. You can't miss it or the smell when the tide's out.'

Ryga withdrew the street map Jenkins had given him and right enough saw it marked as 'Sleeper's Hole' with the word 'Mud' underneath it. It was a wide U-shaped indentation in the harbour.

'Do you know the name of Swinley's boat?'

'Can't say I do off-hand. He probably told me but I can't recall it.'

'It doesn't matter. I'll find someone to ask. I'd like to take a look at it.' Not that it would tell him anything about the constable's death or what had happened to Myra, but it might help him to get a deeper picture of George Swinley. 'It's all right, I shan't need you, Constable, you can carry on with your duties. And if you see the milkman on your travels cancel Mrs Swinley's milk for now.'

'Yes, sir.' Jenkins smartly saluted and strode off.

Ryga turned back and set off at a brisk pace towards Sleeper's Hole.

Five

The pungency of the mud reminded him of rotting food and sewage. He could see why local people called the great U-shaped inlet Mud Hole – that was exactly what it was.

Crossing the railway track, he made for the rough path through the brown-green slime where a couple of rotting wooden hulks, and five small boats – two of them upturned – rested. Ahead of him, almost in the centre of the U, was a landing stage jutting out into the harbour, where one medium-sized sailboat was tied up. To the left, northwards, was a small corrugated-iron hut with a tin chimney emitting a dribble of black smoke. Propped in front of it was a rusting man's bicycle, an old pram piled with bits of wood, an upended tin bath and a wooden beer barrel that was being used as a water butt, not for the watering of any plants, Ryga thought, because there were none, but for washing and maybe even for drinking after being boiled. Ryga couldn't see how anyone could be living in the hut, but since the war he'd seen people living in all sorts of accommodation, including redundant war boats, one of which he could see moored further up the harbour, a Motor Torpedo Boat. There were plenty of those on the Thames at Chelsea, converted into makeshift homes.

Which of these small boats was Swinley's? He felt certain it would be in immaculate condition with the timber well-varnished. But the three upright boats tethered to a buoy were in poor condition while the overturned ones looked about to fall to pieces. He took a chance that he wouldn't sink into mud up to his ankles and stepped off the track to further inspect the boats. He was relieved to find the ground surprisingly firm. Swinley's boat had been unused since November, when he had gone missing, so it was possible that rainwater could have gathered, but the wood on these looked as though it hadn't been cared for in years.

'You the man from Scotland Yard?'

Ryga spun round – he hadn't heard anyone approach. Facing him was a stringy little man of about sixty with a weatherworn face and several gaps in his teeth in a wide mouth where a smouldering pipe was clamped in one corner. He was dressed shabbily in an ancient, patched and mended tweed jacket, trousers and well-worn boots. A cloth cap was parked at an angle on his head revealing wisps of grey hair.

'I am. How did you know?'

'No one comes down to the Hole dressed like that.' The man prised the pipe from his mouth and waved it over Ryga's Trilby hat, Macintosh, smart trousers and stout, muddy brogues. 'And it's about time one of you lot showed up,' he added vehemently, replacing the pipe in its customary corner where, Ryga noted, the mouth tilted down as though it had adjusted itself to the appendage over the years.

'Why do you say that?' he asked, curious.

'Because someone needs to find out who killed George Swinley.'

'You think he was murdered?'

'I do, and so do you, otherwise you wouldn't be here.'

'Why would someone want to kill George Swinley, Mr . . .?'

'Moore. Joseph. Don't know. He was a decent sort but I can tell you this: George knew this harbour and the quays like the back of his hand. Foggy, dark, blindfolded, he still wouldn't have fallen in.'

'He could have been taken ill.'

'Ah, he could, but I don't think he was.'

'Why not?'

'Because he always seemed in the best of health.' Joseph Moore sniffed and looked a little sly before adding, 'Maybe he discovered something.'

'Like what?'

'No idea. But being a policeman, he could have seen or heard something that was against the law, and before you ask, no, I don't know what it was, but some folks are always up to mischief.'

'Anyone particular come to mind?'

'No.'

Ryga wasn't sure if that was the truth. Before he could press him though, Joseph Moore continued, 'George should have been a carpenter or shipwright – he was a skilled craftsman and loved building his boat. Then again, maybe it was best he became a copper

39

because there's not much call for carpenters and shipwrights these days, whereas there's always work for policemen.'

'Sadly, yes.'

'Not sad for you. Keeps you in a job. So who called the Yard in? Not Inspector Holden. He'd not want anyone from London tramping round his patch. Besides, the coroner said accidental death.'

'Mrs Swinley doesn't believe it was.'

'I thought as much,' Moore declared triumphantly.

'She spoke to you about it?'

'No, but I could see it in her eyes at the inquest and the funeral.'

Ryga was sceptical about that but he'd give Moore the benefit of doubt. 'You went to the funeral then?'

'Just said I did, didn't I?'

'Yes.'

'The least I could do was to pay my respects. George and I used to have a fair old chat while he worked on his boat. We'd talk about the sea, the ships, his boat, but never about his work. Man's entitled to leave his job behind him and enjoy his leisure is what I say. I live over there.'

He pointed to the corrugated hut with its dribbling smoke chimney.

'Been there since my house copped it in 'forty-two. All went west including the misses. I was on fire watch at the engineering works over at North Quay.'

'Rough luck.'

Moore shrugged his bony shoulders. 'I'm not the only one. Mrs Swinley was kind to me then and has been ever since. We had no kids, me and Molly, just like her and George. She always asks if I'm eating properly and often makes me up a dinner and brings it over to the hut. My cooking facilities being limited, like. She does a lot of charitable work round these parts at St Margaret's.'

'The church?' Ryga asked, recalling that PC Jenkins had mentioned it.

'Yes, in South Road. I saw that look in Myra's eyes when she watched that coffin being lowered in the ground. She wasn't sad, more like puzzled.'

'That's not unusual. Confusion is a natural reaction to losing a loved one.'

'I know, but it wasn't like that,' Moore said firmly. 'It was . . .' He took a breath and sucked on his pipe as he seemed to search for the right words to describe what he meant. 'It was more like she was anxious. It's difficult to describe.'

Ryga still wasn't sure if Moore was simply making this up to appear interesting and mysterious to the 'Man from the Yard.' He thought Moore was probably lonely and still grieving for his wife. But that didn't mean Ryga should dismiss what Moore said. He could have a critical eye and an insightful knowledge of humanity. And Ryga always considered anyone worth listening to in a murder investigation, *if* George's death was murder, and that was looking increasingly more probable. Besides, Moore was correct in his analysis of Myra Swinley's reaction because she had ended up at the Yard.

He said, 'Mrs Swinley is missing.'

Moore's pipe drooped as his mouth fell open. His lined face creased with concern. 'And that's not all that's missing. George's boat has gone.'

It was Ryga's turn to be surprised. His mind raced with this latest news. He didn't like the sound of this but he just couldn't see Myra going off in it. She had said she was a landlubber. Not that it meant she couldn't, and wouldn't, take her late husband's boat out to sea. But why should she? Could she have done so in order to end her life?

'It was here Thursday night,' Moore declared, 'when I left for the pub about seven, and it's not here now. I can't see Myra taking it out, although I suppose it is possible, but George said she was frightened of being on the sea. And, besides, she wouldn't know how to handle it.'

That confirmed it for Ryga. 'Did you see it when you returned from the pub?'

'It was dark. I didn't really notice.'

'Why didn't you report it missing yesterday?'

'Because I didn't know it was. I went out early and got back late Friday and both times it was dark. I had the chance of a day's work over at North Quay so took it. I was dog tired when I got back. I had something to eat, drank a bottle of beer, which I had fetched from the pub on my way home, read the newspaper then went to bed. I only just noticed it was missing this morning, when you showed up, and I'm reporting it now, to you.'

Ryga wondered if any of the other boat owners or the harbour master had noticed it missing. If so, why not report it knowing that its owner was dead? But then, maybe they thought Myra Swinley had organized its removal or sold it. 'Could it have come adrift on high water?'

'No. It was tethered to that buoy.' Moore pointed to where the two upturned boats lay. And the rope's not been cut. It's probably been stolen by some light-fingered blighter who, knowing George was dead and buried, thought they could help themselves.'

Moore could be right. By now it could have been repainted and renamed. Nevertheless, he asked Moore to describe the boat to him and jotted down the details, noting it was a fairly ordinary, small wooden boat, varnished a mahogany brown, with nothing particularly distinctive about it. There were probably several similar along the shore. The name *Sunrise* was painted on its hull in bright yellow. Moore confirmed it had oars and an outboard engine, a Johnson five-horse-powered one, not terribly powerful but still of value to a thief.

As though reading his thoughts, Moore said, 'George used to take the outboard and oars home in a wheelbarrow, especially during the winter, but he died before he could this time and Mrs Swinley probably didn't think to do it.'

'You could have offered to do it for her.'

Moore looked regretful. 'I could and should have.'

Ryga would ask Inspector Holden if his officers could look out for the boat although he didn't hold much hope of finding it. He said, 'If you hear any news of it will you let me know? You can leave a message at the police station.'

Moore promised he would. 'George would have liked a sailboat. He always said that his next project was to build one, but he won't now.'

No, thought Ryga. 'Was this part of George's beat?

'No. His beat stopped further up Fort Road at the junction with Chapel Street. Then he'd head north instead of coming down here, south.'

'So you didn't see him the night he disappeared?'

'No.'

Ryga thought it worth his while talking to the harbour master who might know more about Swinley and his missing boat. He asked where he could locate him.

'That's Peter Hailsham. You'll find him at the Watch House just over there.' Once again, the pipe came out and Ryga followed its direction to a yellow building with a red roof in the northernmost corner of Sleeper's Hole.

He thanked Moore and headed towards it. Removing his hat, he entered the stuffy building where a smouldering coal fire was giving off more smoke than heat. After introducing himself with a show of his warrant card to a man in his mid-twenties, Ryga asked to see the harbour master. A few minutes later a strong-featured man with a heavily lined face, jutting chin and beetling grey eyebrows under a permanently creased forehead appeared from the backroom. Ryga felt it was difficult to put an age on him. He could have been anywhere between forty-five and sixty-five. He was lean and tall but stooped, and his skin was slightly jaundiced, as were the whites of his eyes. He introduced himself with a firm but brief shake of his hand as Peter Hailsham and asked Ryga to follow him outside. Ryga was glad to do so even though the December day seemed intent on chilling him to his bones, despite his hat, coat and scarf. Hailsham offered Ryga a cigarette, which he refused.

'When was the last time you saw Constable Swinley?' Ryga began.

'The Monday before he went missing,' Hailsham answered, discarding the match and drawing on his cigarette. Ryga noted his heavily nicotine stained fingers.

'He was on duty?'

'No, this was just after one o'clock. He was going down to work on his boat.'

'How did he seem?'

'Same as usual.'

'Which was?'

'Chatty, pleasant. We talked about the weather, the boat movements, the things people find washed up on West Beach.'

'Why the latter?' asked Ryga, wondering if it was of significance but not seeing how it could be.

'It's always a topic of interest around these parts. Sometimes its explosives, sometimes bits of cargo, other times it's what's left of some poor soul who took his life. You've no doubt had a few of them in the Thames.'

Ryga said that sadly he had.

Hailsham continued, 'That's what might have happened to the owner of that.'

He pointed to the Motor Torpedo Boat, which Ryga had noticed earlier from Myra's window. It had been stripped of its weaponry and from the outside looked to have been skilfully converted into a home.

'It was found drifting in the English Channel four weeks ago tomorrow, on the twelfth of November,' Hailsham said. 'The captain on one of the cargo ships spotted her and the coastguard and customs launch brought her back here, to Newhaven. It's not registered here, or at any of the ports on the south coast, but she could have come from further afield, or even from France. She's a lovely craft. I've been on board. She's been beautifully refitted and cared for, but there's nothing to tell us who the owner is. No logbook or papers. No suicide letter either but then maybe the owner didn't feel like writing one, or had no one left to tell,' Hailsham added a little mournfully. Ryga saw the sadness in his eyes and wondered, if Hailsham, like many, had lost loved ones in the war.

Hailsham coughed chestily before continuing, 'Still, you're not here to talk about that but about Swinley. Personally, despite what the coroner said, I can't see George losing his footing.'

'The fog was pretty thick.' Like Thursday night, thought Ryga, when Myra had vanished.

Hailsham sucked on his cigarette.

'When did you last see George's boat, *Sunrise*?'

'A couple of days ago. Why?' Hailsham looked perplexed.

'It's missing.'

'Who told you that?'

'Joseph Moore.'

'Then he should know.' He gazed southwards, frowning in thought, almost as though he was looking for *Sunrise*. 'It was there Thursday morning,' he said after a moment. 'But I can't swear to seeing it after that. Someone must have stolen it.'

'That's what Moore thinks. Any idea who?'

'A few scoundrels spring to mind. I'll pass their names on to the beat constable. They might have taken it further up the harbour into the River Ouse. Whoever took it might have done so just for the engine, which they can sell, but they'd be fools to try and do so around these parts – word would soon get around. They could have taken the boat out of the harbour though, perhaps along Seaford Bay, and put in somewhere there. The lighthouse staff at the end of East Pier might have spotted it. I'll ask them.' He sounded dubious though, and Ryga also thought it unlikely that they would have seen such a small boat in the bad weather.

Hailsham flicked his cigarette on the ground and stubbed it out with his shoe.

'Did you attend Constable Swinley's funeral and the wake?' asked Ryga.

'Only the funeral.' Hailsham looked puzzled. 'Why all the questions, Inspector? I told Inspector Holden and the coroner everything I know, which is nothing. I didn't see George the night he vanished and I have no idea how he ended up wedged by the gridiron over at Railway Quay.' He jerked his head northwards. He took another cigarette from the packet but didn't light it. Ryga noted his shaking hands. 'Has new information come to light?'

'Mrs Swinley has doubts about the manner of her husband's death.'

Hailsham raised his eyebrows as if to say, *And that brought Scotland Yard running.*

'And she's missing.'

Hailsham's eyes widened with surprise, then narrowed. He ran a hand over his chin and frowned. 'I see,' he said slowly. Ryga could see him mentally trying to join up the dots.

'We're concerned for her safety.'

'And you don't think she's gone off and done herself in, otherwise you wouldn't be here. Holden would be on the case.'

'I'm assisting the local police.'

'More like they're assisting you.'

'When did you last see Mrs Swinley?' Ryga asked.

'At the funeral a week ago.'

'And she said nothing to you about her husband's death or mentioned anything that now with hindsight seems curious?'

'No.'

A voice hailed Hailsham. It was the man from his office. 'You're wanted on the telephone.'

He threw Ryga an apologetic glance. 'I'll let you know if I pick up any information about *Sunrise.*'

Ryga watched him hurry away and then consulted his street map. He thought he might get some information about Myra from the vicar, who was also the last person to see PC Swinley before he disappeared on the 7 November.

Six

St Margaret's Church, with a modest spire, was set back off the road behind a concrete forecourt surrounded by a small brick wall which looked as though it had once sported iron railings, no doubt removed and melted down to build spitfires or some such thing connected with the war. To the right of the church was a single-storey building whose brickwork above the solid-looking closed doors proclaimed it was the church hall erected in 1848, while to the left of the church was a detached bay-windowed house set slightly back from the road, which, Ryga saw from the weathered wooden sign in front of it, was the vicarage.

Removing his hat, Ryga entered the dimly lit, cheerless cavern of the church. It felt colder inside than out. In the pulpit was a sparrow-like man in his fifties with sparse grey hair whose lips were moving soundlessly and whose small eyes were focused on the book in front of him. Under his thick, handknitted grey pullover, Ryga saw the clerical collar. Perhaps he was practising his sermon for tomorrow, or simply reading transcripts from the Bible to comfort himself. Maybe he was praying.

Ryga coughed. The vicar gave a startled cry. His pale face flushed and his little eyes darted nervously over Ryga and then beyond him as though he expected hordes of other people to suddenly materialize.

'I apologize for startling you, and interrupting, Vicar. I'm Detective Inspector Ryga from New Scotland Yard. I wondered if you could spare me a few minutes of your time, sir.'

The vicar looked even more alarmed, but he muttered, 'Of course,' and scrambled down from the pulpit running a hand over his grey hair, the same hand which he then limply and briefly offered to Ryga. It was also damp. He introduced himself as the Reverend Isaacs.

'I'd like to talk to you about George and Myra Swinley,' Ryga began, causing the vicar even more stroking of his hair. At this rate

Ryga thought he might soon be bald.

'I don't know that I should—'

'Of course you should, Herbert. Inspector Ryga hasn't come all the way from London for his health.' The sharp voice from behind Ryga made him jump. He spun round to find a small woman in her late forties with short black hair glaring at the vicar with fiery brown eyes. Ryga hadn't heard a sound and he hadn't seen anyone praying in the pews. She seemed to have sprung from nowhere.

'I'm Mrs Joan Isaacs,' she crisply introduced herself. 'That is my husband.'

Ryga almost expected her to add more's the pity.

She was dressed neatly in a fitted navy-blue winter coat, blue gloves, sturdy lace-up shoes but no hat. Ryga thought she would have been an attractive woman if not for her sour expression and the way her mouth had a tendency to turn down.

'But I can't see how we can help you, Inspector, seeing as Police Constable Swinley fell into the harbour after having some kind of blackout and drowned,' she added.

'Did he?'

'That's what the coroner said,' she smartly rejoined, clearly by her tone expecting no dissent.

It wasn't quite what the coroner had said, or so Ryga had been informed, but then he hadn't read the full report yet. He said, 'Nevertheless, there are questions that I would like to ask you and your husband, Mrs Isaacs.'

By now the Reverend Isaacs was looking so nervous that Ryga thought he might start quivering. His lips were moving, as though inflicted by some kind of tic, but no sound emanated from them and he dashed fearful glances at his formidable wife. Ryga had met his type before, a man dominated by a strong woman who had disappointed that woman by not living up to her expectations, which, by now, she realized he never would.

'Oh, very well. You'd better come to the rectory,' she said reluctantly, as though Ryga were a vagrant and not a detective. Perhaps she classed them as one of the same.

He followed them to the double-fronted house where shrubs and even grass in the small square of a limp garden seemed to have abandoned the will to live. Inside, the house was as cold and soulless as the church and it was all he could do to repress a shiver, which became even more difficult when he was shown into an ice-cold front parlour with an empty hearth swept clean and without a trace of coal in sight. Ryga doubted a fire had been lit in here for years. He wasn't offered any refreshment, which was just as well because he would have refused. He wanted this interview over with quickly before frostbite set in! Despite his Macintosh and scarf, the cold seemed to pierce him to the bone. He'd known the same kind of cold in the prisoner-of-war camp. It was more than physical – it seemed to come from within.

It struck him that perhaps Joan Isaacs had invited him here so that he would quickly terminate the interview. She didn't remove her coat but waved her gloved hand at a chair. It was hard and cold, like the woman in front of him. The Reverend Isaacs perched on one opposite, after his wife had sat on a hard, straight-backed chair close by. The room was clogged with heavy, old-fashioned furniture that seemed to have been placed haphazardly without any regard to practicality or comfort. It was as though the occupants might just have moved in, or used the room for storing lumber, and perhaps that's what the Isaacs did because the room smelt of damp and decay and had that dry-rotten odour of neglected and shuttered houses.

'How well did you know Constable Swinley?' Ryga began.

'He was the beat constable,' Joan Isaacs answered tersely.

That wasn't what Ryga had asked but he let it go for now. He addressed the vicar. 'Was he a member of your congregation?'

His wife answered for him. 'Not him,' she said scornfully.

Clearly she had disliked the constable, but then Ryga thought she probably disliked everybody. 'You mean he belonged to another faith?' he asked. Maybe the cause of her derision was that Swinley had been a Roman Catholic and not Anglican. 'Reverend?'

Isaacs ran his hand over his head. 'He might have done.'

'Of course he didn't, Herbert. He was an atheist.'

'We don't know that for—'

'Yes, we do. He didn't come to church and he said that it was impossible to believe in God after six years of war. I told him that God had seen fit to spare him and he laughed.'

I expect he did. Probably with bitterness. Still, Ryga wasn't here to discuss theological matters. 'Mrs Swinley worships here though.'

Again, Joan Isaacs answered. 'Yes.'

'Did she confide in either of you about her concerns over her husband's death?'

'Of course not,' Joan Isaacs declared, as if Ryga had suggested something obscene.

'And you, Vicar?'

'She was upset, naturally, and couldn't understand how he had come to fall in the harbour, which he knew so well. But these—'

'Is she saying there is something suspicious about his death?' Mrs Isaacs sharply cut in. Her lips pursed hard together and she frowned at Ryga.

'When did you last see PC Swinley?' Ryga asked quietly and politely, his glance flicking over them both. He could see that Joan Isaacs didn't like not having her question answered. He already knew that Isaacs had seen Swinley on the night of his disappearance but he saw no harm in asking the question.

The vicar managed to speak before his wife could. 'The night he went missing. I was shutting up the church hall after the Girl Guides had left. It was just on nine o'clock. He was walking his beat. We exchanged a few words about the weather – the fog was getting worse, coming off the river, and it was dark. We spoke for no more than a couple of minutes.'

'The coroner was told all of this, which you'd know if you'd read the report,' Joan Isaacs said accusingly.

'Was there anyone else about?' Ryga continued to address the vicar.

'No. As I said, it was a foul night. The foghorns in the channel were blasting every few minutes. It was getting so that you could hardly see a step in front of you.'

'In which direction did he walk?'

'Southwards.'

'And when did you last see PC Swinley, Mrs Isaacs?'

'I really couldn't say. I'm not in the habit of looking out of the window every five minutes to see who is passing, and I am not one to gossip, unlike some in this town.'

'Was there any gossip about PC Swinley?'

Surprisingly Joan Isaacs flushed. Did that mean there had been something between her and the police constable? Had Swinley become involved with the vicar's wife? No, Ryga just couldn't see anyone setting their cap at Joan Isaacs. From what Ryga had heard, Swinley had been steady, reliable and meticulous and that, to his mind, didn't fit with a man having an affair.

The vicar answered, 'PC Swinley was greatly respected.'

By her expression Mrs Isaacs looked set to differ but she remained silent. Her back was ramrod stiff and her hands folded tightly on her lap. Outside, the sound of children playing and a car struggling to start came to him. A clock in the icy parlour chimed one.

Joan Isaacs made to move, 'If that is all, Inspector—'

'You didn't tell me when you last saw PC Swinley, Mrs Isaacs?'

'I really can't remember. And I can't see that it matters now he's dead and the coroner's verdict given. It was probably some time when he was on his beat.'

'And when did either of you last see Mrs Swinley?'

The vicar looked confused while Mrs Isaacs scowled at the question. She recovered first. 'Why do you want to know that?'

'If you could just answer the question, please.' Ryga didn't waste a smile on her. It wouldn't have softened her. He didn't think anything would. Her husband answered first.

'I saw her on Wednesday. She helps to run a coffee morning in the church hall for the elderly.' The vicar fidgeted nervously. His grey eyes beseeched his wife to hold her vicious tongue.

'And how did she seem?'

'Quiet, but then she is a quiet lady. She looked tired,' he rapidly continued. 'But I shouldn't think she has been sleeping well. She and PC Swinley were a happily married couple. She'll miss him.'

Ryga thought that the vicar might hang out the flags if his domineering wife departed this world. Or perhaps not. Perhaps he would go to pieces. Perhaps he needed someone like Joan Isaacs to look after him.

'And you, Mrs Isaacs – when did you last see Mrs Swinley?'

'The same day, Wednesday, at the coffee morning.'

The vicar dashed a fearful look at his wife. The man clearly lived in dread of her.

'Is Mrs Swinley close to anyone?'

'Ask her yourself,' Joan Isaacs quipped. 'Now, we've got work to do.' She rose.

'So have I, Mrs Isaacs, and at the moment that work involves finding Mrs Swinley.'

'Pardon?' The Reverend Isaacs blinked and smoothed down his hair jerkily.

'Mrs Swinley is not at home and no one knows where she is. We are anxious to find her.'

Joan Isaacs resumed her seat and studied Ryga sceptically through narrowing eyes, as though he was setting them a trap. 'She's missing?'

'It appears so. Is there anyone she might have gone to visit?'

'I know she hasn't any relatives,' the vicar answered, troubled. 'PC Swinley has a sister but she lives in Canada. She married a Canadian stationed here during the war.' He plucked at his lower lip. 'You could talk to members on the local fundraising committee. Mrs Swinley might have told one of them where she was going. She's the chairwoman. In fact, she instigated it during the war when people needed help after being bombed out. We pooled clothes, furniture and everyday essentials. The women knitted for civilians, service personnel and merchant seaman. Mrs Swinley, and the committee, run jumble sales. We had one last Saturday. You see we've continued with the work since the war because, sadly, the hardships haven't ended. In fact, some people are even worse off now than they were then.'

Joan Isaacs sniffed, which to Ryga meant that she disagreed with her husband. But then she seemed to on every count.

The vicar continued, 'Mrs Swinley has a natural flair for organizing things.'

'Bossy, you mean,' Joan Isaacs chipped in, which, Ryga thought, was a bit like the kettle calling the pot black.

'She is enormously energetic,' the vicar added, throwing a pleading look at his wife. Ryga didn't think she would take any notice of it.

'You officiated over the burial of the constable, Vicar?'

'Yes.'

'And did you go back to the house for the wake?'

'Of course. It is expected.' He threw an apologetic glance at his wife.

'Did you attend the funeral, Mrs Isaacs?'

'No.'

'Why not?' Ryga asked curiously and without hostility. He'd have thought it was part of the vicar's wife's duty.

'There were enough of the committee going. I saw no need to add to their numbers.'

From her hard glare Ryga could see she would make no further comment, and he didn't think it necessary to probe her for more. It was clear from her manner that she disliked Mrs Swinley, possibly out of jealousy, not because there was something between her husband and the widow, but that she resented the fact that the Swinleys had been happily married, and had seemed comfortably off with a house of their own and a small boat. PC Swinley would have had a generous salary and pension, a proportion of which Myra would benefit from – *if* she were still alive, Ryga added silently to himself. He didn't know the Isaacs financial situation, but from what he saw of them, and this house, he didn't think the stipend was a lucrative one.

He asked for details of the women on the fundraising committee, jotting down the names and addresses as the vicar relayed them to him. He rose and noted the relief on both their faces. The feeling was mutual. He was glad to leave the cold, forbidding house and the depressing couple. He didn't think the vicar's sermons would be a bundle of laughs. He would interview members of the fundraising committee on another day, if needed, or request that Inspector Holden detail his officers to do so. He was almost certain none of them would know where Myra had gone because he was growing ever more convinced that she had been abducted. However, she might have confided more about her concerns over her husband's death to one of them. And maybe Eva would pick up something from the gossip. He wondered how she was getting on.

He set off down South Street, in the same direction Swinley had taken. At the junction with Chapel Street and Fort Road he halted. Across from him was a narrow alleyway squeezed between a block of four terraced houses on the northern side, facing out into the street, and a small works of some kind on the south behind stout closed wooden doors and surrounded by a high brick wall. There was a streetlight at the entrance of the alley.

From the street map, which he consulted, he could see that it was only a short passage that came out on to the goods train railway track and the harbour. Ryga struck out along it and found himself facing the landing stages with a handful of fishing boats strewn out along it, and across the water, according to his map, was Railway Quays. There were no lights here and neither had there been any along the alleyway. If Swinley had come this way then surely he would have used his torch, and if so it wouldn't have been in his pocket when his body had been found.

For a moment he hesitated over what to do next. Head back to the police station and check out the reports he'd asked Inspector Holden to obtain for him, or view where PC Swinley's body had been found? The gridiron was marked on the street map – always assuming it was the one where the constable's body had ended up – but he couldn't see any other gridiron marked, so he guessed it had to be. He was curious to see it. Not that it would reveal anything. And, despite what Inspector Holden had told him about Sergeant Keaton of the British Transport Commission Police not being in his office on a Saturday, he thought he might as well see if he was while he was that side of the harbour.

He tucked the map away and strode up Chapel Street, taking in the small neat houses either side and the chapel the street was named after, wondering if Swinley had ever got this far on that fateful night. Soon he was at the junction with Dacre Road and could have turned left to return to the police station, but he'd already decided what to do. He continued northwards until he reached Bridge Street where, before crossing the swing bridge to the other side of the harbour, he stopped off to buy some fish and chips. Perched on a high stool facing the window, he ate them while listening to the customers come and go, placing their orders and talking about the weather, Christmas and the rationing, and how you'd never thought we'd have won the war. Nothing was said about PC Swinley's death – that was old news. And the news of Mrs Swinley's disappearance hadn't yet permeated the town's gossip. Soon, though, he knew it would.

Seven

It was two hours off high water. There was little to see at Railway Quays save rusting iron girders, seaweed and seagull droppings. At one time boats had rested here while their hulls were scrubbed. The quay was quieter than usual, it being Saturday afternoon. The cranes had ceased working for the weekend – it was after one o'clock and there were no vessels moored up here, although he'd seen a coaster at North Quay as he'd crossed the swing bridge. At the gatehouse he'd shown his identity to the police officer on duty, who had informed him, contrary to Inspector Holden's information, that Sergeant Keaton was in his office, which was just behind the harbour railway station, close to the Customs House. He had offered to telephone through to the sergeant but Ryga said not to disturb him, he'd find his own way there and to the gridiron.

Turning up his collar against a cold, drizzling rain, which was now sweeping in off the sea, he made his way south along Railway Quay, walking alongside the railway track that carried the goods trains. The transport police office was easy to find. Pushing at the door, he stepped into a steamy, warm office where a uniformed man in his early forties, with slightly bucked teeth and a deep, hollow scar at the corner of his right eye running down to the end of his nose, looked up from a paper-strewn desk.

Ryga introduced himself and said he was there to make enquiries about PC Swinley, which drew a quizzical look but no questions. Instead, Ryga was offered a seat and a cup of tea, both of which he accepted with alacrity. The fish and chips had made him thirsty and he needed something to warm him up. As Sergeant Keaton made tea in the corner of the office, he explained the origin of his scar, not that Ryga had asked or even stared at it, but Keaton either thought he needed to break the ice or it had become a reflex action, saving people the trouble of asking him.

'I'd only been in the RAF six months when the airfield was bombed,' he said, warming the earthenware teapot. He tossed the water into a small tin basin and spooned the tea leaves into the pot. Ryga thought the kettle must be permanently on the boil given the moist atmosphere.

'I was at Biggin Hill on 30 August 1940 when they came over. Couldn't get to the bunker on time. Woke up in a lunatic asylum. Sugar?'

'No, thank you.'

'Just as well because it appears I'm out of it,' he said, peering into a tin.

And it was still on ration, as one of the fish and chip shop customers had bemoaned.

'It's where I met my wife, Irene. She wasn't an inmate but a nurse.' He grinned. 'There was nothing wrong with me, of course. But they wouldn't take me back in the air force.'

Ryga just hoped Keaton wouldn't ask him what he had done in the war. He hated talking about it, the questions, the sympathetic nods, and most of all he loathed that smug look that said you were well out of it.

'So I returned to being a police constable at Tilbury Docks, where I'd started out. I saw plenty of action there.' He pulled a wry face. Ryga knew he was referring to the intense bombing. 'When the docks and railways were nationalized just over two years ago and we all came under the British Transport Commission Police, I transferred here on promotion. Irene comes from the area. But you didn't come here to talk about the war, Inspector, or my police career,' Keaton continued, as he stirred the pot and sat down. 'You're here about George Swinley. He was a decent man – we both liked an occasional drink at The Hope Inn, down by West Pier. And we both liked boats. I go out fishing on mine, but George hated fishing. He'd go out to sea, mainly round Seaford Bay, for the fun of it. Did you know he built his boat? I bought mine off Ivor Tuckett, long since passed on.'

'Where do you keep it?'

'On the other side of the harbour, just off South Road, not far from the swing bridge.'

'And you live in Newhaven?'

'Meeching Road.'

And that was close to the police station if Ryga remembered correctly from studying the map earlier. 'What was George Swinley like?' he asked.

Keaton poured the tea into two tin mugs. 'Steady, reliable, competent. He should have made sergeant years ago but he wasn't ambitious. He liked being on the beat and said he had no intention of sitting in an office shuffling paperwork around the desk. He had a point. It's why I'm working on a Saturday afternoon, trying to catch up.' Keaton waved an arm at his desk. 'But then I expect you have your fair share of it.'

'I do. Were you puzzled when you heard he was missing?'

'I didn't hear it until two days after he went missing, and that was from Joseph Moore in The Hope. He said the police had been asking if anyone had seen George on the night of the seventh of November. I called on Inspector Holden, got all the details and said I would ask my men.'

'Holden didn't instigate enquiries before then around the docks?' Ryga asked, surprised.

'No, but then he didn't have any reason to think that George had come this side of the harbour and he wouldn't have done. It's not his beat. His body ended up here but it doesn't mean he fell in here.'

'I know,' Ryga said. Keaton had echoed his earlier thoughts.

Keaton sipped his tea. His expression was serious as he continued, 'When PC Whitten came running in here three weeks ago to say two boys had found a body by the gridiron I never for one moment thought it would be George, not so that you'd have recognized him by then, save for his uniform.'

Ryga nodded solemnly and drank his tea. It could have been stronger but it was wet, warm and welcome.

'We fished him out, not a pleasant task, or an easy one, as you probably well know. I telephoned to Inspector Holden and he came over in the car. The ambulance was called to take the body to the mortuary.' He shifted and narrowed his eyes. 'Now you being here means there must be more to George's death than it being an accident.'

'Do you think he slipped and fell, perhaps from a landing stage on the other side of the harbour?'

Keaton rubbed at his scar. 'The wood would have been slippery with the wet and maybe he heard something, or saw something, that made him curious or suspicious, went to investigate and lost his footing, but it wouldn't have been like him.'

Everybody was saying the same. It made Ryga wonder why the coroner had brought in a verdict of accidental death. But then there were those headaches. 'Any idea what might have made him investigate the harbour further?'

Keaton shook his head. 'There was nothing untoward going on this side of the harbour that night.'

'Did he mention his headaches to you?'

'Only once when we swapped war stories, and I can tell you that didn't take us long. I told him how I got the scar and he told me about how he'd been wounded at Cassino and left with bad headaches. We both ended up in a mental hospital. Then we just got talking about boats and the sea. It was suggested at the inquest that he could have suffered a blackout. I've never known him to have one but that doesn't mean that he didn't.'

'Did you discuss, or liaise, over police matters?' Ryga knew from his own experience of working with the dock police in London that they must have done.

'Yes. If one of my officers caught a local man pilfering from the docks – and I don't mean just the occasional piece of fruit, which, as you probably know, we turn a blind eye to, I mean more expensive cargo. That generally happens at North Quay where most of the main and more valuable cargo comes in. Or if we caught someone trespassing on the railway, drunk and staggering to God alone knows where then we'd liaise with the local police to secure a prosecution. The daft blighters are lucky to be alive, although not all of them make it. Sometimes it's deliberate – we've had our fair share of suicides along the line from Lewes to Seaford. I have a rail officer policing the stretch, PC Grant, but there's eight miles of track, and that's quite an area to cover.'

Ryga agreed it was. He asked if the swing bridge had opened on the night George went missing.

'Yes, as it usually does at slack water, an hour before and an hour after high water, when the tide's not so strong and the water depth is at its maximum.'

Ryga knew what it meant but made no comment. He said, 'Which was at what time?'

Keaton consulted a chart on his wall. 'Twelve twenty-two a.m. on the night of the seventh of November and two twenty-two a.m. the following morning.'

'It didn't open any other time that night?'

'No. Hold on, yes, it did, at nine fifty-eight.'

That was close to the time of the last sighting of Swinley by the vicar at nine o'clock. 'Did any of the men operating the capstone on the bridge see PC Swinley?' Ryga asked.

'I don't know. I doubt it because no one's mentioned it to me or anyone else and it didn't come up at the inquest.'

'Did anyone cross just before or after that time?'

'There were probably a couple of cars, maybe a lorry or two. I wouldn't expect there were any pedestrians at that time of night and in that fog.'

'But no one has checked?'

'I wasn't asked to,' Keaton said, a little perturbed.

'I'd be grateful if you could ask the men who were working on the bridge that night if any vehicles crossed, round about that time, and if they can remember the registration numbers or a description. Also if anyone went over on foot in either direction. I shouldn't think it has any connection with PC Swinley's death,' Ryga quickly added, 'but I would like to check.'

'Of course.'

Ryga sipped his tea and broached an idea that had occurred to him on the way there. 'I saw the rail track on the bridge. Did a train cross that night?'

'I'm assuming so. There's a goods train that runs at nine fifty-five p.m. from the tracks and sidings at North Quay down to engine sheds near the marine workshops, across the bridge to West Quay, and then all the way down to the West Beach and out to the end of the harbour breakwater. It returns at ten thirty. If the bridge is open to let a ship through then it just has to wait like the rest of us.'

'So on the night PC Swinley disappeared, the seventh of November, the train would have had to wait until the bridge closed again after nine fifty-eight and that could have been another half an hour on?'

'It probably got over just before it opened. No one would have been able to get on board though. That's what you're thinking, isn't it?'

Ryga admitted it was. And that if someone had pushed Swinley into the harbour they might have crossed to this side of the harbour after doing so, or before the act, either on foot, by vehicle or by jumping on the train.

Keaton, with a worried frown, said, 'If it wasn't an accident but foul play, I can't think who would want to kill him. What has alerted the Yard to the fact it could be murder?'

'Mrs Swinley came to see us.'

'Really?' He again rubbed at his scar. 'She's got evidence that someone could have killed her husband?'

'She has serious concerns. Did she mention them to you?'

'No, but then I don't know her. I attended the funeral and passed on my condolences. My wife's spoken to her a couple of times but only to say good morning and pass the time of day while shopping.'

'Did George ever talk about his marriage?'

Keaton looked at him shocked. 'God, no, why should he?'

'They were happily married?'

'I guess so. Like I say, Inspector, we didn't talk about those kind of things.'

Ryga nodded as if to say of course and swallowed some tea.

Keaton said, 'Can I ask what concerns Mrs Swinley has? They must be quite strong to have brought Scotland Yard here.'

'The fact that his notebook and pencil were missing and that his tunic pocket was fastened when the body was found. Swinley's habit, like many police officers, was not to button up his tunic pocket until the notebook was safely put away.'

'You're right, I'm the same. Maybe he did it without thinking because he was distracted by a sound,' Keaton said dubiously. 'But that can't be all that's brought you here?'

'There's been a further development. Mrs Swinley is missing, as is her late husband's boat, and we don't believe she has gone off in it, or elsewhere, of her own free will.'

Ryga noted Keaton's genuine astonishment then bewilderment. He again rubbed at his scar and frowned. 'This all sounds fantastical. George was just an ordinary PC, why would anyone want to kill him and kidnap his wife? That is what you're inferring, isn't it?'

'It is and I don't have any answers, which is why I am here seeking them. When did you last see PC Swinley?'

'On the Saturday before he went missing but he didn't see me. I was here doing the paperwork – it's getting to be something of a habit, which I'll try to break – I'd popped out for a breath of air. It was just after two o'clock and I saw him at the harbour station, which was surprising because I hadn't seen him there before. Newhaven residents usually catch the train at the town station.'

Keaton was right. The harbour station, this side of the water, was a long way from Swinley's house, whereas the town station, which wasn't far from the swing bridge, was much closer. 'Was he catching a train or waiting to meet someone?' Ryga asked.

'I don't know. I didn't speak to him or wait to see. I headed down to the water for a bit of air.'

'But there would have been a train due?'

'Yes, the two fifteen to Seaford. He wasn't on duty, or at least, he wasn't in uniform.'

'What was he wearing?'

'A brown tweed overcoat and soft felt hat.'

Ryga had seen them hanging in the hall.

'You could ask Mr Dakins, he's a customs officer. He was on the platform at the same time. He was probably just going off duty. George Swinley might have spoken with him.'

Ryga said he would.

Keaton said, 'And you say George's boat is missing. Someone could have stolen it.'

'They could have done. Would you ask your officers to keep a look out for it along this side of the harbour?'

'Of course.' Keaton's expression darkened. 'If it's been stolen it's probably been given a new lick of paint and renamed, unless . . .'

'Yes, unless.' Neither man needed to spell out their thoughts. Myra could have been taken out in it, her body dumped in the sea and the boat scuttled out in Seaford Bay.

Ryga drained his mug and rose. He thanked Keaton for his help and made his way to the harbour station where he sought out the stationmaster. Half an hour later – after consulting the booking office clerk and his record of ticket issues – it was confirmed that a return ticket to Seaford had been issued on Saturday 4 November at two o'clock, which coincided with the two-fifteen train. Neither the stationmaster nor the booking office clerk knew PC Swinley but, Ryga, on showing the photograph of Swinley, got confirmation from the booking office clerk that Swinley had purchased the ticket – he wasn't one of their regulars and besides they didn't get many people travelling from there to Seaford, usually more in the opposite direction to Lewes or Victoria, especially those who got off the steamer in the summer from Dieppe to Newhaven. Ryga also got confirmation from the porter that Swinley had returned on the four fifty-five. Nothing suspicious about that. Perhaps the constable had just fancied a breath of sea air along Seaford Bay. But why not catch the train closer to home?

There was one reason, Ryga considered as he walked briskly back to the police station in the rain and gathering gloom – because Swinley had wanted as few people as possible to know where he was going. Now why was that?

Eight

'I've put all the reports you requested on your desk, sir,' Sergeant Williams announced after introducing himself. He was in his early fifties, a burly man with a jovial round creased up face and a slightly florid complexion. 'Inspector Holden has left for home. I'll show you to your office. It's not much, but—'

'It'll do fine,' Ryga quickly answered, following the bulky figure of Williams down a gloomy hall to the room at the back. It was two doors down from Inspector Holden's with a toilet between them and a window giving on to a tiny backyard. But Ryga wasn't here for the view – he'd spend little time in it anyway, or so he hoped. The room smelt of disinfectant and cigarette smoke. It felt clammily cold.

'Does that thing work?' Ryga indicated the gas fire which looked as though it had been installed in the station the same time it had been built probably around the turn of the century.

'Yes, sir.'

'Then light it for me, Sergeant.'

Williams obliged with a match while Ryga divested himself of his coat which he hung up, along with his hat and scarf, on the hook on the back of the door. Soon the little fire was hissing and popping.

Straightening up from the fire, Williams said, 'We usually use this room for interviewing suspects, sir, but Inspector Holden asked me to kit it out for you. I brought your case in here, sir.'

Ryga had already seen it beside the desk.

'I hope you have everything you need.'

On the wooden table that was to serve as his desk there were two letter trays, a neat row of sharpened pencils, along with a rubber, some blotting paper, foolscap-lined notepaper, a buff-coloured folder and a telephone.

'A chair the other side of the table would be helpful,' Ryga answered, taking the seat behind it with his back to the grimy

62

window.

Williams quickly returned with one and placed it carefully on the wooden floorboards in front of the desk as though he was afraid of disturbing Ryga. Ryga got the impression that everything Williams did was executed very carefully. The sergeant made to leave but Ryga forestalled him.

'Have you got a moment to spare, Sergeant?'

Williams looked surprised, probably at being asked so politely, Ryga guessed.

'Of course, sir. PC Charters can man the desk for a while.'

'Sit down.'

Williams looked even more surprised and a little uneasy as if he was about to be interviewed as a suspect.

'It's all right, Sergeant,' Ryga smiled. 'I only want information.'

Williams relaxed and returned the smile. 'Then I'll do my best to supply it, sir.'

Ryga started by asking how well he had known George Swinley.

'As well as I know any colleague,' came the cautious answer. 'We didn't socialize, sir. Not because we didn't want to, but George wasn't a man for the pub or darts.'

'I understand from Sergeant Keaton that George liked to drink in The Hope Inn.'

'Well, yes, on occasions, as do we all, but he wasn't a regular drinker and neither am I,' he quickly added, as though afraid Ryga would get the wrong impression of him. 'I prefer my own home and so did George, except for his boat.'

'Which is missing.'

Williams looked astonished and mystified.

'Is Joseph Moore reliable?'

'I'd say he was.'

'He reported it missing to me this morning. The harbour master, Mr Hailsham, doesn't recall seeing it going out of the harbour or for that matter travelling up it, but it was probably taken in the dark and it's small, therefore not easily noticed. I'd like your officers to keep an eye out for it and to ask if anyone has seen it since Thursday. It seems to have gone missing the same time as Myra Swinley.'

Williams looked concerned.

'I've spoken to the vicar who says he saw Swinley the night of his disappearance at just on nine o'clock.'

'That's right. Reverend Isaacs came into the station early on Wednesday morning, the day after PC Swinley went missing, to report he'd seen him the night before. He was very distressed. You see, by then word had got around. Mrs Swinley, obviously upset and worried, had asked the milkman to look out for her husband on his rounds. She feared he could be lying ill somewhere. We all know that telling Stan, the milkman, is better than announcing anything on the wireless. It helped us because we could then conduct a house-to-house on the rest of PC Swinley's beat, but no one had seen him, which wasn't surprising really because, by then, the fog was thick and it was bitingly cold so everyone was indoors.'

Ryga spread out the map of the town. 'Talk me through his beat from first coming on duty.'

'He came on parade with PCs Allot and Breaton at two p.m.'

'Was it foggy then?' Ryga interjected.

'It was beginning to come in and it got dark early that day because of it. By four o'clock it was like night. I checked the constables had their equipment on them in good order: gloves, truncheon, whistle, notebook, and I read them the reports of what they needed to be on the lookout for.'

'Which was?'

'Can I refer to my notes?'

'By all means.'

He removed his notebook from his top tunic pocket, leaving the button undone, and thumbed through it. 'A stolen lorry from Courtney's, a robbery at Milchesters, and a missing woman who could have been heading for here.'

'Why here?'

'She originally came from Newhaven. She was last seen at Brighton where she worked in a tearoom. Parents killed in the Blitz. Nothing in her belongings at her lodging house to say she'd met anyone or where she'd gone. But she could have got friendly with one of the customers and arranged to go off with him, or she got homesick and decided to return here.'

'Without taking her things with her?'

'Maybe she thought she was just going out for the day but this man had other ideas.'

'Her name?'

'June Abbott, aged seventeen.'

'Did she or her parents have any connection with the Swinleys?'

'No.'

'Go on.'

'The officers then went off on their beats. They come back in at six o'clock for half an hour to eat. We don't have a canteen, it being a small station, so they bring flasks of soup and sandwiches. PC Swinley came in as usual. Nothing was amiss, just a minor road collision. I expected him back at ten p.m., but he never came.'

'Where would he have gone after seeing the vicar in South Road?'

'He'd have headed south down towards the junction of Fort Road and Chapel Street.'

Which Ryga had done earlier. 'There's a passageway there that leads to the harbour with a works one side and four terraced houses the other.'

'That's right, sir. The works closed down six years ago and no one's taken up the premises since. PC Swinley would have checked the gates facing on to the street and those facing the harbour to make sure they were secure. We've never had any trouble there.'

'Were the occupants of the houses adjoining the alleyway on the opposite side questioned?'

'They were. No one saw or heard anything unusual, and we searched the harbour and the railway track there and found nothing.'

'After that where would he have gone?'

'Back up Chapel Street north, straight across Dacre Road, where we are now, sir.'

Ryga followed the route with his finger.

'He'd turn right into Bridge Street, where he'd check the shops and buildings on both sides of the street. Sometimes he'd call in at the hotel.'

'But not on the night of the seventh of November.'

'No, sir.'

'Would he have walked around to the landing stages and that small bridge across to Denton Island?'

'Sometimes, yes. And he'd inspect the buildings and landing stages behind the railway track that runs parallel with Chapel Street just past the swing bridge before coming back into Dacre Street and to the station. We searched that area too after he went missing without finding anything. How much ground an officer covers on his shifts depends on the time and how many people are about.'

'I understand from Sergeant Keaton that the swing bridge was opened at nine fifty-eight p.m. It's possible that the men who opened it might have seen PC Swinley so I've asked Keaton to interview them.'

'I'd have thought they would have come forward by now if they had seen him. They're local men and PC Swinley's disappearance and the recovery of the body was in the local newspapers.'

'You're probably right, Sergeant, but it's worth asking them and checking if they recall anyone else crossing it just before or after that time when the bridge was once again closed. They could consider their evidence unimportant, or they might need prompting, not wanting to get involved with the police. I'd also like the women on the fundraising committee interviewed – Mrs Swinley might have confided in one of them. The vicar's given me their names and addresses and I see there's a Mrs Ida Williams on the list. Any relation?'

'My wife and I can tell you now, Inspector, that Mrs Swinley said nothing to my wife, or the other ladies, because I already asked her, but I'll get an officer to interview them all.'

'No, your word and your wife's are good enough for me.'

Williams looked pleased. 'None of them, including my wife, have any idea where Mrs Swinley could be. When I heard you were coming down, sir, on account of Mrs Swinley being missing, I asked my wife if she, or any of the ladies, could throw some light on it. After speaking to them this morning she said they couldn't. Mrs Swinley has no relatives, and all her friends live here in the town and are involved with the church. My wife, and the others, are adamant that she wouldn't have done away with herself. She's a strong-minded lady, and level-headed.'

'She struck me as being so,' Ryga agreed. 'I'd like to know if Mrs Swinley made or received any calls before she came up to London on Thursday. Could you ask the exchange?'

'That shouldn't take long, sir,' Williams said, rising. 'The exchange is just next door.'

Ryga turned his attention to the reports. He read through them steadily and thoroughly, interrupted only by a stream of several cups of tea brought to him by a young constable. The list of contents of George's pockets confirmed what Myra had told him and Street at the Yard. The two things she didn't mention were a handkerchief and

Swinley's white gloves, no longer white having been in the harbour. On his body was his whistle, torch and truncheon. He was still wearing his cape but there was no mention of his police helmet, which Ryga found a little curious. He consulted the coroner's report on the inquest and found that no one had raised the fact that it had been missing.

He read the pathologist's report noting, as he had originally surmised, that the post-mortem examination hadn't been conducted by a Home Office pathologist, but then no one had suspected murder. Maybe it wasn't, but that didn't answer the question about Myra's disappearance. The pathologist said that PC Swinley had been alive when he had entered the water, as Myra had told him and his chief. There was some evidence of trauma to the skull, which he claimed could have been caused by the body being buffeted against the gridiron. The sea life had feasted on the soft flesh of the eyes, ears, nose, mouth and eyelids but he couldn't find any evidence of trauma to the jaw or cheekbones, so it was unlikely he had been struck across the face and therefore fallen backwards into the harbour. Putrefaction hadn't been advanced – the chilly sea temperature of fifty-three degrees had slowed it down – but it hadn't been cold enough to delay it completely. For that to happen it needed to be constantly under forty-five degrees. The fact that Swinley's clothes were heavy had been deemed to weigh him down in the water for longer than was normal.

Ryga again consulted the coroner's report. High tide on Friday 17 November – a day before the boys had found the body – had been at ten thirty-five p.m. and then at ten fifty-one a.m. on Saturday 18 November. The boys had discovered the body just after one thirty. Therefore, the body could have risen to the surface on Saturday morning on the incoming tide and been swept up and across the harbour where it had become wedged on the gridiron. Or perhaps it had been under the gridiron all the time and had risen to the surface that Saturday morning and got stuck there.

He read the boys statements, which tallied with what Sergeant Keaton had told him. The coroner had dismissed the matter of the missing notebook as having been dislodged from Swinley's hand when he'd fallen.

There was a medical report detailing Swinley's war injury and how it had left him with severe headaches. Swinley had last consulted his doctor about them in 1948, but Ryga thought that didn't mean to say he hadn't suffered a bad head since then. Maybe he'd given up going to the doctor, knowing there was nothing to be done about them, and endured them in silence, although according to Inspector Holden's evidence Swinley hadn't missed a day's work through sickness since his return to duty in 1946.

Ryga closed the file and rose. As he stretched an arm into his Macintosh, Williams entered.

'The exchange says there were several calls to Mrs Swinley on Thursday evening and Friday morning from London, the Yard's number, and only two calls made out last week, both on Wednesday. One was to the Yard on Wednesday morning.'

'To my chief.'

'The other was on the same day at two thirty in the afternoon to a Seaford number.'

Interesting, thought Ryga, on account of the fact that George Swinley had caught the train to Seaford on 4 November, but then it probably had no bearing on the matter. Nevertheless, he said, 'Can you get me the address?'

'Already have,' Williams smartly rejoined, keen to show he was on the ball. 'It's a newsagent's and tobacconists owned by a Terence Collier.'

'Do you know him?'

'No, sir, never heard of him. No call for me to go that way to get my newspaper.'

The same for PC Swinley. And why would Myra telephone a newsagent there? 'Do you have a car I could use tomorrow? I'd like to pay a visit to this newsagent.'

'Inspector Holden usually has the car, but as it's Sunday and he's not on duty, he left it here for you, he said, in anticipation of you might needing it. I'll give you the keys, sir, and I'll leave a map of Seaford in the glove compartment so that you can find Mr Collier easy enough.'

Ryga thanked him, pocketed the keys and made his way on foot to the Bridge Hotel, pondering over the fact that Myra Swinley had telephoned a newsagent's in Seaford just over three miles away and George Swinley had caught the train to Seaford from a station some distance from his home on the Saturday before he went missing.

Nine

There was no answer when he knocked on Eva's door at the hotel. She hadn't been in the bar or in the dining room either when he had looked in there. Surely she couldn't still be taking photographs in the dark, at seven forty-five? He felt a prickling of concern, sincerely hoping she hadn't stumbled into the harbour or that her leg had become so bad she was lying injured somewhere.

He freshened up and decided to have a drink in the bar, warm up by the fire and wait for Eva's return. If she wasn't back within the hour then he would fetch a constable and go and look for her.

The bar was busy, it being Saturday and approaching Christmas. Faded pink, green and orange paperchains had been strung up criss-crossing the ceiling, culminating in paper bells in the corners of the room. Both the chains and bells had seen better days. They looked to be a legacy from before the war. There was some holly in a vase on the mantelpiece above the fire and a small nativity scene, but it was a little too early for a Christmas tree, if the hotel could get one. They too were still in short supply, along with timber, bricks and building material.

He ordered a beer and thought of Sonia in The Quarryman's Arms in Portland. It caused him an ache in the pit of his stomach as he remembered those dark, troubled eyes. Had her husband Sam Shepard tried to approach her? Ryga had left instructions with the local police to be notified if he did but Shepard could easily have slipped under their radar. He hoped she was all right. Maybe he could visit her over Christmas and take something for her son, Steven.

The door opened. There was a slight hush in the bar but conversation quickly resumed. Ryga was mightily relieved to see Eva striding, or to be more accurate limping, towards him. She looked tired. He tried not to show his concern, knowing it would irritate her.

69

'It's freezing out there and even colder in that perishing dark room.'

'What dark room?'

'Miss Green's, the chemist, in the High Street. That's where I've been for what seems like a lifetime developing the pictures I took this morning.'

'Drink?'

'Whisky, a large one.'

He ordered it and she tossed most of it back in one go. 'That's better.'

'Another?'

'Please. Any progress your end?' she eagerly asked.

'Shall we discuss it over dinner?'

'Good idea. I'm famished. I'll just take these up to my room.' She indicated a large envelope and her camera. 'I'll freshen up and be down in a jiffy. Take my drink in and order for me. Anything will do just as long as it's hot, or nearly hot.'

He did so, noting that aside from them there was only one other couple in the dining room, who were in their sixties. The two men at breakfast had either already eaten or left the hotel. The restaurant closed at nine. There was no sign of the censorious Ivy. He ordered oxtail soup and steak and kidney pudding with vegetables from a man who looked as though he should have been picking up his pension years ago and waited for Eva. She wasn't long. She'd discarded the disreputable donkey jacket.

'It'll probably be all suet and very little meat,' she said when he told her what he'd ordered, 'but anything's welcome.'

'Didn't you stop for lunch?'

'I forgot. Don't look at me like that.' But she smiled at his frown. 'And you?'

'Fish and chips.'

'Lucky you. I haven't got much to tell you except that PC Swinley wasn't bad as policemen go and he fell in the harbour. I took photographs on Denton Island, at North Quay and then went on to Railway Quay and got some of where the body was found.'

Ryga hadn't seen her but that wasn't surprising. He had probably been there ahead of her.

'Did you talk to the boys?'

'Yes. I found Tom and Colin where I expected them to be on a

Saturday morning, on the shore on Denton Island, repairing their raft. I'm amazed it hasn't sunk and that they haven't been drowned – it's so flimsy and tied together with bits of old rope. When they discovered that I took pictures for the newspapers and asked me what was wrong with my leg and I told them, they were putty in my hands.'

Ryga could well imagine.

'I got some lovely shots of them before they were aware I was there. The ones I took after that won't be half as good, because they couldn't resist posing. I haven't developed all of them yet. I thought my fingers might fall off if I stayed in Miss Green's dark room any longer. They are two highly inquisitive boys and a little cheeky, but I like that. You've got to have some spirit while you're young, Ryga, before life knocks it out of you.'

'Doesn't seem to have done that with you.'

'Very nearly,' she said solemnly. Their soup arrived. They ate in silence for a moment before she continued, 'They told me their mothers had banned them from ever using their raft again, but as you can imagine that's had the opposite effect – they're more determined than ever to set sail in the harbour or up the river, to see how many more bodies they can discover.'

'Not upset by their gruesome find then,' Ryga quipped, smiling.

'Not the least. They were eager to tell me their story with all the gory details and more added. Have you read the reports yet?'

'Yes.'

'Well, see if it checks out with what they said. They told me that they'd decided to take their raft out into the harbour, despite being ordered by their mothers to stay on the west side of the River Ouse – the Old Arm as they call it because the boats no longer use that. That side of the river was apparently cut off to shipping when the North Cut was made. Being adventurous, inquisitive and rebellious, and not fond of being told where to go and where not to go, their plan was to paddle the raft out with the tide and see how far they could get before the harbour master came yelling at them to get out of the harbour. They'd done it before and said he had to come over and fetch them in his boat and tow them back to the shore. Then he fetched them a clip round the ear.' She'd finished her soup. Ryga had too. There hadn't been much of it.

'They got under the swing bridge, but the tide was playing dirty tricks on them, according to Colin. It was sweeping them out as they had intended but it was also sweeping them over to the gridiron at Railway Quay. I think that maybe they weren't as clever as they thought they were. Tom said they weren't worried because they could easily get themselves off them old gridirons, but his paddle caught on something and stuck and when they looked it was old PC Swinley. Not that they could recognize his features – I got a vivid description of them with the poor man's flesh all eaten away – but they recognized the uniform, minus the helmet.'

Back to that missing helmet. 'I find it strange his helmet was missing. Myra never mentioned it and neither did it come up at the inquest.'

'They probably assumed it had fallen off when he went in the water.'

Ryga considered this as the aged waiter cleared their plates. Ryga almost felt like helping him. He looked as though he'd stumble and smash the crockery before reaching the kitchen. They now had the dining room to themselves.

'Maybe.' But Ryga wasn't convinced.

'It's probably at the bottom of the harbour. That's what the boys think. According to them PC Swinley was always trying to get them into trouble with their parents. Colin said his dad didn't like the police constable. I think because Colin senior might have had a few run-ins with Swinley. He works at the docks, when he can get work.'

'If it's theft then the docks falls under the British Transport Commission Police.'

'It sounded more like being drunk and disorderly. Whenever the boys saw PC Swinley approaching they usually ran away, but sometimes Swinley would creep up on them and give them a clip round the ear for nothing.'

Ryga laughed. 'I seem to have heard that one before.'

'After they found the body, Tom stayed in the raft with the paddle holding on to the corpse while Colin shinned up the iron girders and ran along the quayside until he could find a railway policeman who, as it happened, was talking to some men by the cranes who were waiting to unload a boat. At first the police constable didn't believe him, then he could see it was the truth, probably by Colin's agitated state. He asked a couple of the dock workers to accompany him to the body. They hauled it out and managed to get it on the quayside. The constable told the men to stay by it while he ran to fetch the sergeant with the scarred face who got shot down in the war.'

'Injured on the airfield in August 1940.'

'Well he sent the boys home, much to their disgust—'

'And they didn't do as they were told,' Ryga interjected.

'Of course not. They crossed to the other side of the harbour, goodness knows how in that raft, and watched the activities from there, but, according to Colin – he's the spokesman for the pair – not much happened. An ambulance arrived and carted the body off and that was it. Aside from that I talked to the men working the swing bridge and a couple at North Quay while I took photographs and at Railway Quay. From what I can gather Swinley was generally liked. There wasn't any gossip about him. Some said he had a good war by that I deemed they respected him. So what have you discovered?'

She was as good a listener as Sergeant Jacobs and had a sharp mind and eye, but he had barely got started when their meal arrived. After the waiter had shambled away, and in between mouthfuls, Ryga told her about George's missing boat, his visit to the vicarage, and the fact that Swinley had caught the train to Seaford on the Saturday before he went missing and Myra had called a Seaford number on the day before she had come to the Yard.

'They might have friends there.'

'At the newsagent's?'

'Why not?'

'Well, I'll soon find out. I'm paying Mr Collier a visit tomorrow morning, and yes, you can come,' he quickly added, seeing her glance.

'Good.' She tucked into her steak and kidney pudding.

Ryga thought Eva had been correct in her analysis of the meal. There was hardly any meat in the pie, but the flavour was appetizing.

'Did you discover anything interesting in Myra's house?' she asked.

'There was no sign of her handbag, or the coat and hat she wore to London. The bedroom curtains weren't pulled across the window and it would have been dark when she arrived home.'

'So she didn't go upstairs to change before getting some tea. Unusual that, wouldn't you say?'

'Maybe she was too hungry or too thirsty to bother.'

'It was tea and not the remains of breakfast things on the table?'

'From the condition of the house, which is spotless, I'd say yes.

Myra is not the type of woman not to clear away immediately after a meal.'

'Anything else?'

'There was a faint smell of perfume on her raincoat on the hall stand. I don't remember that in my chief's office, but Street does puff away on his pipe all day and it's hard to smell anything but that.'

'And?' she prompted when he paused.

'Something's nagging at me but I don't know what. The house was cold as though—'

'She'd gone for ever.'

'Yes.' He pushed away his empty plate. But there was more. It was something that he had seen but not registered, or rather not realized the implications of.

Eva finished her meal and sat back. 'Did you search the house?'

'Not thoroughly, but from what I managed to see there was nothing to give any indication of what might have happened. No life insurance policy and no wills. PC Swinley has a sister living in Canada, and if she does inherit, I can't see her popping over to kill her brother and abduct his wife. George's clothes are still in the house, and his shaving tackle is in the bathroom. Myra obviously can't bear to part with anything of her late husband's yet.'

'Find any sleeping pills or nerve tonic?'

'No. Should I have done?'

'According to Miss Green, the pharmacist with the dark room, yes. She was reluctant to tell me anything at first, that kind of information being confidential, but when I told her that Myra was missing she said that she regularly made up prescriptions for Myra for sleeping tablets and for something to calm her nerves. Myra has been on nerve tonic for about five years.'

'She didn't strike me as being a nervous person.'

'The tonic obviously works then,' Eva said slightly sarcastically.

Ryga thought he deserved that. 'She must have been prescribed both not long after her husband got injured at Cassino. He returned to his former job here in 1946. I wonder why she was still on them.'

'Perhaps she found it difficult to adjust to her husband being home again. He could have changed a lot from the man she had known and married.'

Ryga knew it happened. He too had changed. Sometimes he wondered how the men he'd been imprisoned with, and their wives, were coping after four years spent in a POW camp. Some men might have returned to find their marriage was over.

Eva said, 'Or perhaps the headaches turned George into a different man, made him moody maybe even violent. Maybe she kept her nerve tonic and sleeping pills in her handbag. Or went upstairs to fetch them to take them out with her. Miss Green says that a large cocktail of the tonic and tablets would be enough to put her to sleep permanently. Myra anticipated Scotland Yard's response to her request to look into her husband's death. She might have seen from your expressions, or heard in your voices, that it was hopeless, and the more she thought about it as she headed home on the train the more convinced she became that you wouldn't take her seriously. She tried to shake it off, made herself a cup of tea and a sandwich, intending to settle down and wait for the telephone call but the house became more and more oppressive, her anxiety grew as she waited for the phone to ring, her thoughts became more suicidal until she couldn't stand it any longer and she took off.'

Ryga mulled this over. It was possible. As he'd said, Myra hadn't struck him as someone suffering from nerves, but people could be awfully adept at disguising their real emotions when necessary. He'd seen several strong-minded men collapse under the nervous strain of an incarceration without a sentence, not knowing what the future held, if anything. He'd also seen men at sea go to pieces in the silence and solitude. But Myra hadn't been alone. She'd had a husband. And he too had medical problems. Perhaps headaches weren't all he suffered. There might have been flashbacks, tremors, nightmares, but he had been too frightened to confide in a doctor. Perhaps he thought it would make him appear weak and he wouldn't have wanted his colleagues to know of it. Had Myra been giving her nerve tonic to her husband?

He said as much, adding, 'George Swinley took too much, he become dazed, disorientated and fell into the harbour. Myra came to Scotland Yard claiming her husband had been killed because her conscience wouldn't allow her to accept she might inadvertently have caused his death.'

'That doesn't explain the missing notebook or why he'd buttoned up his tunic without replacing it.'

'He could have heard something, removed the notebook to jot down the time and what he'd heard. The tonic he'd taken made him confused, he thought he'd put the notebook away and automatically did up his tunic before falling in.'

The ancient waiter shuffled over to remove their plates and asked if they'd like anything further in a tone that indicated he sincerely hoped not. They humoured him and plumped for coffee in the lounge. The wireless was playing softly. The rain was lashing against the windows. They had the room to themselves. Eva picked up where they had left off.

'Miss Green said that she had dispensed strong painkillers containing morphine for George.'

'For his headaches?'

'Yes. But she hadn't made any up for about two years.'

'Which bears out what the doctor said at the inquest. He hadn't seen George for two years.'

'So maybe the headaches had stopped, or he was getting drugs from elsewhere.'

'I don't like the sound of that. And why should he obtain them illegally when he could get them on the National Health Service? He'd have to pay for them from other sources.'

'Maybe not in monetary terms.'

'You mean he'd turn a blind eye to a crime that was being committed.' Ryga liked that even less.

'Perhaps he became addicted to these drugs because they were the only ones which could stop the headaches, but he couldn't get more of them under prescription, or the quantity he needed, so he looked elsewhere.'

Ryga had come across such a situation before with men who had served in Burma. On account of their terrible experiences they'd become addicted to morphine to try and obliterate what they had seen, or at the least eradicate the pain of the memories, and sadly some had died of an overdose, sometimes deliberately, other times accidentally.

Their coffee arrived. Eva popped up to her room to fetch the photographs she'd taken and developed. On her return she spread those of the boys and of the gridiron at Railway Quays on the table in front of them.

Ryga's breath caught in his throat as he viewed the pictures of the boys she had taken before they had been aware of her presence. Their rapt expressions as they repaired their makeshift raft tore at his heart. Their too-tight jackets over short trousers with socks rolled down and their shoes caked in mud. Their thin bodies tending their pride and joy. He thought of Sonia's son, Steven, and remembered his intense, delighted expression when he had shown him the contents of his murder case. Ryga ached to see that same joyous expression again, and hoped that if, and when, they found his father, and Steven learned of the truth about him, it wouldn't spoil life for the boy.

These children had little of material value in their lives and here they were finding joy in something so basic yet so precious to them. This raft was all these boys had and they had made it themselves from old bits of wood and rope found along the shore. Eva had captured that raw joy and pride with her camera so well that it brought a lump to his throat as he thought of all the children lost during the war. He sniffed and pulled himself together. Maybe Eva sensed his sorrow and his emotions because she said nothing. He liked her even more for it.

The waiter coughed noisily and glared at them with a rheumy eye. Eva shuffled up the pictures. 'I think we've outstayed our welcome.'

Ryga consulted his watch. The bar would be closed by now; besides, he didn't want another drink and Eva looked as though she was ready for her bed, not that he would say as much. It had been a long day. Rising, he said, 'Let's catch the newsagent before he can rub the sleep from his eyes. Always the best time to interrogate a suspect, not that Terence Collier is one.' But then who could tell?

Ten

It was dark when they set out on the deserted road towards Seaford the following morning. A cold mist clung to the streets and swirled around the streetlights. They had agreed to forgo breakfast in the hotel as, being Sunday, it wasn't served until eight thirty. Eva sat quietly beside him, her camera in the boot, along with a bag containing not only her rolls of film and flashlight but also a flask of coffee which she'd persuaded the night porter at the hotel to make for them. 'When I told him it was for Scotland Yard he couldn't do it quick enough,' she'd joked. There were also a couple of biscuits which the porter said he had sneaked in.

Soon they were on the outskirts of the small coastal town, and from what Ryga could see on first impressions it looked to be more respectable and middle class than its neighbour, Newhaven. He changed his mind, however, when he turned off not far from the railway station into rows of small terraced houses fronting directly on to the pavement. Some were neat and trim others looked run down with threadbare net curtains and scratched front doors. There was no one about.

Colliers Newsagents and Tobacconists straddled the corner of two streets. It had clearly seen better days. So too had its proprietor. Collier, a smallish man in his early sixties with a drawn, heavily lined and pock-marked face, paused in his task of sorting through a pile of newspapers on the counter, while another stood on the grubby floor. He eyed them with a mixture of surprise, suspicion and guarded hostility. A single lightbulb shone on his balding head, casting a sickly beam over the worn linoleum covered in dust and grime. A strip of fly paper twirled from the light flex with dead flies on it. The tiny, cramped, dusty shop smelt of tobacco, grease and dirt.

'You from the press?' he growled.

'Should we be?' Ryga answered.

'You look like it but who and what you'd be after round here I can't imagine. Nothing ever happens unless you count the missus running off with a cigarette salesman. Has he done her in? Wouldn't blame him if he has. Felt like it myself many a time.' His wide mouth split into a grin showing bad teeth.

Ryga thought it was time to flash his warrant card, which caused Collier's skin to blanch. 'I was only joking. Christ, you don't mean—'

'It's all right, Mr Collier, it's not about your errant wife that we're here.'

'Well, thank Gawd for that. The man she run off did me a favour. I always said—'

But Ryga didn't wait to hear what the newsagent always said. 'Did you receive a telephone call from a woman on Wednesday?'

Collier looked sly. 'I get lots of calls from women.'

'I doubt that,' Ryga said evenly. 'This one probably gave her name as Mrs Swinley.' Ryga saw instantly that Collier recognized it. 'What did she ask you?'

'I can't remember.'

'Oh, I think you can if you try, sir, and I would hate to deprive your customers of their Sunday newspapers and tobacco by you having to close the shop and accompany me to the police station.'

'All right, keep your hair on.' Collier rubbed a hand over his balding head. 'This woman phones, she says who's that when I answered the phone. I says you should know, you telephoned me – it's Colliers the newsagent's. That seemed to take her back a bit because she went silent and I thought she'd rung off. Then she asked whether a man called George Swinley had visited the shop. I said we get a lot of visitors – they don't give their name. She says I must remember strangers though, and this man Swinley would have been one. She described him but I said I'd never set eyes on him and she rang off.'

'This is the man she mentioned and described.' Ryga produced the picture of George Swinley.

'A copper? I don't know any coppers except the local bobby and that's not him.'

'Take a closer look,' Ryga insisted. 'Think of him in civvies and without the helmet.'

Collier squinted at it closely and scratched his unshaven chin. When his bloodshot grey eyes flicked up, Ryga saw in them wariness and apprehension.

'You know him, of course,' he said casually when Collier seemed to have lost his tongue.

'Not know exactly.' He squirmed.

'But he has been in your shop.'

'Yes, he's been here. What's he done?' Collier asked hesitantly.

'He was found dead on Saturday eighteenth of November.'

Collier's eyes widened in alarm. He swallowed hard. His protruding Adam's apple went up and down. 'Blimey! You mean someone's done him in?'

'Why did he come here?' Ryga pressed. He half expected Collier to say, *Why do you think? To buy a box of matches.* But he didn't.

Looking troubled, Collier said, 'Look, I just acted as a letter box.'

'For what?' Ryga felt a frisson of excitement.

'How the blazes do I know? I didn't open the packages. I was just asked to hold on to them and hand them over to a man called George Swinley.'

'He showed some identification?' Eva interjected.

'His ration book.'

'That could have been stolen,' she persisted.

Collier shrugged. 'So what if it was? That was none of my business.'

'How many packages did he collect?' Ryga asked, his voice betraying nothing of his keenness to get the information.

'Three.'

'So he came here three times?'

'I just said so, didn't I?'

'He might have come more often without collecting any packages.'

'Well, he didn't.'

'The dates? And don't tell me you don't remember.'

Collier sniffed and reached for a date calendar hanging up behind him. He flicked back the months to October. 'The first was on Monday the thirtieth of October.' Ryga could see a cross on the date. Collier flicked over the page. 'The second was Saturday the fourth of November.' When Swinley had been seen catching the train to Seaford. 'And the last one was Tuesday the seventh of November.' When Swinley had disappeared.

'So who gave you these packages?'

Collier took a cigarette from behind his ear. 'A woman, which was why I didn't say anything to the other one who telephoned me last Wednesday, because I thought she might be the wife and I don't want to get mixed up in any domestic squabble.'

Ryga was growing more intrigued. He didn't have time now to think through the implications of this. He needed information. 'Describe the woman who left the packages.'

'Smart, well dressed,' Collier answered, looking Eva up and down, and by his expression disapproving of her trousers and old donkey jacket. 'Fur coat, hat, gloves, high heels, not a tart, didn't speak, look or act like one. Foreign, if you ask me.'

'She spoke with an accent?' Ryga asked, noting down what Collier was saying.

'No, posh, but she looked like a foreigner. By that I mean she had a dark complexion, not suntanned, a bit swarthy. French maybe, or Spanish, or could have been Italian, but then again she could have come from Brighton for all I know. One thing I do know, though, is that she had unusual eyes – bright blue with dark circles around the blue. It made them stand out. And she smelt nice.'

'How nice?' Eva asked.

Collier's cigarette stayed perched in the corner of his mouth unlit. 'Like . . . I don't know, soft.'

'Describe her coat.'

'I said it was fur.' He looked at Eva as though she was deaf or stupid.

'Brown? Black? Grey? Long? Short?' she pushed. 'You don't see many fur coats in here, Mr Collier. You must have noticed it, an astute man like yourself.'

He looked momentarily stunned at the compliment, which Eva had probably intended cynically, but after a moment he melted. 'Brown, glossy, short. It swung round after she walked out.'

'A swagger coat then,' Eva directed at Ryga. 'Over trousers? A skirt?' she addressed Collier.

'Skirt, black, matching her stockings, nice pair of legs and a tight skirt too because I thought how can she walk in it and those heels? Like I said, a nice party.'

'Did she give a name?' Ryga asked.

'Nah, and I didn't ask it.'

'But you can remember the hat?' Eva said.

'Hats,' he said pointedly. Eva rewarded him with a smile, which seemed to melt the newsagent because he expanded. 'It was a different one each time. I noticed because my missus had a thing about hats, spent a fortune on them, and if she'd have seen these she would have been green with envy.'

'Can you describe them?' Eva asked gently.

'Now you're asking. I don't know anything about hats.'

'Have a stab at it,' she encouraged brightly.

He cackled hoarsely, emitting the smell of bad breath, but Eva didn't flinch. She had him well in hand. 'Righto,' he said brightly, obviously completely won over by her charm. The unlit cigarette came out of his mouth. 'First time I didn't pay much attention to her hat because I was looking at her legs.' He grinned. Eva smiled back. Ryga silently shook his head in admiration of her technique. 'It was a sort of turban but not like the women wear in the factories – this one was made of velvet or some such silky material, and it was pushed back off her head with a veil over her face.'

'But you still noticed her eyes.'

'Yes. The veil, or what do you call it, was like netting so I could see right through it. The hat was black. The second time she wore a green one. It was like a beret but square and it had a veil the same as before.'

'And the last time you saw her?' Eva prompted.

'A funny kind of thing – looked like straw but wasn't, and it had a knot and a feather sticking out of the top. No veil.'

Eva's eyes travelled over the magazines on the shelves. 'Do you stock the magazine called *Vogue*?'

Collier shook his head looking baffled, as though he'd never heard of it and Ryga thought he probably hadn't. Not much call for an elite fashion magazine in these parts.

Eva continued, 'Or do you get it in as a special order for anyone in the neighbourhood?'

'No.'

Ryga addressed the newsagent. 'Tell me what happened when she first visited you.' So far, they hadn't been disturbed by early morning customers or the return of the newspaper boys. He hoped it stayed that way for a bit longer.

'She came in the Friday before he collected the first package.'

'Friday twenty-eighth of October.'

'Yes. She asked if I could act as a letter box for her, said she needed to leave some correspondence for someone to collect. I've done it for a few people in the past and I *always* make sure there is nothing dodgy about it – you know, illegal.'

How? wondered Ryga. Did he open the correspondence to find out? He said he didn't and Ryga knew he wasn't bothered just as long as he got paid.

'She said it was documents – felt like it too. It was about a quarter of an inch thick, a large brown envelope, foolscap size with handwriting on the front, *For personal collection by George Swinley only*. She said Mr Swinley would be in to collect on Monday and he was.'

'What time did she arrive with this package?'

'About seven thirty in the evening. She came at the same time on the other two occasions.'

When it was dark and unlikely anyone would have seen her.

Eva said, 'What made her choose you?'

'No idea and I didn't ask. The man, Swinley, came in. I handed it over and he left. I didn't know he was a copper. Was he up to something dodgy? Is that why he was killed?'

'How did she pay you?'

'Cash. A pound note each time.'

'Do you still have them?' Ryga thought they might be able to trace the numbers but Collier shook his head.

'Paid into the bank.'

Ryga said an officer would be round to take his statement, which he would be asked to sign, and that he might also return if new information came to light. Collier looked nervous at that. Ryga also instructed Collier to inform the local police, or himself at Newhaven police station, if he saw the woman again.

Outside Eva took a couple of photographs of the shop then climbed into the car. They said nothing until Ryga pulled over on the seafront. Eva fetched the flask of coffee and biscuits from the boot. The mist had morphed into a freezing fog, but despite that they took their coffee to a small shelter on the deserted esplanade.

'Why choose Seaford?' Eva mused, pouring the hot, steaming liquid into two small flask cups. 'I can understand them not wanting to fix Newhaven as the delivery and collection point because obviously neither wanted this activity to be noticed and remarked upon, but they could have selected Lewes or Peacehaven.'

'Perhaps she lives here, oh, not round Collier's streets, but in a more select area and couldn't be seen in her own neighbourhood. She's obviously well-off.'

'And fashionable if Collier's description is right and I'd say it is – tight-fitting pencil skirt, swagger fur coat and three hats! She was hardly dressed to blend in with the scenery, although she did visit the newsagent's at night. But someone around there might have seen her and they'd have noticed her.'

Ryga agreed.

Eva continued, '*Vogue* magazine is not the regular reading matter of Collier's clientele, as we discovered, but those hats might help me find out more about her. If I can track down the milliner I might be able to get a name because I don't think our mystery lady bought those hats from a department store.'

Ryga knew that Eva had extensive contacts in the fashion industry, having been engaged on photographic shoots for various magazines.

Eva said, 'Her coat sounds as though it would be genuine fur – mink, most probably. Know anything about fur coats, Ryga?'

He gave a wry smile and sipped his coffee. 'I should do, we have a spate of robberies from furriers in London, and last Monday night the Alaska fur factory in London was robbed.'

Eva raised her eyebrows. 'I don't think this one was stolen but then you never know. Was Swinley involved in investigating the fur thefts?'

'No, although a circular has gone out to all police forces to be on the lookout for furs being sold illegally in their areas. But it's more likely they're being passed on in London.'

'Maybe this woman was giving Swinley information on them and that last package was the final link. He was about to come to you with the case solved.'

'It doesn't seem likely. But it could have been drugs in those packages, as we discussed. From what Collier said about Myra's telephone call, it sounds as though she came across a piece of paper in one of her husband's pockets with the telephone number on it and wondered about it. She rang out of curiosity.'

'Would Swinley have written such information down?'

Ryga recalled what PC Jenkins had said, that Swinley had been a stickler for recording information. 'I think he would but not in his police notebook.'

'Why wouldn't he have written down the address, as well as the telephone number?'

'Perhaps the mystery woman only had the opportunity to give him the number. She might have telephoned it to him or passed it to him on the piece of paper, saying to call there to collect the packages. Swinley got the address by telephoning the number without announcing himself to Collier. He pushed the paper back in his pocket and forgot it was there, or it got caught in the lining. If Myra believed Collier then perhaps she dismissed it of being of no consequence hence her not mentioning it to us at the Yard.'

'So what happened to contents of the packages?' Eva mused, biting into a biscuit.

'If it was drugs then perhaps after picking up that last package Swinley got a message to the woman saying he didn't want any more. He'd go to his doctor and admit he had a drug problem only the woman, or whoever she works for, decided he'd become a risk.' Ryga drained his coffee and Eva poured another. 'I need to speak to the local police.'

'I'll take a walk around the streets close to the newsagent's and make casual enquiries while snapping away with my camera – always a good cover. I'll meet you back at the police station. Where is it, by the way?'

Ryga had already consulted the map Sergeant Williams had left for him. 'Close to the railway station. I'll also ask the staff there if they remember seeing an attractive woman in a swagger fur coat alight from a train or embark on one on the dates Collier gave us.' They finished their coffee and Ryga dropped Eva back on the corner of the newsagent's street before making his way to the railway station.

Eleven

He drew a blank. It being Sunday and fewer trains, there was only one man to ask who, in the small station, acted as ticket collector, porter and guard, and he hadn't been on duty on the days in question. Ryga thought he might have more luck if he returned on a weekday. Tomorrow he'd call at both the town and harbour stations at Newhaven to try and ascertain if Swinley had caught the Seaford train from either of them on the other two occasions. After all, he must have got to Seaford to collect his packages somehow. There was the possibility he could have walked there and back though. It was about three miles in each direction. Eva didn't make any progress either, except she said she was pleased with some of the pictures she'd taken around the streets of Seaford.

Ryga drove back to Newhaven in the thick, grey, enveloping fog that made him feel as though he would drive forever without coming out of it. Traffic signs were no use, as the moment they appeared they disappeared. He knew the way but fog on land could be as equally disorientating as at sea, and he was aware that he could easily drive off the road, or into a brick wall or over a cliff. It took all his concentration, and Eva seemed content to pass the journey in silence.

The air had grown colder still when, just after eleven, he parked the car at the police station with a sense of relief. It was eerily silent, even more so than the night, he thought, with the exception of the rhythmic regular boom from the lighthouses and a foghorn out to sea, both of which only served to make it more ghostly. The smell of the mud of low tide was like thick boiled molasses and wet socks. It seemed to waft towards them in the mist.

Eva turned to him. 'I'm going to return to London. I'll develop the pictures I've taken today in my own dark room. I can't impose on Miss Green on a Sunday, and besides I prefer to use my own equipment, which is better. My dark room is also much warmer than hers. Tomorrow I'll make some enquiries with my contacts in the fashion industry about the mystery woman's hats. I'll keep my room on here. I'll be back as soon as I can. Meanwhile, if you find out anything more call me at my flat.'

'I'll drive you to Lewes.'

'Not in this weather – it will take forever. It'll be easier and quicker for me to get the train from here and change at Lewes. I'll get something to eat on the train – hopefully there'll be a refreshment car or a Pullman. There's nothing I need from my room – I've got plenty of toiletries and clothes in my flat. I'll get going now.'

'Then I'll drive you to the Town Station.'

Eva made the eleven thirty. After consulting the guard, Ryga established that she'd be able to get the eleven forty-seven from Lewes to Victoria and be in London by one thirty. He made some inquiries at the booking office to see if George Swinley had travelled to Seaford on 30 October or the 7 November but was told to come back Monday when the man-in-charge could look it up in the records. The ticket collector couldn't say if Swinley had travelled from there on those occasions as he had been on the late shift.

Ryga headed back to the hotel for Sunday lunch where Ivy served him. She seemed far more amenable than she had at Saturday morning breakfast. Word had circulated on who he was and why he was there. She asked about Miss Paisley and Ryga said she'd had to return to London but she'd be back within a day or two.

'You'll be here that long then, sir?'

'Maybe.'

She gave him two extra roast potatoes to make up for the lack of meat, she said, it still being on ration.

'Did you know PC Swinley?' asked Ryga.

'He used to look in sometimes. Always cheerful and polite. You can't think someone has murdered him!' she said, dropping her voice to a whisper so the other diners wouldn't hear.

'I don't know, Ivy, that's what I'm trying to find out. Do you know Mrs Swinley?'

'Only to say "hello" to if I pass her in the High Street.'

Ryga ate his meal, chewing over the revelation about the packages and the mystery woman, but nothing new occurred to him. It was mid-afternoon when he entered the police station, lit his gas fire and warmed his hands and back against it. When Sergeant Williams brought him a cup of tea, Ryga relayed what he and Miss Paisley had discovered from the newsagent, which drew a startled then worried look from the sergeant. Williams confirmed that Swinley's visits to Seaford could have nothing to do with any current police investigation of theirs. Ryga made no mention of the theory of drugs, which he and Eva had discussed, but he told Williams that Eva had returned to London to see if she could get any information about the mystery woman from her fashion friends.

Ryga then asked about Swinley's shifts for Monday 30 October and Saturday 4 November when he had called at the newsagent's. He knew Swinley's shift on 7 November. On Monday 30 October, Williams said Swinley had been on the morning shift from six a.m. to two p.m. So he could have caught the train to Seaford, say after three p.m., given that he would have returned home to change out of his uniform before doing so. His rest day had been Saturday 4 November when he had caught the two fifteen to Seaford. He'd started his two p.m. to ten p.m. shift on Sunday 5 November, and had been working it on Tuesday 7 November when he had picked up his final package, which he must have done in the morning. Ryga realized he had omitted to ask Collier, the newsagent, that. So what had happened to the contents of the packages? If drugs had been inside them Swinley couldn't have taken all of them in the last package before being killed. Not unless he had taken them with the intention of ending his life. Could he have left a suicide note in his notebook on the side of the harbour somewhere and then, overcome with the drugs, fell or threw himself into the water? Ryga hadn't seen any packages as described by Collier in Myra's house.

He wrote up his interview with Collier. At least they had a new lead to follow up, and tomorrow he would call through to Jacobs and Street at the Yard and update them. He switched off the gas fire, donned his hat and coat, and carried his cup and saucer out to the front desk where he said goodnight to Sergeant Williams, who said he was also leaving shortly after handing over to the six p.m. shift sergeant.

The fog closed in around Ryga as he made for the hotel, making him feel claustrophobic. Yellowing car lamps loomed out of the dark, startling him, the fog muffling the sound of their engines. The icy drops of water dripped off his hat and settled on his shoulders. It was difficult to see a yard ahead. It was bad enough here but it must be awful in London, he thought, where the fog would once again have turned to a thick, nauseating, choking sulphuric stink, clawing at your throat and stinging your eyes. He didn't envy Eva being back there. By now she was safely ensconced in her apartment, buried in her dark room, busy at work. He wondered what her apartment was like. Modern, he thought, not ostentatious, practical, possibly even untidy. But then she might have someone who came in to 'do' for her.

A ship's hooter sounded so loud that Ryga started and thought he must have walked right down to the quay without realizing it. He hadn't though, because here was the entrance to the hotel. But the sound had triggered a thought. Could Swinley's killer have slipped into the harbour on a boat during the late afternoon of 7 November under cover of darkness and fog, waited for the constable, killed him, and then slipped out again on a rising tide much later that night or in the early hour of the morning? Could that same person have repeated the process on Thursday 7 December, luring Myra to one of the landing stages and killed her?

It was a theory that he warmed to as he stepped into the welcoming heat of the hotel bar and reception. It was deserted. A fire burned in the grate. Ryga removed his hat, shook the damp from it and crossed to it to warm himself. His thoughts took him to another burning coal fire in a pub in Portland, and he was filed with an impulse to talk to Sonia.

He made for the hotel's telephone cubicle, which was thankfully vacant. Taking some coins from his pocket, he put them in the slot and pressed button A as the telephone was answered. He felt a quickening heartbeat at the thought of hearing Sonia's voice. But it was a man who answered. She must have help, he thought, although it was Sunday and usually the quietest day of the week for the pub.

'I'd like to speak to Mrs Shepherd. It's Mr Ryga.'

'She's not here,' came the reply, surprising Ryga for a moment, but then why shouldn't she have an evening off?

'Do you know when she'll be back?'

'She won't be.'

'I'm sorry?' Ryga asked, bewildered.

'She's no longer the landlady.'

Ryga's heart lurched. My God, had Sam Shepherd returned to Portland and persuaded her to leave with him? No, the brewery must have dispensed with her services. Knowing of her husband's desertion, and his record of helping himself to the profits, which Sonia had replaced, they'd sacked her and forced her and her son from their home. His body stiffened with fury. 'Has she been moved to another pub?' he asked, hoping that was the situation.

'No. She handed in her notice and left on the thirtieth of November.'

This Ryga hadn't expected. Why should she do that? Why not tell him? But then why should she? There was nothing between them. She didn't know he would be in contact; in fact, he hadn't given her any indication that he wanted to see her again, for which he cursed his sluggishness and stupidity.

'Do you know where she's gone? You must have a forwarding address.' He heard the desperation in his voice.

'No idea. You could try the brewery.'

Ryga would but he'd get no answer until tomorrow, Monday.

He should have anticipated this. She could have taken flight because she was terrified that her husband would come to her. He tried to tell himself that his concern was professional but his churning stomach was saying different. Maybe she had met a man, and she had happily gone off with him. The ache inside him told him he didn't much like that thought either. Why did he feel it should be his role to banish those dark circles from under her eyes? He had to know where she was and make sure she was all right. And if the brewery didn't know then someone at the railway stations in Portland and Weymouth might know the train she had caught and to where. Now he had two missing women to find, and one was someone he knew he cared about deeply.

Twelve

Monday

Before leaving the hotel the next morning, Ryga rang the
brewery who, after some delay, said they had no idea where
Mrs Shepherd had gone. She hadn't left a forwarding address.
Maybe she had considered running away was her only option, she had
a son to raise and a secret to keep, that her husband was a deserter and
conman. He knew he couldn't simply leave it there. He had to know if
she was all right. At the station, in the privacy of his little office, he
put a call through to Weymouth police station and asked for Sergeant
Daniels.

'Hello, Skipper.'

Ryga smiled despite his concerns about Sonia. He liked Daniels
and the way he addressed him, a hangover from Daniels' brief days in
the Royal Air Force at the end of the war. He also admired Daniels'
breezy cheerfulness and his dedication to his work. Ryga told him that
he wanted to trace Sonia Shepherd who had left The Quarryman's
Arms with her son.

'Have you news of her husband?' was Daniel's natural assumption.

'No, but if, or when, we get it, we need to know where she is so
that we can communicate with her.' It was partly the truth. 'Make
enquiries at the railway and bus stations, Daniels – someone must
have sold her a ticket and try to establish what train or bus she took,
and to where. The brewery says she didn't leave a forwarding address
but see if she did at the post offices either on Portland or in
Weymouth.'

'Righto, Skipper, where can I contact you?'

Ryga gave him the telephone numbers of the Newhaven police
station and the Bridge Hotel. That done, he asked Sergeant Williams
where Inspector Holden was. Ryga thought he should report to him

what he had discovered over the weekend, but he was greeted with the news that the inspector had gone down with this dreadful flu. Ryga said he was sorry to hear that while silently hoping Holden's germs weren't floating around waiting to lay him low.

He made his way to the Watch House, having decided to check out boat movements before calling in at the town railway station. He also wanted to have a word with the customs officer who Sergeant Keaton had mentioned, Mr Dakins, who had been with Swinley on the platform of the harbour station on Saturday 4 November.

The fog had lifted but what had replaced it wasn't much better. A cold, grey clamminess seemed to hang depressingly over everything and everyone. He found Hailsham in a haze of tobacco smoke in his office. Ryga asked him if any boats had come into the harbour on the late afternoon or night that Swinley had disappeared, Tuesday 7 November and on Thursday 7 December when Myra had gone missing.

'They could have done, but whoever would have been at the helm would need to be a first-rate seaman in that weather on both nights.'

'Or know the harbour well.'

'There is that. I went off duty at six thirty on Thursday so I wouldn't really know, but you could check with customs across the harbour – they'll have been alerted by the lighthouse staff if any vessel came in, that is if it was showing a light.'

And if murder had been the pilot's intention, thought Ryga, the boat wouldn't have been. He made to leave when Hailsham said, 'I can take you over to the Custom House if you like. It will save you walking all the way around.'

Ryga agreed with alacrity. It would feel good to be back on the water, even for a short trip. As he climbed on board he nodded at the Motor Torpedo Boat. 'Any further news on the owner?'

'Nothing.'

'I'll ask someone at the Yard to check with the Chelsea Yacht and Boat Company. It might have come from there given that there are quite a few moored up there. If she didn't hail from Chelsea someone might recognize her by her number. Twenty-one,' he said, reading the number painted on the side. Then he frowned, puzzled, as something struck him. 'That's strange. As far as I'm aware there wasn't a number twenty-one. She is a sixty-footer, isn't she, Mr Hailsham?'

'She is.'

'Didn't they only go up to number nineteen?'

'They did. She was probably given that number to fool the Germans into thinking we had more of them than we did. It was common practice in the war.' Hailsham started the engine. It throbbed into life and he swung out into the harbour. 'She's also been renamed *Constance*.'

It seemed a waste to let her lie here unlived in, Ryga thought as they motored away from her.

Hailsham said, 'Maybe her owner will wash up somewhere along the coast at some time. That's the Customs House.' He pointed at a two-storey building facing on to the northernmost berth on East Quay. Ryga could see two tugs and a small rowing boat. The latter he recognized as the one which took a line across to the West Quay to be attached to a strong hawser which helped to pull the ships round so that they faced out to sea. Hailsham pointed down the harbour out to sea where a powerful motor launch was heading towards them.

'And that's the customs launch,' he said, bringing his boat round to the landing stage.

Ryga jumped nimbly off while Hailsham kept the engine running.

'Anytime you need a lift across, Inspector, just ask me or my assistant if I'm not around.'

Ryga said he would. He waited for the customs launch to come alongside and throttle down. Hailing the uniformed officer at the helm, he said, 'Throw me a line, I'll tie off for you.'

'Thanks.'

That done and the engine silenced, the officer alighted. He was a couple of years older than Ryga – about mid-thirties – a slight man with tired hazel eyes, a wide mouth and a wind-blown countenance.

'Preventive Officer Leslie Dakins. Can I help you?'

'I hope so.' Just the man he wished to speak with. 'Inspector Ryga, Scotland Yard. I'm looking into the death of PC George Swinley.'

'I thought the constable's death was accidental,' Dakins said, clearly bemused.

'New information has come to light. Did any craft unknown to you come into the harbour on the night of the seventh of November when PC Swinley went missing?'

'Not that I remember. Has someone said one did?'

'No. I wondered if it was possible that PC Swinley had witnessed smuggling, or seen or heard something suspicious and had been attacked and pushed into the harbour as a result by someone from a boat.'

'That can't be. We would have known about it,' Dakins confidently asserted.

'The boat could have been a very small one that got past you and the lighthouse staff without being seen.'

'I doubt it,' Dakins answered in a friendly tone, and yet Ryga sensed a slight arrogance about the man. 'You mentioned new information had come to light, Inspector, hence you being here. Can I ask what that is?'

'PC Swinley's wife is missing and we're concerned for her safety.'

'Oh. I'm sorry to hear that. But if it's suicide then surely it can't have any bearing on PC Swinley's death being suspicious?'

'I didn't say it was suicide.'

'No, of course not. I just assumed,' Dakins easily replied with a sheepish grin.

'Do you know if any vessels unknown to you came into the harbour on Thursday night, seventh of December?'

'Is that when she went missing?'

'Yes.'

'Well, again the answer is no. It was a quiet night, save for the foghorns. I'm sorry I can't help you, Inspector.'

'It was just an idea. But you might be able to help me on another matter. Sergeant Keaton told me that PC Swinley caught the train to Seaford from the harbour station on Saturday the fourth of November and that you were on the platform at the same time. Did you speak with him?'

Dakins looked bewildered by the question but he answered, 'I did. Only briefly. I was just going off duty and I wasn't feeling too bright. I'd been up since before five a.m. and it had been a busy day rummaging craft just off Seaford and further along the coast for contraband goods: tobacco, alcohol, drugs, and with nothing to show for it. PC Swinley said he was going for a walk on the Downs.'

'According to Sergeant Keaton, he wasn't dressed for walking.'

'Now you mention it, no, he wasn't. He had his best suit on, under his overcoat, and ordinary shoes but I didn't think to question him.'

'No, of course not,' Ryga replied smoothly to Dakins' slightly tetchy remark.

'It wasn't exactly suitable walking weather either, damp and chill, like this,' Dakins added. 'But there's no accounting for taste, and it wasn't my business to pry. Besides which, he was, shall I say, a little standoffish. He obviously didn't want to make polite conversation and neither did I. When the train came in, he bid me good afternoon and made for the first carriage. I got in the last one. When we alighted he was ahead of me. He struck out towards the Downs, along the esplanade. My lodgings are on the seafront, almost at the end of the esplanade. I saw him turn off on to the path that leads up to the Downs. It was raining by then, drizzling.'

'Well, thank you, Mr Dakins, that's most helpful.' Ryga shook the customs officer's hand, noting it was damp and limp. He headed for the railway station where he sought out the stationmaster. Within minutes he had discovered that Swinley hadn't caught the train from there on either the 30 October or the 7 November. So he must have walked or gone from the town station.

As Ryga made for the latter he considered Dakins' remarks about Swinley wearing his best suit. You wear your best suit to see a solicitor, to visit friends or relatives, not to collect a package from a grubby backstreet newsagent and tobacconist. Dakins could be mistaken, though – after all, how did he know which suit was Swinley's best? Then there was the fact that Swinley had struck out towards the Downs, the opposite direction from Collier's. Maybe he just wanted to stretch his legs and get some sea air before collecting the package.

At the town station Ryga explained that he was interested to know if PC Swinley had caught the train to Seaford on Monday 30 October or Tuesday 7 November. Dunton, the stationmaster, couldn't remember seeing him, but he asked Ryga to accompany him to the ticket office where the clerk confirmed, after checking his records, that he hadn't sold a ticket to PC Swinley on those dates, or any others, only a day return to Mrs Swinley last Thursday to London.

'That's right,' Dunton reiterated. 'I took her ticket when she alighted.'

Ryga didn't know if the news that Myra was missing had spread around the town. 'What time was that?'

'Ten past six; the train was five minutes late.'

'Did you speak to her?' Ryga asked.

'Only to say "good evening" but she hardly noticed. In fact, she didn't even reply, she was too deep in conversation with someone.'

'Who was that?' Ryga asked, thinking that Myra might have said something more to this local person about her journey to Scotland Yard, and her concerns over the cause of her husband's death.

'No idea, never seen her before,' was Dunton's surprising answer. 'Very attractive woman, smartly dressed, fur coat, veiled hat and pearls. Not from round these parts. Foreign looking.'

Ryga stared at him in astonishment. This he hadn't expected. My God, the mystery woman with Myra Swinley. It had to be her. The description fitted Collier's perfectly. 'Where was the other woman's ticket from?'

'Same place as Mrs Swinley's, London Victoria.'

'Return or single?'

'Day return.'

'And did she return?'

'Not while I was here. I left just after six thirty. I'll ask the night porter when he comes on duty at six and telephone to the police station to let you know if you think it's important.'

It was, very. Ryga said he'd be obliged if he could do that and made his way back to the police station, considering this new surprising development. Had Myra known the mystery woman? Collier, the newsagent, had said he hadn't known the woman's name and that he had said nothing to Myra Swinley about her. Had he lied? Or had the mystery woman contacted Myra and arranged to meet her in London or on the train? It couldn't have been a chance meeting, surely, on the part of the woman in the fur coat. That would be too fantastic.

He recalled that faint smell of perfume on the coat stand in the hall which he hadn't noticed in Street's office on Myra Swinley and now he knew why. It wasn't because of the smell of the gas fire or Street's pipe tobacco but because Myra hadn't been wearing any. The woman in the fur coat had accompanied Myra home and perhaps hung her coat on the stand or brushed up against it. And the visitor would account for Myra not going upstairs and changing before making the tea. But something more rankled with Ryga. Why hadn't there been two places set for tea? Had the mystery woman refused refreshment? Why had she made contact with Myra? Was it to lure her away and kill her or have her killed? It seemed a possible explanation because shortly afterwards Myra had vanished, just as her husband had done, and Ryga was of no doubt that just as Swinley's body had eventually risen to the surface so too, eventually, would that of his poor wife.

Thirteen

After collecting his murder case from the station, Ryga made for Myra's house. He wanted to see if he could lift any prints from it that might belong to the mystery woman. There would be plenty of Myra's, possibly others from the wake, but knowing Myra to be house-proud he was certain she would have dusted, and thoroughly polished, after the mourners had left. And the mourners would have been entertained in the front parlour. It was possible Myra had shown her visitor in there. He might also find some hairs from the mink coat which would prove she had entered the house. Neither the fingerprints – if they existed – nor any hairs from the coat could lead them to the mystery woman's identity though, not unless her prints were on file.

As he let himself in he thought the house seemed colder than before, not because a fire hadn't been lit for three days but it was the chill of finality. He knew that Myra Swinley wouldn't return.

He lifted prints from the crockery on the table, again considering the fact that only one place was set. Had the mystery woman washed up her plate, cup and saucer and put them away to make it appear as though Myra had been alone? It was a possible explanation, but why then let the ticket collector see them together? She hadn't exactly been secretive about her meeting with Myra. On the contrary, the ticket collector had said they'd been talking.

He poured the dregs of the dark brown sludge of tea and tea leaves from the tea pot into a small glass jar, sealed it, wrote on the label and put it in his case. Next he lifted some fingerprints from the mantelpiece and another set from the kitchen. He did the same in the bedroom, pausing to look out of the window where he could see the red roof of the Watch House, the Motor Torpedo Boat, Sleeper's Hole and Joseph Moore's hut. He made a mental note to ask Sergeant

Jacobs to check out the Motor Torpedo Boat with Chelsea Yacht and Boat Company when he rang him after six o'clock.

Descending, he took prints from the arms of the chairs at the table and examined them with his magnifying glass. They matched the others in the house, so they had to be Myra's. And there were none in the front parlour save Myra's. He picked up Myra's raincoat from the hall stand and sniffed. The smell of perfume had worn off. There seemed no point in sending it up to the lab but perhaps they could find just a trace of it and some hairs which belonged to the mystery woman, or even to the mink!

He wrapped the coat in brown paper, a supply of which he carried in the murder case. Then he conducted a search of the downstairs cupboards and the more unlikely places for where George Swinley might have hidden the contents of the packages – the inside of the piano, under the aspidistra, in Myra's knitting bag, under the cushions of all the chairs, he even looked under the mattresses upstairs. Nothing, which didn't really surprise him. Swinley must have disposed of them.

He locked up and made his way back to the station in the gathering gloom of the afternoon. There he gave instructions to Williams to despatch the items and fingerprints to the Yard. Then, with the hissing gas fire full on, he wrote up his reports of the day. The telephone rang just after six. It was Dunton, the stationmaster, with the news that the mystery woman hadn't caught the train back to Lewes for her onward journey to Victoria that night. Ryga had half expected that.

He put a call through to Sergeant Jacobs, pleased to find him still at his desk. The sergeant said he had been working on the fur thefts, reviewing all the reports, hoping for a breakthrough. One idea had occurred to him: they had all taken place in premises close to the river. 'It's possible the furs could have been got away by boat. That last robbery at Alaska's Furriers is at Fountain Dock and close by is East Lane Stairs, with West Wharf further up the river. The other robberies weren't far from the river. A fast car down to a landing stage would have got them there in minutes. And the weather on the nights of all the robberies was either fog or heavy rain making visibility poor, so not a lot of movement on the river. Beat officers and the River Police are making enquiries with the wharf men.'

'Talking of fur coats,' Ryga said, 'I've got a mystery woman wearing one who I would very much like to locate.' And swiftly Ryga updated him, telling him about the newsagent and the packages. Jacobs agreed it could be drugs.

Ryga continued, 'This woman, and whoever she works for, couldn't risk Myra stirring up trouble.'

'But hang on sir, they've had plenty of time to silence Mrs Swinley since her husband disappeared and since his body was found, so why wait until now?'

'Because somehow they've discovered she went to Scotland Yard. Or Collier, the newsagent, knows more than he's saying and tipped off this mystery woman after Mrs Swinley's phone call to him last Wednesday. The mystery woman and Myra were seen together leaving the station. Myra must have told her that she was waiting to hear from us as to whether or not we would investigate her husband's death.'

'This woman and her confederates should have waited then to dispose of poor Mrs Swinley because the answer was no and Myra would have had no choice but to accept the coroner's verdict.'

'Yes, but they couldn't take that risk. The fact that the mystery woman didn't use her return ticket indicates that someone met her in a car or a boat. And I think it's the latter. Somehow they got Myra on board, killed her, ditched her body in the sea and also took her husband's boat. They scuttled it to make it appear like suicide. I know there are several blanks, Jacobs, but between us and Miss Paisley let's see if we can fill them in. Instigate enquiries at Victoria Station around the time of Myra's train. I'd like to know if the woman approached Myra on the platform, or if they entered the station together, and if they boarded separately or together. She's very striking looking so would probably have been noticed.' Ryga knew that patient questioning of the porters on duty at the time could yield a result. He gave Jacobs a detailed description.

Jacobs said, 'I'll also locate the guard on that train. He might be able to give us more information.'

'Oh, and check with the Chelsea Yacht and Boat Company if they had a Motor Torpedo Boat, number twenty-one renamed *Constance*, moored there at any time.'

'Connected with the investigation?'

'No, it's moored here at Newhaven, but its owner is missing and no one knows who that is. It looks like a possible suicide or accident.'

'Righty-oh. Shall I update the chief for you?'

'Please.' Ryga told him about the samples, prints and raincoat he was sending up for the lab to analyse, then rang off.

He thought of telephoning Eva then decided to hold back a while. He sat deep in thought. A remark made by Dakins, the custom officer, niggled at him. It was that best suit of Swinleys, which might not have been his best anyway, but Swinley had been smartly dressed. Where had he told Myra he was going dressed like that and on three occasions, always given that he wore his best suit the other times he collected the packages? Wouldn't she have suspected something? Maybe she had, which was why she had telephoned the number she had found in her husband's trousers or jacket – his best perhaps. She'd have been surprised, and perhaps relieved, to find it was a newsagent's and not a woman. She might also have been puzzled but pushed it aside to consider more fully after her visit to the Yard. But why would Swinley dress so smartly to visit a rundown newsagent's? Maybe he always liked to look smart. Or perhaps he had donned his best suit on that Saturday only.

Then there was the fact that Dakins had seen him walk right to the end of the esplanade and turn on to the lane that led over the Downs. The opposite direction to Colliers. Here, then, were some of those blanks he'd mentioned to Jacobs. Ryga knew he would have no peace until he looked into the matter more thoroughly. Tomorrow he would retrace Swinley's footsteps along Seaford esplanade and towards the Downs, and he'd call again on the newsagent.

That decided he headed back to the hotel, where he ate an indifferent meal, missed Eva's company, worried about Sonia's whereabouts and spent an uncomfortable night in a chilly room with a lumpy mattress and a dog somewhere nearby which seemed intent on barking all night.

It was a relief to get up and after eating lukewarm scrambled eggs and burnt toast and swallowing three cups of tea he was glad to strike out towards the railway station. He could have used the police car but had decided that taking the train and following in Swinley's footsteps might be more productive, and at the same time he could ask the railway station staff and train guards if they remembered seeing Swinley or the mystery woman. No one had.

It was just after ten when he stopped off at Collier's before following in Swinley's footsteps along the Seaford esplanade. The scruffy, shuffling newsagent swore on all he held scared that he didn't know the 'young attractive woman's' name who had deposited the packages and therefore couldn't have told it to the woman who phoned him last Wednesday. Neither had he described her. And no one else had contacted him or come calling or deposited or asked about any packages save him.

Collier said that Swinley had collected the package on Saturday 4 November at about four o'clock, when it was dark. That had given Swinley plenty of time to walk along the esplanade and up on to the Downs. On Monday 30 October, Swinley had again arrived about four p.m., but on the 7 November, Swinley had shown up late morning at about eleven. The times fitted in with his shifts.

Ryga set off along the esplanade wondering how the woman had first made contact with Swinley to tell him about the packages. Had they met somewhere to make arrangements? Or was it as he and Eva had discussed – she had telephoned Swinley? That brought him back again to how they had known one another.

Despite the damp cold wind coming off the sea it was a pleasant walk, and he practically had the esplanade to himself save for a couple of people walking their dogs. The white chalk cliffs of Seaford Head were shrouded in mist and he thought back to Saturday 4 November when Swinley had walked this way in the drizzling rain. Perhaps Swinley, like him, enjoyed walking as it helped him to think and often threw up new ideas. Or perhaps he had just been killing time until it was dark enough to collect the package.

The esplanade gave on to a narrow single tarmacked lane to the left. Ryga followed it, twisting first northwards and then east. Low hedges bordered small fields either side of him. Just as Ryga considered turning back he saw a substantial brick house built in a mock Tudor style on a slight knoll behind the hedge, and a little further on a wide gap in the hedge which led into a driveway.

He halted and stared up at the large house set in landscaped gardens of bare branched trees and shrubs. To the left was a substantial garage complex in front of which were two cars, a low-slung modern sports number and a Rolls-Royce. A man in grey overalls was wiping down the latter. It was the sort of house in which an expensively dressed fashionable woman in a mink coat would reside and where Swinley would have donned his best suit to visit. Had he come here to meet her face-to-face? But if she lived here then why leave the packages with Collier? All right, so she didn't want to risk anyone seeing her give them to Swinley. Her husband perhaps? This was all supposition, but now that he was here he thought he might as well check it out.

Fourteen

'Can I help you?' the wiry man in the overalls asked politely as Ryga drew level with him.

'I'm a police officer,' Ryga announced, extracting his identity card. 'I'm trying to trace the movements of a man who I believe passed this way on Saturday 4 November, and I wondered if anyone residing here might have seen him.'

'Now you're asking something,' the man cheerfully replied, glancing briefly at Ryga's warrant card. 'That's quite a while ago and a lot of people pass this way on their route up to the Downs. What's he done? Robbed a bank? Scotland Yard and all that,' he joked. Ryga put him about mid to late thirties. His dark eyes were set deep in a face that was lean and lined and looked as though it had seen some hard times. He was of average height, a little under five feet ten inches.

'No, he was a police officer.'

'Was?'

'George Swinley. His body was found in Newhaven Harbour on the eighteenth of November.'

'I read about that in the paper. And you say he came here?' The man put the wet cloth on the bonnet of the Rolls-Royce and threw a worried glance over his shoulder at the house.

'He came this way. He might have called in here.'

'Why would he do that?'

'Are you the owner of the house?' Ryga asked, side-stepping the question. He could see his action wasn't lost on the man.

He laughed. 'No. I'm just the chauffeur, gardener, handyman, jack of all trades. I live in the flat above the garage. Neil Broxham.' He stretched out his hand. Ryga took it and unlike Dakin's this man's handshake was extremely firm and dry. 'The owners are Major Charles Ashmore and Mrs Valerie Ashmore.'

Immediately Ryga wondered if Valerie Ashmore was his mystery lady. 'How long have the Ashmores lived here?'

'Three years. They also have an apartment in London.'

'Were they at home on Saturday the fourth of November?'

'No. Mrs Ashmore was in the Midlands visiting relatives and Mr Ashmore was in London on business. I drove him there and stayed there. He's a property developer.'

'Is Mrs Ashmore at home now?' Ryga was keen to see her.

'Yes. Mrs Doulton is the cook housekeeper and lives in. She might remember if your police officer called here or walked past.'

Ryga removed the photograph of Swinley from his notebook and asked Broxham if he recognized him or had seen him around the area at any time, adding that PC Swinley hadn't been in uniform when he walked this way. Broxham studied it closely.

'No, I don't remember seeing him on any occasion.'

'Thank you. I'll just check with Mrs Doulton and Mrs Ashmore.' Ryga was tempted to give Broxham a description of the mystery woman and gauge his response but he'd see for himself soon enough if it was the mistress of the house.

The brass bell echoed throughout the property and a couple of minutes later a stout, no-nonsense-looking woman in sensible shoes and a plain grey dress and in her late fifties, answered the door with a dour look on her round face.

Ryga removed his hat and showed his warrant card while introducing himself. The woman studied it closely before her shrewd eyes examined Ryga's face as though summing him up. It looked as though he'd passed muster. She curtly introduced herself as Mrs Doulton. He explained the purpose of his visit and showed her the photograph of George Swinley. She stated quite categorically that she had never seen him before, and that he certainly hadn't called at the house on that Saturday, or at any other time. That seemed to be it. Swinley had simply been filling in the time with a walk up to the Downs before collecting his package from Collier. But Ryga had to check if Mrs Ashmore was his lady in the fur coat.

He asked if he could speak to her.

'I'll see if she is at home,' Mrs Dolton replied stiffly and reluctantly, it seemed to Ryga, and invited him to step inside. Asking him to wait in the hall, she disappeared into a room down the passageway on his right. The hall was expensively furnished in a modern style with some nice paintings, some of which to his semi-trained eye looked to be valuable. He crossed to examine one more closely. It was of a wild, stormy seascape with a couple of wave-tossed fishing boats and two men looking on concerned from the quay with a hill in the distance. It reminded him of Eva's aunt's paintings in the small stone cottage on the Island of Portland, which in turn made him think of Sonia. But he had no time to dwell on that as Mrs Doulton reappeared and showed him, silently, into the lounge at the rear overlooking an extensive landscaped garden, currently drenched in a damp, drizzling rain. Like the hall, it was expensively furnished and in a modern style that seemed to have come right out of a stand at the Ideal Home Exhibition. There was nothing shabby, second-hand or pre-war here. There were some abstract paintings on the walls and Valerie Ashmore was not his mystery lady. She was blonde, with a narrow face, a petulant, discontented mouth and sharp blue-grey eyes which examined him haughtily. She was smoking, in her mid-thirties and slender to the point of thinness, although the wide-skirted, brightly coloured patterned dress gave the illusion of her having hips.

'I can't think why you want to see me, Inspector,' she said crisply, scrutinizing him in a manner that made him think she was short-sighted but too vain to wear spectacles. She didn't bother to rise from the sofa, in front of which was a low modern coffee table and magazines. And she didn't invite him to sit. 'Mrs Doulton said you're making inquiries about a police constable found dead in Newhaven Harbour. I have no connection with any police officers and I can't spare you much time. I have to go out shortly.' She spoke with a slight lisp.

'I'm sorry to trouble you, Mrs Ashmore, and I won't keep you any longer than necessary,' Ryga politely apologized. He noted that her eyes narrowed as though she was trying to work out if he was being sarcastic. 'I wondered if you might have seen this man in the neighbourhood.'

He again removed the photograph of PC Swinley from his inside coat pocket and handed it to her. 'He wouldn't have been in uniform.'

She took it in her slender, well-manicured fingers as though it might be contaminated and peered at it closely, confirming to him that she was short-sighted. His eyes flicked over the magazines. *Vogue* was one of them.

'I've never seen him before.' She thrust it back at him.

He noted the Midlands accent, which she tried to disguise by over pronunciation. It reminded him of a stage hall act.

'Well, thank you for your help.' He made to leave but stalled. Mrs Ashmore was clearly a fashionable lady and she read *Vogue* magazine. That didn't mean she would know the mystery woman but she might recognize the description of the hats. He also wondered if the mystery lady had chosen Seaford as the drop off and collection point because she was a friend of the Ashmores and had visited here on a number of occasions.

He said, 'You might be able to assist me with one more matter, Mrs Ashmore. I'm trying to locate the whereabouts of a fashionable, smartly dressed lady who seems to have a link to Seaford. There is a chance that you might have come across her.' Ryga described the mystery woman in detail, including the striking eyes and the hats. As he did so he watched Valerie Ashmore's reaction carefully and with growing interest. It changed from haughtiness to surprise and then apprehension. It was clear to Ryga that Valerie Ashmore recognized the description and she was bright enough to know that she had betrayed herself.

'She sounds vaguely familiar,' she eventually answered, averting her gaze in order to lean forward to stub out her cigarette in the ashtray. When she looked up her eyes held his only briefly then flitted away. 'I'm not saying it is her, but your description is remarkably like a mannequin I know of.'

Ryga felt his pulse quicken. 'Her name?'

'I'm not in the habit of socializing with mannequins,' she smartly rejoined.

But the faint flush under her skin told him she knew this one. 'Maybe you heard her being addressed by someone,' he prompted.

'If I did I can't remember. It's not something one pays any attention to.'

Ryga's dislike of Valerie Ashmore deepened but he didn't show it. That wouldn't get him anywhere and what he thought of her personally was neither here nor there.

'I've seen her a few times at shows in London,' she elaborated when Ryga didn't speak. 'And her picture has been in fashion magazines. I don't take any notice of who shows the clothes.'

'Has she been in *Vogue* magazine?' Ryga asked, indicating it on the coffee table.

'I expect so. But why are you interested in her? What's she—'

The door opened and a tall, slender man in his mid-thirties wearing an expensive grey lounge suit and an expression of irritation and unease on his angular face entered. Valerie Ashmore gave a slight start and there was a flash of something between her and the man that Ryga interpreted as a warning of some kind.

'Major Ashmore,' he crisply announced, not offering his hand. 'Broxham tells me you're a police inspector from Scotland Yard enquiring about the constable who was found dead in Newhaven Harbour. I can confirm what Broxham told you: I don't know the man. Neither have I seen him before, nor has my wife.'

Major Ashmore was too defensive and too quick with his denial. He hadn't even seen the photograph yet. Not unless he recalled it from a newspaper article.

'I've already told him that,' Valerie Ashmore quipped. She looked about to say something more, then snapped her lips tight together.

Showing nothing of his quickening interest, Ryga went through the ritual of handing Ashmore the photograph of Swinley but he barely looked at it.

Crossly, he said, 'As I've already said, Inspector, I've never seen him before.'

Unlike his wife, Major Ashmore had no discernible accent, although Ryga thought he heard the faint twang of the Londoner in it. Ryga didn't think he was from the upper class but had worked hard to hide his origins, which he suspected were working class. Perhaps his promotion to major had been earned during the war.

'I'm also enquiring about a woman, dark-haired, about mid-twenties, slightly dusky skin, striking blue eyes, fashionable, wearing a swagger mink coat.'

Ashmore looked stunned, but quickly tried to cover his shock, by saying, with what sounded to Ryga, false indifference, 'Could be any number of women. There are lots like that in London.'

'I didn't say she was from London.'

'I assumed . . .' He floundered and reached for a cigarette from the box on the coffee table. Again that glance between husband and wife.

'Mrs Ashmore thought she might be a mannequin.'

Ashmore froze in the act of retrieving the cigarette. His lips tightened.

Defensively and sulkily, Valerie Ashmore said, 'I only vaguely recognized her. As I said, Inspector, there are lots of mannequins like that.'

That wasn't what she had said but Ryga let it go. 'Of course. If either of you do remember her name or if you see her again, Mrs Ashmore, in a magazine or at a fashion show, or in London, Mr Ashmore, perhaps you could telephone Newhaven police station or Scotland Yard.'

'Why are you interested in her?' Ashmore asked, straightening up and trying to sound unconcerned, but to Ryga's finely tuned senses he heard alarm. It was the question his wife had been about to ask before her husband entered.

'Just routine enquiries,' Ryga answered with a smile, taking a little pleasure in seeing the irritated expression cross Ashmore's face and a worried one on his wife's. 'Thank you for your help, Major Ashmore, Mrs Ashmore.' Ryga made for the door. Ashmore quickly gathered himself together and got there ahead of him.

'I'll see you out, Inspector.'

In the hall as he crossed to the front door, Ashmore said, 'Why are Scotland Yard involved? I understood that the police officer you're asking about fell into the harbour. That's what the newspaper said.'

'They don't always get it right.'

'No, but the coroner's inquest said accidental death. I read that too,' he hastily added.

'New information has come to light.'

'Connected with this woman in the mink coat? But how can she be involved?' he persisted.

'It's too early to say, sir,' Ryga gave another of his stock answers and registered Ashmore's worried and puzzled expression. He paused on the threshold. 'But PC Swinley's wife is missing and we're very concerned about her. The last sighting we have of her is with the woman I described to you.'

'But that's . . . You can't think that . . . How would they know one another?' Ashmore stammered.

'They probably don't, they just happened to be on the same train to Newhaven last Thursday,' Ryga fudged. 'We thought the lady might be able to tell us if Mrs Swinley said anything to her about where she was going or what she was concerned about.'

'Oh, yes, I see, of course . . .' Ashmore's relief was palpable. 'My wife and I will let you know if we come across her but I shouldn't think we will.'

'Is your chauffeur around, sir? I'd like to ask him if he has seen or knows the lady.'

'No, he's taken the Rolls to my boat. I need him to get some provisions for it. I'm hoping to take it out later this week, weather permitting. He won't be back for some hours. I'll ask him and he can contact you if he recognizes the woman's description.'

'Thank you, sir.' Ryga replaced his hat and walked down the driveway knowing that he wouldn't receive any telephone call from Broxham or the Ashmores. Equally he knew that husband and wife had recognized the mystery lady but were too afraid to admit to it.

Fifteen

Tuesday

There were two messages awaiting him on his return. One from Sergeant Daniels at Weymouth and the other from Sergeant Jacobs.

He called Jacobs first and was pleased to learn that he had tracked down the guard who had been on the Victoria to Portsmouth train Thursday night – the one Myra Swinley and the mystery woman had caught.

'They got on separately in different carriages. The guard remembers this because the attractive young woman in the fur coat almost missed the train. He helped her in. Said she had lovely blue eyes and she smelt nice. Expensive. The next time he saw her she was in the compartment with the other woman I described to him. Mrs Swinley. There were a couple of other people in the compartment. He said they didn't seem to know one another and yes, they both got off at Lewes. They would have caught the five fifty-three from Lewes to Newhaven, arriving at the town station at five minutes past six. The guard on that train today is the same one who was on duty on the seventh of December.'

Good. Ryga would speak with him.

He told Jacobs about the Ashmores and asked him to look into their backgrounds and find out if there was a mannequin in London fitting the mystery woman's description, adding that Miss Paisley was checking it out with her friends at *Vogue* magazine.

'Then she'll probably have more success than us,' Jacobs replied.

Ryga called Sergeant Daniels at Weymouth police station. A few minutes later Daniels' bright, cheery voice echoed down the line. His news wasn't so cheerful. Sonia Shepherd had left no forwarding address either at Portland or Weymouth Post Offices and no one remembered her buying a ticket at the railway or bus station. Ryga felt uneasy. Had Sam Shepherd got hold of a car and driven her away? Or perhaps she had met another man and had decided to go off with him.

It appeared that Sonia had decided he had no part to play in her life. It wasn't surprising. After all, he was a policeman and would do his best to capture her husband and put him in prison. Sonia and her son would bear the humiliation and shame of it. How could she even feel remotely drawn towards the man who would be responsible for that? Of course, he wasn't the only police officer in the country, and it was unlikely he would be the arresting officer, but that didn't make him feel any better. He didn't blame Sonia for wanting to get away and make a fresh start, but he'd very much like to be the officer who would break the news to her when her husband was caught, if he ever was, and help support her.

He telephoned Eva at her London apartment but there was no answer. He wrote up his interview with the Ashmores, had another cup of tea, and left in plenty of time to reach the railway station. The air had grown even colder, the drizzle had ceased and there was a moderate breeze stirring. The sounds of the harbour reached him as he crossed the swing bridge. The water lapped against the hulls of the ships lining the quayside to his left along North Quay and to his right along Railway Quay. He could hear the creaking of the mooring ropes as the current and wind gently jostled the vessels. Somewhere from further down the harbour came the deep throb of a boat's engine and the shunting of a train. The cranes were silent; the dock workers had gone home. Buildings beside him loomed up out of the dark. There was the smell of the sea, fish, oil and a musty scent of rotten wood, conjuring up memories of his former life before the war. He reached the station in plenty of time but had to hang around as the train was late. Eventually it arrived with a hiss, a flurry and a clanging of doors. Ryga quickly hailed the guard and showed his identity.

'Yes, I remember the two women,' came the welcome reply. 'They boarded together at Lewes.'

'Were they friendly?'

'They seemed to be.'

Ryga could see the platform guard eyeing him impatiently, his flag in his hand and whistle in his mouth. A railway carriage door slammed and someone ahead of them put his head out of a window.

'Did you overhear any of the conversation?' Ryga asked, not really hopeful.

'Only a few words when they alighted. I was standing not far from them. I heard the young woman say, "You must have them." She didn't sound angry or upset, just sort of matter of fact. The older woman didn't answer, or if she did, I didn't catch what she said. I got called away.'

'Did you see anyone take more than a usual interest in them?'

'No.' The guard looked puzzled by the question.

Ryga doubted he'd get more from the man. He stepped back, saying, 'If you remember anything more call Scotland Yard. Sergeant Jacobs.'

'Will do,' the guard shouted back through the open window as the train began to pull away, adding, 'You might get something more from Sergeant Keaton. He was on the train.'

Ryga watched the train disappear into the darkness. Keaton hadn't mentioned that or that he had seen Myra Swinley. Maybe he hadn't recognized her, but he would have done because although Keaton had said he didn't know her he *had* attended the funeral. But why should he have mentioned it? Ryga hadn't asked him for his last sighting of Mrs Swinley, only of George Swinley, which had been on the harbour station on that Saturday 4 November. And Ryga hadn't told Keaton when Mrs Swinley had visited the Yard, so there had been no need for him to make the connection between her getting off a train from London and the Yard. But Ryga was eager to know what Keaton had seen and remembered and he would ask him tomorrow.

What did he make of that remark the guard had overheard? *You must have them.* The packages? The drugs? It seemed likely. And maybe Myra did have them but hadn't realized what they were. The mystery woman could have accompanied Myra to her house, retrieved the packages and passed them on to a confederate. Was that person Major Charles Ashmore? Had Ashmore then taken the woman back to London by car? The more he considered it over half a pint of bitter at the Bridge Hotel the more he thought it possible. He'd liked to have discussed it with Eva over dinner. There was no message from her. He called her London number from the hotel's telephone cubicle and got no reply. He missed her company.

In the morning, after breakfast, he made straight for Sergeant Keaton's office, where he was again offered tea. Again, he accepted.

The office was just as steamy and stuffy as before, but Keaton was looking a little more jaded. 'I've got another officer down with this blasted flu,' Keaton explained. 'That makes four. At this rate I'll be handling all the track and port single-handed.'

Ryga empathized and said Inspector Holden had succumbed to the ailment. 'Does this mean you haven't had time to question the men operating the capstone on the night of Swinley's disappearance?'

'No. I've managed that with the help of PC Whitten. I was going to telephone the station to leave a message for you but now you're here.' He handed Ryga a mug of tea and sat down opposite across his untidy desk. 'A lorry and saloon car crossed just before the bridge opened at nine fifty-eight and only two cars and a van crossed when it closed after that. No pedestrians, which is understandable given the late hour and the foul weather.'

'Was one of the cars a Rolls-Royce or a sports car?'

'No. Both were saloon cars. The van was the local baker's. Is it important?' he asked anxiously.

Ryga shrugged and sipped his tea. It ruled out Ashmore's vehicles but he could have been parked on the eastern side of the swing bridge. If so, that would have meant the mystery lady walking across it, which clearly she hadn't done. Ashmore could have used a different car, he supposed, but Ryga thought it unlikely, although he wasn't ruling anything out.

After a moment, he said, 'I understand you were travelling on the train from Lewes last Thursday night which arrived at the town station at ten minutes past six.'

'No, I wasn't,' Keaton answered, perplexed.

'But the guard said you were.'

'Well, he's right and he's wrong. I'm sorry, I'm not being very clear. I got on the train at the town station and travelled to the harbour station. I'd received a telephone call from Plumpton, up the line, to say that a drunken man had forced his way past the stationmaster without a ticket and had run for the train. I thought he might have been at the races but they said there wasn't any horse racing that day. It was cancelled on account of heavy frost. They made to stop him but they were taken aback and both are, shall we say, past their prime. The porter also has a bad leg so the train was pulling out before they could get to it. I went to Newhaven Town Station to see if the fare dodger had changed trains at Lewes. The Plumpton train runs from Haywards Heath to Lewes and terminates there. The Lewes to Newhaven train was running five minutes late so he could have switched from one train to the other quite easily. I got to the town station just as the train was pulling in. I was looking for a youngish man, in his thirties, dishevelled, wearing a cap. I got on the middle carriage. There was only one man in it who was in his forties so I stuck my head out of the window and called out to the guard, "Has anyone else got off?" He said no and the train began moving away.'

Ryga remembered the guard saying that he'd been called away soon after the women had alighted.

'There was no sign in the train of the man I was after. Why do you want to know about that?'

'Did you see Mrs Swinley alight?'

'I didn't know she was on the train,' he answered, surprised.

'She was with a striking-looking woman who I'm keen to trace.' Ryga described her.

Keaton rubbed at his scar. 'I was concentrating on finding the drunken fare dodger but now you mention it, when I put my head out of the window I did see the backs of two women, which must have been Mrs Swinley and her companion. You could ask Mrs Isaacs. She got off the train as I got on it.'

'The vicar's wife?'

'Yes.'

He would speak to her. It wasn't an interview he was particularly looking forward to because it would probably be another frosty exchange.

He left Keaton and walked down to the landing stage where the customs launch was moored up. He was hoping for a lift across the harbour if he could attract the harbour master's attention, but there didn't seem to be anyone about on the other side of the water. Nevertheless, Ryga lingered, considering Keaton's story. It sounded like the truth and the Plumpton stationmaster and porter could back it up. Mrs Isaacs hadn't mentioned that she'd seen Myra Swinley on the train, probably because they had been in different carriages and, according to Keaton, Mrs Isaacs had alighted first and would have handed in her ticket before the two women.

He watched a fishing boat chug steadily into the harbour, trailed by a long row of bleating and screaming seagulls. The men must have gone out in the early hours of the morning before the high water.

From what he could see they looked to have had a sizeable catch. He decided that no lift was forthcoming and made to turn when a voice came from behind him.

'I'm just going out do you need to get across?'

He turned to find the customs officer, Dakins. 'If it's not too much trouble.'

'None at all, Inspector.'

Ryga let off the lines and climbed on board as Dakins started the engine. They swung out into the harbour and Dakin's, following Ryga's gaze, said, 'She's a lovely craft, the *Constance*.'

'I understand from Mr Hailsham that you and the coastguard went out to her.'

'Yes. Sadly, she was deserted. The coastguard brought her in and I followed. I've searched her since but I didn't find any contraband and nothing to tell us who the owner is. Looks as though Mr Hailsham has been having another nosy around her,' Dakins added as they came along the landing stage.

Ryga saw Hailsham climbing off the *Constance*.

'Any progress with your investigation, Inspector?' Dakins asked.

'Some but it's slow work.' He saw no need to mention his trip to Seaford and subsequent interview and interest in the Ashmores. 'Thank you for the lift.'

Ryga made for the vicarage. There was no answer to his knock and the church was deserted. He thought he'd try the church hall. There he encountered a small group of women sitting around a trestle table in the middle of the chilly hall with their coats and hats on. He didn't blame them – it was colder in than out and that was saying something. All eyes swivelled to him but it was Joan Isaacs' he registered, showing first surprise and then fury.

Ryga stepped forward, removed his hat and hastily apologized for intruding.

'If I might have a quick word, Mrs Isaacs?' he said pleasantly, his gaze holding hers. If looks were electricity he'd have been scorched on the spot and the entire hall would have been floodlit. Clearly she'd like to refuse him but she must have judged agreeing was better than further embarrassment. With a sniff, she scraped back her chair and strode out of the church hall, leaving Ryga to give an apologetic smile to the ladies and follow her.

'How dare you embarrass me in front of those women,' she

launched.

'I'm sorry, Mrs Isaacs, but I tried the vicarage and the church. I didn't know you would be in a meeting,' he said, hoping to mollify her a little. But it was a vain hope.

'What do you want?' she demanded.

'Last Thursday, the seventh of December, you got off the train at the town station at ten minutes past six.'

'That's not a crime.'

'No.' He paused, holding on to his patience. 'Mrs Swinley was on that train and I wondered if you saw her and spoke to her.'

'I didn't. I didn't even know she was on the train.'

Ryga wondered why she made everything sound so hostile and defensive. He pitied the poor women in the church hall. They probably hoped she wouldn't return before their meeting ended. He saw the vicar scurrying towards them with a concerned frown on his narrow hatchet face.

'Where did you go on that Thursday?' he asked her in as friendly tone as he could muster as the vicar drew level.

'I don't see that is any business of yours,' came the answer he had half expected. He sighed inwardly.

'The reason I am asking, Mrs Isaacs,' he said patiently, 'is because on that day Mrs Swinley visited us at Scotland Yard to express her concerns about her husband's death, and that evening she disappeared. She was seen at the town station with a smartly dressed young woman wearing a fur coat, who I would like to trace. If you saw Mrs Swinley, or this woman in London, or on the train, you might be able to give us some information which could help us to find out what has happened to both of them.'

'I really can't see that anything I have to say can possibly help you find Mrs Swinley or this woman. I didn't see her or the woman either in London or on the train.'

'Then you were in London.' Ryga had wondered if she had been in Lewes for the afternoon and had boarded the train there.

She looked put out that she had betrayed herself. The vicar threw his wife a concerned glance and then transferred it to Ryga.

'I have a meeting to get back to.' She tossed a furious glare at her husband, who seemed to visibly flinch before she marched back into the hall.

'You must forgive my wife, Inspector,' Isaacs said wearily. His nose was red and running with the cold, but he made no attempt to wipe it. He wasn't wearing an overcoat, just an old suit jacket over his cassock. His fingers looked blue from the cold. 'She doesn't mean to be so curt. There is a reason why she didn't want to tell you she had gone to London. She went to visit her brother, Jonathan.'

'There's no crime in that.'

'But there is in Jonathan, or I should say there was. He's serving time in Wormwood Scrubs.'

'Oh.'

'And my wife is, shall we say, somewhat overdefensive about it.'

That explained her hostility towards him, Ryga guessed, and the angry, fearful look she'd given him on entering the hall. She'd been terrified he might have dredged it up in front of the women.

'Jonathan has always been a bad lot, Inspector. He went to prison during the war for dealing on the black market and he was again caught stealing and selling petrol last year, for which he is serving another term in prison. Joan won't desert him, though. She tries to reform him but, well, let's say Jonathan is one of those who seem to defy all attempts at saving.'

'I understand. I'm sorry if I caused her distress.'

'She'll be all right.'

But the way he said it, wearily and without hope, made Ryga believe that Joan Isaacs would never be all right. He felt sorry for the vicar and for Joan Isaacs. It must be hard work keeping up such a hostile manner and her life must be empty and lonely. Underneath her anger and bitterness was frustration and a desperate unhappiness. Ryga watched him scuttle away, a nervous, weak man but well-meaning and kind-hearted.

He returned to the police station where he asked the exchange to connect him to Plumpton railway station and once through he received confirmation of Sergeant Keaton's story.

Inviting Sergeant Williams into his office, Ryga asked him about Mrs Isaacs's brother.

'Jonathan Grimley. A bad lot,' was the sergeant's opinion. 'Not that Mrs Isaacs will agree. She dotes on him. Grimley came here in 1946 after serving a stretch for four years for dealing on the black market. You'd have thought he would have learned his lesson but that sort never do. He got up to his dirty tricks almost the moment he was released and was caught filching petrol. He was sent down for six years. He was the only boy of six and the last, and thoroughly spoilt by his mother and sisters, no doubt.'

'Have you any children, Sergeant?'

'Two boys, and they know right from wrong, I can tell you,' Williams said proudly.

'I expect they do. Are either going to follow in your footsteps?'

'The eldest, he's thirteen, is enthusiastic. But then he might change his mind. The youngest, he's nine, wants to fly aeroplanes but I expect he'll grow out of it.'

'And the Isaacs, do they have children?'

'No. The vicar was an army chaplain during the war. They moved here from Bognor Regis in 1946, after he was demobbed. Grimley moved in with his sister on his release from prison.'

That, thought Ryga, would go some way to explaining her hostile, defensive manner. Everyone in the town knew about her errant brother and with her being the vicar's wife tongues would wag and the gossip she so despised would flow freely. He felt pity for her and for the reverend.

Williams said, 'Mrs Isaacs and the vicar tried to reform him but it was no use. Jonathan was soon up to his old tricks. There are some people you simply can't help, despite all your efforts.' An opinion the vicar had already expressed.

Williams fetched Ryga a cup of tea and the rest of the day was spent waiting for reports to come in. It was mid-afternoon when Sergeant Williams reported that none of the bus drivers, conductors or taxi drivers remembered seeing George Swinley on either the 30 October or 7 November. He must have walked to Seaford then. And it was early evening when a telephone call came through from Sergeant Jacobs.

'The Ashmores own a swanky apartment in Mayfair, the building of which they also own along with others dotted around London. They've also got a motor cruiser, *Liberty* registered at Dover.'

Ryga recalled that Ashmore had mentioned his boat. An interesting fact to tuck away for the moment.

'Major Ashmore has been on the up since after the war. He has a reputation for buying land and property in the right place, at the right time and price and either selling it on for development or developing it himself. He's not top drawer. No references to him or his family that we can find in the usual, Debrett's and so forth. Probably got his majority during the war. Whereas Valerie Ashmore is a wealthy woman in her own right, heiress of her late father's manufacturing business in Birmingham, which made a nice tidy packet in the war and was sold to one of those conglomerates that seem to be gobbling up everything. They were married in 1948. That's as far as we've got but we're working on it. Nothing from the photographic agencies on the mystery woman so far. And we're still waiting to hear back from the Chelsea Yacht and Boat Company about the Motor Torpedo Boat.'

Ryga walked slowly back to the hotel mulling over what he had learned during the day. Nothing that seemed to progress his case much further, but the information was amassing. Somewhere along the line and at some time he hoped it would begin to join up, make sense and give him a motive for the murder of George Swinley and the possible abduction and murder of his wife, and with that the identity of a killer. He was almost outside the hotel when he spotted a parked pale blue-green, two-seater MG TC sports car. Eva's. His spirits lifted. He pushed open the door to find her in the bar, drinking a whisky. She looked up with a smile which warmed him more than any liquor or tea could.

'I thought you weren't meant to drive,' he said, crossing to her.

'We're not meant to do a lot of things, Ryga, but we do. I've found your mystery woman,' she declared triumphantly, her blue eyes sparkling.

'She's a mannequin.'

'You know!' she said with a mixture of surprise and disappointment.

'But not her name.'

'Then I have the better of you,' she said gleefully. 'And what's more I also have a picture.'

She handed across a photograph of a slender, beautiful woman with short dark hair, immaculate make-up and a pixie face, wearing a fur coat and smiling down at a row of women dressed in working clothes. The caption made him start. The women were workers at Alaska's, the factory which had been the victim of the latest thefts of furs. There was no mention of the model's name in the photograph but Eva furnished it. Feline Perrier.

Sixteen

'She's in great demand as a model.'

'I can see why,' Ryga answered after he had bought himself half a pint of bitter and they had moved to seats by the fire. Eva had refused a second whisky. The bar was thankfully quiet. There were, aside from themselves, only three middle-aged men in suits who, judging by their appearance and the snatches of conversation Ryga had heard while he'd bought his beer, were commercial travellers staying at the hotel.

'She has an apartment in Eldon Road, Kensington, and she also has a car. An Austin 8. She keeps it at a garage just around the corner from her apartment. It's there now. I spoke to the garage proprietor.'

'We need you at the Yard.'

'Be glad to oblige anytime.' She sat forward. 'It's a pre-1943 model, produced before Austin shut down production for the war, except to manufacture for military use, so it wouldn't have stood out in the streets of Seaford around Colliers newsagent's because it's quite old. It also looks rickety, although according to the garage proprietor it is in perfect working order.'

'But Feline didn't drive to Newhaven to call on Myra Swinley – she caught the train instead,' Ryga said and quickly relayed what he had discovered from the stationmaster and the guard. 'Feline must have known that Myra would be on that train and perhaps she also knew she'd been to Scotland Yard.'

'But how?'

Ryga swallowed some beer. 'I haven't got the answer to that yet. Did you ask the garage proprietor the last time Feline used the car?'

'Yes. It was on Saturday the fourth of November.'

'When Swinley caught the train to Seaford and collected the package. And when he also walked past the Ashmores' house.'

'Who are they?'

121

Ryga told her and explained it was how he had arrived at the conclusion that Feline was a mannequin.

'You have been busy and so have I,' Eva said. 'Let's see if any of the pieces fit together.' She took a sip of her whisky before continuing. 'I began, as I said I would, by visiting the fashion editor of *Vogue*.'

'Which is where Valerie Ashmore recognized her from,' Ryga interjected. 'That and at various fashion shows. But she claimed not to know her name.'

'That could be true. Or she might have heard it at some time and forgotten it.'

'Judging by the Ashmores' manner, my experience tells me they knew exactly who she was. The fact they covered it up must mean they are implicated in this somewhere, but for the life of me I can't think how.'

'It'll come to you,' Eva said brightly, as the men at the counter guffawed.

'Go on.'

'I described the hats to the fashion editor and she said they were the work of a milliner called Jacqueline Chasewater. I called on Miss Chasewater and she confirmed that the three hats were all her designs. She showed me pictures of them, and of the model wearing them. It was our mystery woman – beautiful, short dark hair and stunning eyes. Miss Chasewater said that Feline had shown the hats at an outerwear fashion show last year. Orders had been taken for them, and for other exclusively designed headwear, and at the end of the show the model, in this case Feline, got to keep the hats.

'I then called on the modelling agency, Opal, which is owned by Angela Salcombe. I've worked with Angela, and some of her models, before but never with Feline, otherwise I would have recognized her from the description Collier gave us. Feline Perrier is one of their top models. She's worked a great deal in Paris and Milan, more so than in England, which explains why I haven't come across her before. She's been away on a three-week fashion shoot and returned on 1 December. Angela spoke to her on Saturday 2 December. She hasn't seen or heard from her since.'

'Was she meant to?'

'She tried to get in touch with her last Friday for a modelling assignment, but there was no answer when she telephoned. Angela said she tried several times that day with no result, so she assumed that Feline had gone away for a few days.'

'That's worrying,' Ryga said, concerned.

'Yes. I called at Feline's apartment. There was no answer.'

'Did you manage to talk to any of Feline's neighbours?'

'Only one, who happened to be leaving her apartment as I was ringing Feline's bell. She said she hadn't seen Miss Perrier since last Thursday lunchtime. She said, "good afternoon" and that was it. Feline was wearing a swagger mink coat, and a black velvet turban hat with a veil, the one Collier described to us, a pencil skirt, and she was carrying a handbag and wearing black gloves.'

Ryga didn't like the sound of this. 'So where has she been for the last six days after being seen with Myra Swinley? Has she gone into hiding after getting what she needed from Myra? Does Charles Ashmore know where she is?'

'Maybe he does. When I pressed Angela for more information about Feline, she said that before she left for her last modelling assignment on the eleventh of November she had seemed distracted and uptight.'

'Boyfriend trouble?'

'No, brother trouble. He lives on a boat at Chelsea boatyard although he's rarely there. He takes it out to sea a lot.'

Ryga froze with his beer halfway to his lips. 'It doesn't happen to be a converted Motor Torpedo Boat?'

'I don't know. It could be. Why?'

'There's one in the harbour, which was found drifting in the English Channel on the twelfth of November with no one on board, and nothing to say who the owner is.'

'Could it belong to Phillipe Perrier, Feline's brother?' Eva pushed her hand through her hair.

'I've asked Sergeant Jacobs to make enquiries. He's waiting to hear back from Chelsea. It could explain why Feline hasn't heard from her brother, but it doesn't mean he's involved in this case. It's just coincidence his boat was picked up drifting in the English Channel and taken into Newhaven.'

Eva looked doubtful. Ryga was himself. 'The boat was reported drifting five days *after* George Swinley collected the last package, and that's five days *after* he disappeared, so how could he be involved, *if* the boat is Perrier's?' Ryga mused. 'The timing seems wrong. Did you get anything else?'

'Of course. Feline is twenty-three. She, her brother and mother, came to England in 1939. Their mother was English. Their father French.'

'Was the mother's name Constance?'

'No. Lucy.'

If it was Phillipe's boat, he hadn't renamed it after his mother or sister.

'Feline's father, Maurice, died in 1940, or so Feline discovered after the war. He was a renowned art historian. And a Jew.'

Eva didn't need to say anything further on that score. Ryga could guess the poor man's fate.

'Phillipe is a talented painter. He's also an expert sailor, the family having owned a boat in France before the war. He served in Coastal Command during the war as a pilot.'

Coastal Command had protected lightships and convoys carrying vital food and weapons the country needed. Phillipe would have spent hours flying over the oceans with his crew relying on instrumentation and observation, no landmarks in the Atlantic, and he might not have seen land of any kind for nine-tenths of the patrol. Phillipe Perrier would have needed the same sense of direction as that of a sailor or a homing pigeon and could easily navigate a boat in the fog as, according to Eva, he was also a competent sailor. An accident on board was looking less likely and suicide a stronger possibility, but why? And just because he was missing – as were Myra and Feline – it didn't mean he was mixed up in this.

'Feline's mother lived in London and joined the ambulance service as a volunteer as soon as she arrived in England. She was killed during the Blitz. Feline lived with an aunt in Hastings who's now deceased.'

Ryga sat back, deep in thought. There was so much he didn't understand. Was Phillipe Perrier involved in this? Was the Motor Torpedo Boat moored up in the harbour his? If so, was he dead and how had he died? What had become of Feline? What had been in those packages?

Before he could express any of his questions the door flew open and a uniformed officer burst in, his young face flushed. His eyes alighted on Ryga and he hurried forward.

'We've got a body, sir,' he began. The men at the bar instantly fell silent.

'Let's discuss this outside,' Ryga said quietly, rising and picking up his hat, scarf and coat from the chair beside him. Eva grabbed her jacket from the back of her chair. They stepped out into the bitterly cold still night.

'It's a woman,' the constable said.

'Myra Swinley?' Ryga asked, his heart lurching.

'I don't know, sir. Sergeant Williams asked me to run and tell you. Joseph Moore came into the station in a right state, said he'd tripped over her in Sleeper's Hole. The sergeant couldn't get any more out of him except that she's by the upturned boats. Moore's a gibbering wreck so the sergeant's left him having a cup of tea with PC Benton and sent me to fetch you. Sergeant Williams has gone ahead of us. He said I was to take you there.'

Ryga said nothing more. There wasn't anything he could say. His mind was racing with thoughts and with speculation on what they were going to find. At the end of Fort Road they crossed the railway track and turned on to the short rough footpath almost in the middle of the U-shaped Sleeper's Hole towards the landing stage. Ryga's torch, and the young constable's, lit their path. Ahead Ryga could see the beam of Sergeant Williams' torch and beside him the two upturned boats which he'd noted on his previous visit here on Saturday.

As he came level, the sergeant's usual jovial round features showed consternation and sorrow. Williams didn't speak but nodded to where a dark, lifeless bundle was lying beside one of the boats that was now the right way up. Ryga crossed to it and with bated breath played his light over the body. His heart skipped a beat. The constable beside him retched and staggered away. Ryga heard Eva let out a long, slow breath. The fur coat was sodden and bedraggled. The once beautiful face was covered in mud and seaweed, and the lively, startling eyes stared out at them, sightless. There was no mistaking who it was. Feline Perrier.

Seventeen

It was very late when Ryga got to bed; in fact, it had hardly been worth going because for the few hours left to him by the time he returned to the hotel he knew he wouldn't be able to sleep. Not only was he haunted by the image of Feline Perrier but he was also plagued by the myriad of questions regarding her death and that of the fate of Myra Swinley. As Eva had been, she admitted the next morning over breakfast. They could discuss them all day – as they had last night when heading back to the hotel – and they'd still not get the answers. Those lay in the gathering of information.

Last night Eva had taken photographs of the body fully clothed in situ with the aid of a powerful flashlight and torches, and in the mortuary at the local hospital. Her presence had caused a bit of a stir with the mortician and the police doctor, who both clearly thought the task was no job for a woman, but Ryga had quietly insisted that she stay, while Eva had simply got on with the job. Ryga barely needed to tell her what was required. It was a solemn and distasteful task but necessary. He felt sorrow and anger at such a violent and wasteful end to a young life.

The police doctor officially certified death and confirmed that in his opinion the cause appeared to be the blow to the head, but he couldn't say whether that had been inflicted by the killer or by a fall. Ryga had asked for the body to be undressed and this was again photographed by Eva. Ryga noted how Feline was still wearing all her clothes including her gloves, so the flesh was remarkably untouched by the ravages of nature because not only had she been protected from the elements and the birdlife under that upturned boat – which was where it was obvious her body had been hidden since Thursday night – but she'd also been fully clothed. However, where the flesh had been exposed – the face and neck – there were distasteful signs of decay caused by sea lice and crabs, not to mention the maggots that had hatched in the body. Her small black hat with the veil had been slightly askew on her short dark hair. The fur coat carried a label, *Alaska Furriers, London*, the one she had been modelling in the photograph Eva had obtained. Eva said that Feline's clothes were exquisitely made, not chain store, and her underwear was silk and of the highest quality. She said she'd probably be able to trace who had made and supplied them but that wouldn't solve the mystery of who had killed her because, despite what the doctor said, that blow to the head hadn't been caused by any fall.

Ryga had called Superintendent Street at his home. Street said he would request the autopsy to be conducted by a forensic Home Office Pathologist who would hopefully arrive that day. He asked if Ryga wanted Jacobs down there to assist but Ryga said the sergeant would be more useful in London obtaining information about Feline Perrier and her brother, who was also missing, because the Chelsea Yacht and Boat Company had confirmed the Motor Torpedo Boat moored in Newhaven Harbour was Phillipe Perrier's and that it had left Chelsea on 11 November. Ryga said he would use Sergeant Williams and his officers to assist. He also mentioned the role Eva had already played and said she would continue to help with the investigation. Street seemed perfectly happy with that. The clothes had been wrapped up in paper and were that morning being despatched to the Yard laboratory for examination.

The air was bitingly cold as he and Eva stepped outside and made for Sleeper's Hole. The dawn had arrived late and dismally grey. At least Ryga assumed it was grey – he couldn't see it. He could barely see the other side of the harbour, the fog was so thick. Eva said she was wearing two sweaters under her faithful old donkey jacket and she wore a pair of fingerless mittens. Ryga was sorely tempted to buy a jumper from the local menswear outfitters but didn't.

It was two hours after high water. Joseph Moore, now recovered from the trauma of falling over the body, was drawing on his pipe, sitting on the remaining upturned boat. He greeted them solemnly, said he couldn't believe what had happened and that he hadn't slept a wink all night for thinking of the poor woman. He looked on incredulously as Eva set about photographing where Feline had lain and the surrounding area.

'Not much point doing that now the body's gone,' he volunteered. 'Fair gave me a turn seeing it there. My foot struck against it. Thought it was a bit of old wood washed up, and blow me if it wasn't a woman. Who is she?'

'What time did you go out last night?' Ryga asked.

'About seven o'clock.'

'To the pub?'

'Yes. Had a beer and came back just before ten.'

That beer had lasted him a while. 'Did you hear or see anything unusual?'

'Like what?'

Ryga looked pointedly at him.

'No, nothing out of the ordinary,' he said. 'A coaster came in and another made its way down from North Quay.

'When did you notice this boat had been turned up the right way?'

'Not until I walked into the poor dead woman. I think it was upturned all of yesterday, but I can't swear to it.'

Ryga wondered if Hailsham would remember.

Moore pushed back his cap. 'How long has she been under there?'

'Since last Thursday night, we believe.'

'Good Gawd, a week, and there's me walking round the poor creature! Who could have put her there?'

'Who owns that boat?' asked Ryga.

'No idea. It's been here for years.'

He could see that, by its sorry state. Ryga was amazed it hadn't fallen to pieces when the killer had lifted it and dragged Feline under it, and then when he had again lifted it up and moved it slightly to the right and exposed her body. One man could easily have done it alone. But while Feline was being killed, where was Myra? At home still? Or had she too been knocked out, put in her husband's small boat, and after the killer had hidden Feline, been taken out into the harbour?

Ryga opened his murder case, drawing a wide-eyed look from Moore and a gurgle of his pipe. Ryga tried to get some prints from the ends and the sides of the boat, where the killer would have lifted it, but there were only smudges. Either the mud and rain had obliterated any prints or the killer had worn gloves. He took samples of the mud around the boat and where Feline had lain, another activity that caused Moore to shake his head in wonder. Eva took more pictures.

To Moore, Ryga said, 'We'll need your fingerprints for elimination purposes.'

'I haven't touched the boat.'

'Nevertheless.'

'Want to take them now?'

'No, call in at the station as soon as you can.'

Eva nodded to say she had all she needed. She addressed Moore. 'Could I take some photographs of you and your home later?' She jerked her head in the direction of the corrugated-iron edifice, adding, 'I don't work for the police. At least not all the time. I'm usually just a nosy photographer.'

'I can't see why you'd want to photograph it, or me. It's nothing to look at and neither am I.'

She smiled. 'Ah, but you are, Mr Moore, and I'd love to see inside your home. Both you and it fascinate me.'

Moore's mouth fell open before he visibly preened himself. 'Then call in and have a cup of tea, miss, whenever you like.'

'I will. Thanks.'

'So that's how you do it,' Ryga said, as they walked to the landing stage where the Motor Torpedo Boat the *Constance* was berthed. 'Charm and flattery.'

'Works most of the time, but not always. And those who don't like being photographed are often the people I would like to – the interesting ones, with hidden depths,' she said, glancing at him. He remembered he had told her he was averse to being snapped after she had done so without his knowledge while he'd been on the isolated Church Ope Cove on Portland Island trying to fathom out why a man in a pinstriped suit had ended up dead in it.

They'd arrived at the boat. Ryga was looking forward to seeing if the interior was as exquisitely kept as the exterior.

Eva said, 'I see what you mean about her being lovingly restored. Phillipe's disappearance and Feline's deaths must be connected, Ryga. What on earth were they up to, and how and why involve George Swinley?'

'Let's hope something inside can tell us that, or at least give us some ideas.' Ryga did, however, think that Sergeant Jacobs' enquiries at the Yard into both Feline and Phillipe's backgrounds, and the search of Feline's apartment, would provide a better chance of that.

He would need the boat keys, which he said he'd get from Hailsham, but as he was about to make for the Watch House, Hailsham emerged from it and came hurrying towards them.

'I've just been told the news about the body. It's not Myra Swinley, is it?' he asked, alarmed.

'No. It's a woman who was seen alighting from the train with her last Thursday.'

'This is a terrible turn of events. Who is she? Why would anyone want to kill her?' Hailsham removed his cap and ran a hand over his head. Replacing his cap, he reached for a cigarette from his jacket pocket and offered the packet round, eyeing Eva curiously. Ryga introduced her but made no explanation of her role. They both refused the cigarettes.

Ryga said, 'This boat belongs to the dead woman's brother, Phillipe Perrier.'

Hailsham's jaw dropped. 'Then what has—'

'I need to see on board.'

'Of course. I'll fetch the key.'

While he did, Ryga climbed on board with Eva. The exterior of the boat had been stripped of all the weaponry. There was a metal plaque above the hatch telling them she had been built in Portsmouth, probably, Ryga thought, by Vosper Thorneycroft based there.

Hailsham returned and handed over the key which was on a piece of stout string tied to a float.

'I'd like to retain it for a while,' Ryga said. 'Did you or your staff see or hear anything unusual yesterday evening?'

'No. I left here just after eight o'clock. My assistant had already gone home. I had some paperwork to attend to, otherwise I would have gone sooner. Nothing came in this side of the harbour after three p.m. and that was only a small fishing boat. A couple of coasters went up after that to North Quay.'

So no one about, no Joseph Moore or harbour staff to see him unveil a corpse from the upturned boat. But why do so? A question he, Eva and Sergeant Williams had already considered without any answer, save the killer had a prick of conscience. Sergeant Williams had said that maybe the killer wanted to be caught. Ryga had replied that he wished then the culprit would turn himself in, it would save them all time. Maybe he was too afraid to confess, proffered Eva. Or the killer could be taunting them in the belief that he was clever enough not to be apprehended. Why not let Feline rot there for a very long time, until the trail had grown completely cold?

'Did you notice whether that wooden boat was upright or still upturned yesterday?'

Hailsham puffed at this cigarette, his face screwed up as he tried to remember. After a moment, he shook his head. 'Sorry, Inspector, I can't say. Those two boats have been in the Hole for so long that I've stopped noticing them.'

'Do you know who owns it?'

No. It's just one of those fixtures. Like the other one. I don't know who owns that either.'

Ryga thought he'd get much the same answer from the officers at the police station.

He said, 'As you've been on board this boat, Mr Hailsham, I'll need your fingerprints, just so we can eliminate them from our enquiries.'

'Of course.'

Ryga would also have to ask Dakins for his. 'If you could call into the station at your convenience, sir.'

Hailsham took the hint that he was no longer required. 'You know where to find me if needed,' he said, alighting, sounding slightly put out.

Eva took some photographs on deck while Ryga entered the Bridge, which was now a galley with gleaming polished wooden units, a sink and small gas hob. There was cutlery in the drawers, clean crockery in the cupboards and also some basic food provisions. The main operations room was now the salon with a rug and two small armchairs, along with a table and two chairs. It was cosy. In the cupboards, which Phillipe or someone else had built around the side of the salon, he found charts of the English Channel, the Solent, the North Sea and France. He could see nothing marked up on them.

Eva joined him and began to photograph the interior. 'I love this boat. It's got a lived-in, much-loved feeling. Found anything interesting?'

'No.'

The wood panelled captain's cabin contained a double bed, made up, and a locker that held some clothes. The porthole window gave out on to the harbour. The wireless room – still bearing its name in a brass plaque on the solid wood door – was the lavatory and washroom. Towards the prow, there were still the bunks where the crew used to sleep.

Ryga returned to the salon.

'What do you see, Ryga?' Eva asked, just as she had before on their case in Portland in a shabby little jewellers shop.

'A neat man, ordered, meticulous, clever with his hands, someone who likes his own company.' He sniffed. 'I can't smell any perfume but it could have evaporated by now if Feline had been on board. Although I don't think she got this far.'

'She could have been struck after leaving the boat. This could have been the bait that lured her across the Hole from Fort Road. Someone told her that her brother's boat was here and, excited, she hurried here hoping to see him. The porthole is open. Was it open when it was brought in? The killer could have opened to erase the scent of Feline's perfume.'

Ryga said he would ask Dakins, the customs officer. 'It doesn't strike me that this is his main residence. There's not enough clothes, food or personal items here for that.'

'Perhaps he liked to live with the barest essentials. Or perhaps he hasn't any belongings. Many people lost everything in the war and, given what happened to his father, it wouldn't be surprising if Phillipe liked to live with just the minimum required.'

Ryga knew that Eva was right. He kept his possessions to the minimum.

'I wonder if he worked, and if so what he did for a living. His money must have come from somewhere,' Eva mused.

'His sister perhaps? Or perhaps some criminal activity, which is what he had decided to expose via his sister and those packages. Whoever is behind it killed both brother and sister. Yes, I know, why did she give the evidence to PC Swinley? The obvious answer is that Swinley and Perrier must have known one another.'

'From the war?'

'They were in different branches of the services. Swinley was with the Royal Artillery, Anti-Aircraft Division while Perrier was Coastal Command. Myra said her husband was moved around to different places – Dundee, Belfast, the Midlands, London. Perhaps they came into contact but why, if Perrier wanted to expose a criminal activity, did he involve his sister? Why not come straight to us at the Yard with what he knew? Let's take a look at the engine room.'

It was, like the rest of the boat, spotless. Returning to the salon, Eva said, 'Could Feline have seen her brother's boat moored up here on the way from the railway station to Myra's house?'

'Not from the road, no. She would have seen it from Myra's

bedroom window though, but by then it was dark and foggy. I'll see if I can lift some fingerprints and conduct a search. After that I'll ask Hailsham to take me across to the Customs House to speak to Dakins, if he's on duty.'

'I'll get these photographs, and the ones I took last night of Feline, developed and suffer the cold of Miss Green's dark room, as I know you must be keen to have them.'

Ryga began his painstaking work. He took prints from various surfaces across the entire boat including the engine room, while at the same time combing the surfaces and the floors for hairs, fibres and in particular for fur or feathers the latter of which could have come from Feline's coat and hat. He found some fibres on the deck of the salon that looked like fur, carefully placed them in a small paper bag and put them in his case. Even if they had come from Feline's coat, though, it didn't mean she had been on the boat on Thursday evening. They could have been there for some time, before she had gone abroad to work. There were some varying prints which Ryga knew must be Dakins, Hailsham, and the coastguard who had brought the boat in. Once they were ruled out the remaining ones would probably be Perrier's.

He went up on deck. Perrier could have deliberately set his boat adrift on 12 November then returned to shore in a tender he had kept on board, his purpose to make his confederates believe he was dead. He had gone into hiding, fearing for his life, waiting until his sister returned to England. He then had told her to find out if Myra had the packages his sister had left at the newsagent's. Someone had discovered this, or extracted the information from Perrier after tracking him down, and had lured Feline here to kill her. And if so, then Perrier by now was probably also dead. Perhaps Feline, after hearing from her brother, had inadvertently told the very person her brother was trying to expose.

Ryga stared around the deck. The bow was long enough to accommodate a tender and it would have had oars and an engine, like George Swinley's missing boat. There was no covering of any kind lying around. There were two double cleats close to the bow, one on the portside, the other on the starboard side. Both had lines curled around them with two of the starboard lines tied off on the cleats on the landing stage. There were also two double cleats at the stern, with a line again fastened to the landing stage on the starboard side.

He crossed to the bow where the anchor rested on deck and faced south looking down the harbour, out to sea. He could see nothing, and the cold cut through him. The rattling, grinding and throbbing of the harbour at Railway and East Quays sounded a ghostly accompaniment to the foghorns.

There was a steel pole directly in front of him about two feet high. Aside from that the deck was open, broad and long, with two eighteen-inch redundant torpedo tubes either side of the bridge. On the lines connected to the torpedo tubes there were two white buoys on the deck on the port side, and two further buoys attached to lines on the starboard side which were protecting the hull from the wooden landing stage. But Ryga noted two extra lines fixed to the torpedo tubes with nothing attached to the end of them. They were curled up neatly on the deck. There was also a line wrapped around the pole that stood between him and the bridge.

With a quickening pulse, he surmised that their purpose had been to secure a tender. And on close examination of the wet deck – which necessitated him dropping to his knees and causing damp patches on his trousers – he detected that the paint was a slightly lighter shade of grey in a large area of the deck confirming his suspicions.

Ryga returned to the salon. There were two places he hadn't searched – under the cushions of the two seats. Nothing. Hold on, though. His hand reached deep down inside the left-hand seat and struck against something. It was only part of the chair's construction but he hadn't felt it on the first chair. He tried the first chair again, no nothing there. Returning to the second chair, he knelt and pushed his hand deep down inside it. Yes, definitely something there, not that he felt it was of significance – it wasn't paper or wood but a thin rod of some kind. He reached down further, so that his chin was almost resting on the seat of the chair. Any further and his hand would connect with the deck, he thought. Then his fingers curled round it, and with some considerable manipulation, effort and time, he finally managed to bring it to the surface. Astonished and bemused, he found himself holding a size-nine steel knitting needle. It was the last thing he had expected. Carefully, with gloved fingers, he placed it in an evidence bag.

Eighteen

‘ W here's the other one?'
       'Good question, Sergeant Williams, and the first I
       asked myself.'
Ryga had postponed his visit to the Customs House and had called
in at Myra's house where he had made straight for the knitting bag.
He'd found several knitting needles, including a pair of nines, but no
single ones. Along with the grey skein of wool and the navy-blue balls
of wool he'd seen on his earlier visit, he'd found a few more balls of
assorted colours in the depths of the bag, but there wasn't any knitting
in progress and no knitting patterns. Perhaps Myra had recently
finished a knitting project and hadn't the heart to embark on a new
one with her husband gone. There was no longer that need or desire to
knit jumpers, gloves or hats for him.

'The other questions I asked myself, Sergeant, were what was it
doing on board a boat owned by Phillipe Perrier? How did it get there,
how long has it been there, and does it have any significance to this
case?'

'It must have, especially as the other one's gone missing, and that's
because the other one is the murder weapon.'

'And where did the killer get the knitting needles from?' posed
Ryga. He had already speculated on this, but he was interested to see
if the sergeant would come to the same conclusion. He did.

'Myra Swinley's house. He took a pair of them, stabbed Feline
Perrier with one of them, mislaid the second one and took off because
he didn't have time to look for it. Could be the brother.'

'Then where has he been since the twelfth of November? And why
not leave by his boat after killing his sister?'

'Too foggy.'

Ryga had checked in with Hailsham on his way back to the police
station from Myra's and Hailsham had confirmed there hadn't been a

135

tender on board the *Constance* when it had been brought in. And Ryga kept coming back to the same point – why abandon such a lovingly restored and maintained boat?

'Perhaps the knitting needle has been there for some time,' Ryga said, 'and has no significance at all. It could belong to a friend of Phillipe Perrier's from Chelsea boatyard. It could be his sister's. I saw the body, Williams, and there was no puncture wound in the chest.'

'Might be so small you didn't notice it, sir. Or maybe she was stabbed elsewhere on the body, in the back, for example.'

'Not that I could see there either but then I didn't examine it closely.'

'There you are then. It could have been the head, of course.'

'There was that blow to the head, so it's possible that disguised a stab wound, but it would take some force to stab someone with this through the head!'

'And a cold-blooded villain at that,' Williams agreed sadly.

'Does Mrs Williams knit?'

'Of course, she's always got something on the go,' Williams answered, slightly puzzled by the question.

'Does she always knit from a pattern?'

'Mostly. I see her marking it and tutting at it sometimes, although scarves she can knit blindfolded she's done that many, and balaclavas. She knits for the church's fundraising committee. But I can't see how a knitting needle belonging to any of them could have ended up on Perrier's boat.'

'Neither can I. Nevertheless, send it up to the Yard as soon as you can, Sergeant, along with these other samples.'

'Will do. Oh, and a message came for you earlier, sir, to say the pathologist was driving down from London. He should be at the mortuary by three o'clock.'

That gave Ryga an hour. He'd like to speak to the pathologist before he began the autopsy. 'Is the car available for me to use, Sergeant?'

'Yes, Inspector Holden is still poorly. His wife said he tried to come into work this morning, especially when he heard a body had been found, but he was too weak. He sends his apologies. I expect he's annoyed at not being here to be involved.'

'Better he stays where he is and gets fit instead of spreading his germs around.'

'That's what I said. Is there anything more you need, sir?'

Ryga said there wasn't. He had already given Sergeant Williams orders for his officers on the beat to instigate routine enquiries. An appeal in the local newspaper had gone out, which also might encourage someone to come forward, but Ryga was positive he'd get the same answers as he had from Moore and Hailsham – that it had been too cold for many to be abroad last night and to have witnessed anything.

Sergeant Williams returned within a minute and placed a package wrapped in greaseproof paper on Ryga's desk. 'The wife made them for you,' he said shyly. 'Cheese and homemade chutney sandwiches. She's won prizes for her chutney,' he added proudly.

'Thank you, that's extremely kind of her,' Ryga said gratefully. He was, he realized, hungry, not having eaten since breakfast, and that had only been two pieces of toast. He hoped Eva had managed to get something to eat. He could tell by Williams' expression that he wouldn't be happy, or budge, until he had tried one.

'I'm not surprised she's a prize winner. The chutney, and the sandwiches, are delicious,' Ryga announced after biting into the wedge of bread. And he meant it.

'I'll tell her that,' Williams said, pleased and proud.

The sergeant brought him in cup of tea. Sometime later, Ryga, checking his watch after finishing off his reports, saw it was three-twenty and time he made for the mortuary.

He found Dr Plumley, a broad, squat man with a balding head, hair in his ears and nose, and a frown on his podgy fifty-year-old face, already gowned and gloved, inspecting the body of Feline Perrier. Ryga thought there was something a little obscene about his critical and obsessive gaze but quickly checked his revulsion and irritation. This was the doctor's job. And wherever Feline was now she wouldn't worry.

The body hadn't been washed. With unaccustomed crispness, caused partly by his anger at Feline's fate and Plumley's manner, Ryga updated the doctor on the finding of the knitting needle. He asked if it could have been the murder weapon. This caused Plumley's bushy grey eyebrows to rise in his broad high forehead. Sarcastically he replied, 'I have no idea, Inspector Ryga. I will, of course, look for puncture marks and other indications of the cause of death. It is my job so to do.'

It was as though Ryga had questioned his ability. 'Thank you,' he answered politely, thinking it pointless being frosty with a man who, he surmised, wouldn't notice the difference between politeness and sarcasm anyway. 'Can you give me an estimate of time of death?'

'From what I've seen of the evidence of maggots, which I'd say were in their first stage of development, she's been dead about five days.'

'The last time she was seen alive was a week ago.'

'Then you have the advantage of me. Anything else you've omitted to tell me?'

Plumley appeared to be a prickly soul but Ryga didn't mind that, just as long as he was proficient at his job.

'She was discovered in Sleeper's Hole close to the harbour, a mud inlet off the harbour,' he explained. 'It's probable that she was placed there after being killed, rather than being washed up. If there is any evidence of this I'd be interested to know it.'

'That might be difficult to tell, Inspector, certainly initially. I'll take samples of skin and internal organs, which will be analysed, but you won't get those results for some days. Now if you don't mind, I'd like to get on. I want to be back in London tonight.'

Ryga asked to be notified at the police station when he had finished, which he estimated would be at approximately seven p.m. Ryga hoped Plumley wouldn't rush on account of his haste to return to London and therefore miss anything vital.

Next he drove across the swing bridge to the Customs House and found Leslie Dakins with another man who he introduced as his boss, Chief Preventive Officer Harold Leemings. Leemings was a tall, thin man with potato-coloured skin, a discontented expression and a hint of hostility in his grey eyes. Ryga quickly ascertained from Leemings that last night only he and Dakins had been in the Customs House.

Requesting a private word with them both, Leemings showed Ryga into a small staff room where a gurgling tea urn was creating a damp, steamy atmosphere. Taking the offered seat but refusing refreshment, Ryga told them about the death of Feline Perrier and where and how her body had been found, drawing startled and concerned looks from both men. Neither claimed to have seen or heard anything unusual last night, although Dakins said that he had been out on the customs launch for two hours on receiving notification that a cruiser was making for Cuckmere Haven.

'It turned out they had got lost in the fog, the sailor's nightmare – it slowed them down and took them off course. I said they were lucky to get back at all, and safely. Some idiots go out no matter what the weather. I helped escort them back to Seaford, arrived here just after nine, then signed off.'

'I'd just left when the call came through at seven,' Leemings said a little sourly. 'Otherwise I would have stopped Dakins from going out because of the weather.'

Dakins threw Ryga a slightly apologetic smile. Ryga could guess what he was thinking. Fog made the perfect cover for smugglers, and members of the Waterguard had to go out no matter what the weather.

'I alerted the coastguard who accompanied me,' Dakins said with a slightly weary tone as though he'd said this already, several times.

Leemings' lips tightened and his body stiffened.

Ryga quickly interjected. He asked if they had seen an abandoned tender anywhere along the coast. 'Not George Swinley's small wooden boat,' he added. 'I think this one might have been launched from the Motor Torpedo Boat *Constance*.'

They hadn't. Ryga requested they look out for it. 'We also need your prints, Mr Dakins,' he continued. 'The dead woman's brother owns that boat. We're trying to trace him to give him the news, but he could have taken off in that tender and . . . well, you don't need me to spell it out to you.'

'No, sadly.'

'You'd better take my fingerprints as well,' Leemings chipped in, frowning more heavily than previously and looking out of sorts. Perhaps he was ill, thought Ryga. 'I went on board while she was moored up here, before Dakins took her over to the landing stage by the Watch House.'

Dakins looked stunned. 'You didn't say.'

'I don't have to report to you, Dakins,' came the sharp rely.

Dakins' lips tightened but he said nothing. Ryga could see there was no love lost between the two men.

'Can I ask why you went on board, sir?' Ryga asked as smoothly and pleasantly as he could. By the gleam in Dakins' eyes Ryga could see it was the question Dakins would have liked to have asked his boss.

'It's part of my duty,' came the stern and surly reply, along with a glare at Dakins as though daring him to comment. Dakins had more sense.

Ryga opened his murder case. 'Then I'll take both your prints.' He did so. No one spoke during the process. Ryga could hear a phone ringing somewhere and men's voices but couldn't make out what they were saying.

'Was the salon porthole open when either of you went on board?'

Leemings frowned. 'I can't remember.'

'I think it was,' Dakins said. 'But I can't swear to it. I didn't really look.'

He asked who had piloted the *Constance* back to the harbour. Perhaps he had noticed.

'The coastguard, Godfrey Lawes,' Dakins replied.

Ryga said he would contact him. As he made to leave, he said, 'Was there anything that struck either of you as unusual on the *Constance*?'

Dakins answered first. 'Only that it was remarkably tidy and clean and well maintained. I thought it must belong to an ex-serviceman, Royal Navy most probably, someone who might have served on such a craft during the war.'

Leemings threw Dakins a look that Ryga thought was distaste or was it disgust?

'And you, sir?' Ryga addressed Leemings.

'The logbook was missing,' was his sole comment.

Dakins had also told him that. He showed Ryga out. Quietly he said, 'You'll have to forgive Mr Leemings, Inspector. He's not in the best of health. He's a bit forgetful but he doesn't like anyone to point that out. I think he's afraid of losing his job.'

'Does he live in Newhaven?'

'Yes. Not far from Myra and George Swinley's house in Fort Road. I shouldn't say this, but his wife left him just after the war. It was a terrible blow to him. They lost their only son in the war. He was in the navy. Leemings took his wife's desertion badly. He had a breakdown. He's only been back on duty for eight months.'

More fractured lives, thought Ryga, making for the British Transport Commission Police office where he repeated his questions to Inspector Keaton who, like Leemings and Dakins, claimed not to have seen or heard anything suspicious the previous night. Keaton had knocked off at seven thirty and had never been on board the *Constance*, so there was no need for Ryga to take his prints.

He hadn't been back at the police station long when Eva arrived with a bulky envelope, but before she could speak the telephone rang. It was Sergeant Jacobs at the Yard.

'There were only two photographs in Feline's apartment, one of her and her brother as children and one of them with their parents, Lucy and Maurice Perrier, taken before the war.'

Both now deceased.

Jacobs said, 'There were no letters or diaries. Her apartment is well kept, looks expensively furnished and is in a respectable area. The neighbours say she'd lived there for about eighteen months but wasn't always at home on account of her modelling work. Feline was friendly, polite, kept herself to herself, was no trouble and always beautifully dressed. I'd say her wardrobe bears that out, fashionable and expensive clothes, shoes and hats and three furs, a fox fur stole, a short mink and a full-length sable. I've become something of an expert,' Jacobs added, tongue-in-cheek.

'Any of them stolen?'

'Not by the labels. None of them come from any of the furriers who have been robbed.'

'Only the one she was wearing when her body was found. It was a swagger mink, the same one Collier the newsagent said she had on when she dropped off the packages and when she alighted from the train with Myra. It was from Alaska's.'

'They don't sell them direct but go through a retailer.'

'She might have modelled one there. Can you check that out, Jacobs? Perhaps they gave her one.'

'That would be mighty generous of them if they did!'

Eva studied him curiously as she sipped the tea Sergeant Williams had brought her.

Jacobs continued, 'She was either very well paid or had a generous boyfriend. Not that the neighbours have seen her with a man but she rented the apartment, as do all the occupants, and the building is owned by . . . you might wish to guess.'

'Ashmore,' Ryga said triumphantly.

'Bang on target. Ashmore Property Developments.'

'Might not be the same Charles Ashmore who lives at Seaford.'

'It is. Major Ashmore designates the collecting of rent, and the management of the building, to an agent. I've spoken to the agent, who confirmed that Miss Perrier paid her rent as opposed to having it paid for her or being given the apartment rent free.'

'It doesn't mean that Ashmore personally knows all his tenants.'

'But he'd know the names.'

'Yes, and he denied recognizing Feline's. There was a decidedly frosty look between husband and wife. He looked angry that his wife had admitted recognizing her.'

Ryga wondered if Broxham, the chauffeur, would admit to knowing or recognizing Feline. Perhaps he had seen her with his boss in London. And perhaps Feline had been to Ashmore's house on the days when she had dropped off the packages at Colliers – Friday twenty-seventh of October, Friday third of November and Monday sixth of November. If she had been there, Ryga felt confident that Mrs Doulton would tell him even if the others lied. He asked Jacobs to check with the garage if Feline had used her car on those days, recalling that Eva had ascertained from the garage that she had used it on Saturday 4 November. He then told Jacobs about the possibility of Phillipe's boat having had a tender on board. 'Check that out with the Chelsea Yacht and Boat Company. Did you find any knitting in Feline's flat?'

'No. Should I have done?'

Ryga told him about finding the knitting needle buried deep down in one of the chairs on board Perrier's boat. Eva was listening with an intent expression. Jacobs was of the opinion that it could have been stuck down in the chair for years and could have belonged to a previous owner. That was possible because the chairs could have been bought second hand.

When he came off the line, Ryga swiftly updated Eva, after which she spread her photographs out on the desk. The ones of Feline's body made gruesome viewing.

Ryga said, 'Tomorrow I'll re-interview Ashmore if he's at home. I'll also speak to the chauffeur and housekeeper.'

'I wish I could come with you, but even if you said I could I'm due at the hospital for this wretched leg wound. I might not be able to get back tomorrow evening. My father will expect me to report back to him, and while I'm a big girl now I don't want to cause him any more distress than I already have so it might be a case of duty calls. But will you promise to let me know if you make a major breakthrough or arrest anyone?'

Ryga said he thought either highly unlikely.

The phone rang. Sergeant Williams said that Dr Plumley was on the line. Ryga listened carefully, then thanked the doctor and rang off. To Eva, he said, 'The knitting needle is not the murder weapon. She was asphyxiated after being struck on the back of the head. There was mud in her mouth and trachea.'

'Poor woman.'

'The blow to the head was enough to stun her, then, according to Doctor Pumley, her face was pushed down into the mud and held there. Plumley estimates the time of death to have been between eight thirty p.m. and midnight on the seventh of December. I think it more likely to be closer to eight thirty, after she left Myra's house. I'm certain she was inside it because of the perfume on Myra's coat on the stand.'

'But she didn't stop for tea,' Eva said. 'There was only one place setting.'

Again, something nagged at Ryga. Tea. He stared at the cup and saucer Sergeant Williams had brought in for him earlier, a pale green, while Eva's cup and saucer was white with a floral pattern on it and clearly a notch above that given to police officers, probably only reserved for distinguished visitors.

Suddenly he got it. 'Of course, the best china,' he cried. 'I should have noticed it before. Myra used her best china. It was from the set in the front parlour.' There was another thing that also struck him. There had been no tea cosy on the teapot. Ryga wouldn't mind betting that on his return to Myra's house he'd find an earthenware teapot just like the one Sergeant Keaton had used and a tea cosy in the kitchen. 'Myra was out to impress Feline and invited her into tea. The fact there was only one place setting means that either Myra cleared one away when Feline left, which I think unlikely, or the killer returned to Myra's house and cleared one place setting to make us believe that only Myra had been in the house. And that she left suddenly. Distraught over her husband's death, she took off in her husband's boat with the intention of killing herself, taking her nerve tonic and sleeping pills with her.'

'And *before* she could take a telephone call from Scotland Yard. The best china doesn't get us much further forward.'

'Everything is a factor in the case. Little by little it will all add up somewhere along the line,' he optimistically replied. And tomorrow he hoped to have more from the Ashmores that could take him a few steps closer to catching a ruthless, cold-blooded killer.

Nineteen

His early morning visit to Myra's house confirmed to him that the china on the table was that taken from the set in the front parlour, and there was an earthenware teapot in the kitchen under a handknitted, multi-coloured tea cosy. That done, he drove to Seaford. It was yet another foggy day and bitterly cold. Eva had left for London after breakfast and he hoped she reached there safely. He also hoped that the Ashmores were at home and that he hadn't had a wasted journey, but even if they weren't there would at least be the housekeeper, Mrs Doulton, to interview. However, as he turned into the driveway, he was pleased to see the Rolls parked in front of the garages. It meant that at least one of the Ashmores was at home, a fact which was confirmed by Mrs Doulton, who let him in with an even more disgruntled look than before. He would interview her in due course, but first he wanted to see what Valerie Ashmore had to say about Feline Perrier.

Mrs Doulton asked him again to wait in the hall while she informed Mrs Ashmore of his request to speak to her. She was in her bedroom. Mr Ashmore was in London. He had travelled up there alone in the sports car yesterday. That meant the chauffeur handyman, Broxham, was around. Mrs Doulton confirmed he was and the way she said it made it clear to Ryga there was no love lost between them. Maybe a sour disposition was Mrs Doulton's natural manner or perhaps she was unhappy in her work, or with her employer.

He twirled his hat in his hand and thought over how to approach the interview. He'd not given it much consideration on the journey here on account of the treacherous driving conditions caused by the fog which had required all his concentration. His thoughts were soon interrupted by the return of Mrs Doulton, who curtly announced that madam would be with him shortly and he was to wait in the drawing room. She showed him into the same room as before. Ryga postponed asking Mrs Doulton questions. He didn't want to be interrupted by the arrival of Valerie Ashmore. While he waited, he heard the telephone give a small jingle – someone was making a call and it didn't take a detective to work out it was Valerie from her bedroom. And neither did he think she was calling her dressmaker. Unless he was mistaken, she was getting instructions from her husband on what and how much to tell the man from Scotland Yard. He was tempted to lift the receiver of the phone on the table close to the mantelpiece but resisted and two minutes after the tell-tale ting from the phone that the call had ended, Valerie Ashmore entered the room.

She was immaculately and fashionably dressed and a little over made-up with almost the same disgruntled expression on her face as Mrs Doulton had displayed.

'I can't think why you want to see me, again,' she said, crossing to the coffee table in front of the large sofa. 'My husband is in London on business.'

'It's about Miss Feline Perrier.'

'What about her? I told you I don't know her. She's just some model I've seen occasionally.' She flushed and quickly leaned over to retrieve a cigarette from the ornate box on the table, knowing she had betrayed herself.

Ryga felt a stab of triumph. On his last visit he hadn't known Feline's name.

'You remembered her name then, Mrs Ashmore,' he said lightly.

She busied herself lighting the cigarette. Ryga remained silent.

'It came to me earlier this morning,' she said, after inhaling and puffing out the smoke quickly.

A likely story. Ryga, keeping his expression serious and his voice neutral while carefully studying her, said, 'Her body was found on Wednesday night in Sleeper's Hole. She'd been murdered.'

Her hand froze as she made to draw on her cigarette, her body tensed, then her eyes fell before she turned away from him and crossed to the window. 'I still don't see why you're here,' she said with an attempt at indifference, but Ryga, with years of practice, could hear the fear in her voice. He remained silent, forcing her to turn to face him. There was anxiety in her eyes.

'She rented an apartment in a property owned by your husband's company, just off Kensington Gardens.'

'My husband owns a lot of property.' She picked some tobacco from her teeth and continued trying to look indifferent, but her eyes were flicking all over the place save at him.

'He claimed not to know her when I asked him the previous time I was here.'

'Then he doesn't. He can't possibly know all his tenants.'

'It's an unusual name, and she was an attractive woman. I would have thought he would have remembered her.'

'Why should he? He doesn't interview tenants, that's what he pays an agent to do. My husband has much more important and more valuable business matters to attend to.'

Ryga left a short pause. 'Was your husband at home on Wednesday night?'

'Well, really! What are you implying?' she hotly declared, puffing angrily at her cigarette.

'I'm simply asking you a question.'

'And I refuse to answer it. I resent your manner, Inspector. You're treating us as if we are suspects. I've told you, my husband and I have nothing to do with that girl. Now if you've finished.' She marched to the mantelpiece and pressed a bell on the wall beside it.

Aside from her initial shock she showed no emotion at Feline's death. Was she really that cold and self-centred? He thought so. She hadn't even asked how Feline had died.

'I'm sorry if you feel that way, Mrs Ashmore. It is not my intention to offend but to discover who brutally murdered Feline Perrier.'

'Well, you'd better get on with it. You won't find her killer here. And I'll thank you not to trouble me or my husband again.'

Ryga held her gaze. 'I will have to if more evidence comes to light which you are withholding from me, and,' he quickly added as she opened her mouth to retort, 'I will need to speak to your husband. When is he due back?'

'I have no idea.'

'Then one of my colleagues will interview him in London.'

'You can't do that!'

The door opened and Mrs Doulton stood on the threshold.

'I assure you, Mrs Ashmore, we can and we will. Don't you want us to find Miss Perrier's killer?' Ryga saw Mrs Doulton's expression darken.

'Well, of course I do.' Valerie Ashmore shifted. Her lips tightened. 'But you won't find him here. Mrs Doulton, show Inspector Ryga out.'

'I'd like to speak to Mr Broxham.'

'He's not—'

'He's in the kitchen, sir,' Mrs Doulton broke in, earning a furious glare from her mistress. 'I'll show you the way, Inspector.'

'Thank you.'

He took delight in Valerie Ashmore's furiously petulant expression and the fact that Mrs Doulton had upstaged her.

'Was Mr Ashmore at home on Wednesday night?' he asked Mrs Doulton as they headed across the hall.

'No.'

'Do you know where he was?'

'Broxham will.'

'And Mrs Ashmore was she here?'

'She said she had a headache and retired to her room.'

'What time was this?'

'Straight after dinner, eight thirty.'

'And she didn't go out at all that night?'

'Not that I'm aware of, Inspector. I didn't hear her car.'

Ryga couldn't really see Valerie Ashmore uncovering the body of Feline. She wouldn't want to get her fashionable clothes dirty and her perfectly manicured nails muddy. And she would no more know where Sleeper's Hole was than she would Timbuktu. But she could have asked someone to do it, just as she could have asked someone to kill her. Motive? Jealousy, if her husband had been having an affair with Feline? But that didn't square with why Myra was missing and the packages Swinley had collected from the newsagent.

Ryga stilled Mrs Doulton as she was about to enter the kitchen. 'Have you seen this woman?' He showed her the picture of Feline which Eva had acquired.

'No.'

She pushed open the door into a large kitchen at the rear of the house where Broxham was sitting at the table. He showed no surprise at seeing Ryga. Obviously Mrs Doulton had told him about his arrival because Broxham wouldn't have recognized the car, not unless he was familiar with Newhaven Police Station or knew Inspector Holden.

'Tea, Inspector?' Broxham said, indicating the pot.

'Thank you, yes.' Ryga sat and placed his hat on the table.

'Don't mind if I get on with the rooms,' Mrs Doulton said. 'Otherwise, she'll be complaining.'

'When isn't she?' Broxham rejoined, pouring Ryga a cup of tea. He waited until Mrs Doulton had left the room.

'She's handing in her notice after Christmas,' Broxham said. 'I think she'd go now given half the chance.'

So that explained why she wasn't bothered about upstaging her mistress. 'Why is she leaving?'

'I wouldn't have thought a detective from Scotland Yard needed to ask that.'

'I sensed some hostility between the two women.'

'Mrs Doulton thinks Valerie Ashmore is spoilt and rude. And she's right. She's also selfish, self-centred and vain.'

'I'm surprised you don't hand in your notice.'

'Charles and I go back a long way. We served together in the war. Is it true that Feline's been found dead?'

'Yes. How did you know?'

'It made yesterday's *Seaford Gazette*.'

Then Valerie Ashmore obviously hadn't read the paper.

'It's a sad business,' Broxham continued. 'I can't think who would want to kill her or why.'

'You knew her?' Ryga asked. He extracted the photograph. There hadn't been one in the newspaper.

Broxham studied it his expression sorrowful. 'Yes, that's her, and yes, I knew her and so did Charles, despite what he told you before.'

Ryga sipped his tea. There was a soft shuffling noise from the hallway. Ryga didn't think it was Mrs Doulton.

Broxham rose. 'Let's talk outside.'

Ryga swallowed another mouthful of tea and hastily followed Broxham. They crossed to the garages in the freezing fog.

'This weather reminds me of when I was stationed in the Bay of Lubeck with the Second Army, after the war, in the winter of 'forty-five and 'forty-six. Bloody freezing it was there too, and chaotic. Dealing in black market goods was a way of life.'

'For you?'

'Not on a major scale. I dabbled in dealing the odd two or three items, cigarettes, alcohol, but then we all did, including Charles. We were stationed there together.'

'He was your commanding officer?'

Broxham threw back his head and laughed. 'No, the major thing is a phoney.'

Ryga wondered why Broxham was being so forthcoming. Maybe he'd discover that later.

'Ashmore was a lowly corporal. I was a private.'

'Does Mrs Ashmore know?'

'*I* haven't told her and Charles won't. He knows when he's on to a cushy thing, money-wise. They met in 1947 and married a year later. Valerie's wealth helped to kickstart his property empire, although he's paid for it. Being married to Valerie is not the easiest arrangement in the world. It suits Valerie to tell her friends her husband was a major, and Ashmore plays along with it because it makes him more credible and trustworthy in business circles. Nobody bothers checking anyway. If they did, they'd find a Frederick Charles Ashmore. Fred doesn't seem to fit with this.' Broxham waved his arm at the grand house behind them, only partly visible in the wet, clinging, icy fog. 'He's clever with money and has a shrewd eye for the main chance. He's also clever at cultivating the right contacts and developing them. Not like me. I just drive him around.'

Ryga didn't think that was all Broxham did by a long chalk, but how far his activities extended he didn't know, or how legal they were. Ryga thought that Broxham was blackmailing Ashmore by threatening to expose his past which could ruin Ashmore's marriage and stem the flow of finance. His business reputation would also suffer a blow and he could lose some valuable contacts such as those who tipped him the wink about land ripe for forthcoming building developments.

Broxham made no attempt to open the garage doors or lead the way up the outside steps to his flat above the garages. 'Charles had an affair with Feline.'

'Had?' Ryga had already guessed that might be so.

'It finished at the end of October.'

When the packages to Swinley began. So was it Ashmore who Feline was exposing? Ashmore had three motives for wanting her dead – his marriage, his reputation and his wealth. And perhaps Feline had evidence of some shady deals Ashmore had done along with some dubious characters he had associated with. Ashmore feared that Feline had given that evidence to PC George Swinley, so had killed him. Fearful that Swinley had told his wife, Ashmore also had to kill Myra. And perhaps Ashmore was afraid that Feline had confided in her brother so had arranged for him to have an accident on his boat. But why would Feline have given the evidence to PC Swinley? How did she know him? Not through modelling. Myra wouldn't have been able to afford the clothes and hats Feline had shown. Had Swinley known the aunt in Hastings who Feline had lived with after her mother's death?

'Where was Ashmore on Wednesday night?'

'I'm sure you've asked Valerie that.'

'I did, and she refused to tell me.'

'She's an idiot. You'll ask Charles, of course, not that he had anything to do with Feline's death and neither did I. We were both in London, and yes, we have alibis,' he said, smiling. 'Charles and I were at The Pelican Club, Mayfair.'

Ryga raised his eyebrows. It was expensive and exclusive. 'You're a member?'

'Charles signed me in.'

Ryga left a thoughtful pause. 'And Thursday evening, seventh of December?'

'In London. I drove Charles there. He stayed overnight as did I. I have a small flat there.'

By the manner in which Broxham said it, Ryga surmised that Ashmore paid for that, or that he had given Broxham a flat in a property he owned in return for his silence about their army career.

'Do we need alibis?' Broxham enquired, seemingly not the slightest bit concerned but Ryga's antennae sensed a slight shift in tone.

'It would help.'

'On the other hand, it might not,' Broxham said lightly. 'The concierge at Charles' Mayfair apartment might be able to vouch for him but my block doesn't have one. Still, someone might have seen me. I garaged the Rolls at Vintners, around the corner in South Street, at about eight o'clock. You can always check with them.'

Ryga took his time writing this down, waiting and wondering if Broxham would elaborate on his movements that night. He didn't.

'Does Mrs Ashmore know about her husband's affair with Feline?' he asked. Judging by Valerie Ashmore's manner during their earlier interview it was already clear to Ryga she did.

150

'She told Charles to finish it or else she'd leave him and take her wealth with her. Charles is clever, manipulative and shrewd in business dealings, but when it comes to women he's not strong. We all have our weak points.'

'And yours is?'

Broxham laughed. 'Avoiding responsibility and lack of ambition, which is why it suits me to be a chauffeur and not a businessman.'

And Ryga guessed that being a chauffeur to Ashmore was not the same as being a chauffeur to anyone else. Broxham's claim of lack of ambition was a lie. The job was a cover because Broxham had carved out a nice life for himself. He had access to an expensive luxury car – and probably Ashmore's boat when he wanted it – a flat here in Seaford but more importantly one in London. Broxham was also probably on a very generous salary.

Broxham said, 'It was actually Feline though who finished the relationship with Charles.'

Was that the truth? Ryga wondered. 'Why did she do that?'

'Because she found someone else.'

'You.'

'We didn't mean it to happen.'

Oh, but he had. Broxham had drawn great delight in taking Feline away from Ashmore. In fact, Ryga was beginning to wonder just who had the upper hand in the relationship, Ashmore or Broxham? He thought the latter. An idea dashed into his head and stayed there. Could Broxham have killed Feline in order to frame Ashmore for it? Was there an enmity between the men that went right back to war? Did Broxham want to get even with Ashmore for some injustice or perceived injustice? Was Broxham his killer? Had he uncovered Feline's body so as to draw the investigation towards Ashmore and frame him for her death?

He let the thought go for the moment as he needed time to consider it, plus he was certain that if Broxham was his killer then, unless he had cast-iron evidence to prove it, the man would slip out of his clutches.

'Did Feline speak to you about her family?'

'She told me her mother was dead and that she didn't know what had happened to her father. She was trying to find out but wasn't having much success. He was one of the hundreds of thousands of people who disappeared under Hitler's regime. She spoke about her brother, Phillipe, said he was in Coastal Command during the war and that he lived on a boat at Chelsea boatyard when he wasn't travelling.'

'A converted Motor Torpedo Boat which is now moored in Newhaven Harbour.'

'Really!'

'You didn't know?' Ryga said lightly but kept his steady gaze on Broxham's face. He looked surprised but then Ryga knew he was dealing with a clever man, one far more astute than Ashmore. 'It was found drifting in the English Channel on the morning of the twelfth of November with no one on board. Where was Mr Ashmore on that day?'

'In London, as was I.'

'And on the seventh of November?'

'Why then?'

Ryga scrutinized him carefully. Was it a bluff? 'It was the night PC Swinley disappeared and was killed.'

Broxham showed no emotion. He answered smoothly. 'Charles was here. I was in London.'

'Can anyone vouch for that?'

'Valerie can for Charles. I was with Feline.'

'All day?'

'No, just for the evening and night.'

And Feline wasn't around to confirm that. 'Did anyone see you between nine p.m. and midnight?'

'Only Feline.' He grinned. Ryga didn't reciprocate. His expression remained impassive and he was silently pleased to see that it ruffled Broxham a little. 'Do you think Phillipe's disappearance and Feline's death are connected?' Broxham asked.

'Do you?'

'I can't think why anyone would want either of them dead. If Phillipe is dead.'

'Maybe someone has something to gain by their deaths.'

'You mean financially?'

'Not necessarily. Perhaps Feline and her brother were party to information that could ruin or harm someone if it came to light.'

'Well, I don't think that's Charles. He might be a bit on the shady side but he's not a killer.'

'Not even when he served in the army?'

'That's different. He certainly wouldn't have killed Feline.'

'He could have got someone to do it for him.'
'Well, don't look at me,' Broxham joked.
But Ryga thought that maybe he should.

Twenty

Ryga drove back to the station at a snail's pace. There was no other speed he could drive with the fog thicker than ever. Broxham had told him that Feline had not been there on Saturday 4 November. Ryga wasn't sure if he believed him. Along with Charles Ashmore, Ryga thought he could add Neil Broxham to his list of suspects.

He postponed the many questions and theories buzzing around in his head to concentrate on driving. He needed to arrive in one piece, without a scratch or dent in the car, otherwise Inspector Holden would have something to say about it when he recovered from his influenza. He was pleased to find that Sergeant Williams' wife had once again provided him with sandwiches. This time it was ham inside great wedges of white bread spread liberally with her homemade chutney. There was also a pickled egg and an apple.

'She doesn't think Scotland Yard detectives get enough to eat, and she says you can't live on fish and chips every day. I told her you were staying at the Bridge Hotel, but she seemed to think that made matters worse.'

Ryga laughed. 'She's got a point. I'm very grateful to her. Please thank her for me.'

'I will. I'll bring you in a cup of tea.'

As Ryga ate his lunch he considered his conversation with Mrs Ashmore and what Broxham had told him. Maybe all three of them – Charles Ashmore, Valerie Ashmore and Neil Broxham were involved. He needed to verify the alibis for Charles Ashmore and Neil Broxham for Wednesday night when Feline's body was uncovered, and for the Thursday before last when she had been murdered. According to Broxham they had been in London on both dates. But Feline could have seen either of them there on the Thursday and told them she was going to Newhaven with Myra. One or both could have driven to Newhaven, killed Feline and also Myra. But Ryga kept returning to those questions that bothered him. How had Feline known Myra would be on the London train? Feline must have telephoned Myra before Thursday and Myra told her she was going to the Yard.

He put in a call to his chief and finished his sandwiches while he waited to be connected. When the call came through Ryga updated Street, adding what was troubling him about his conversation with Broxham. 'He was too forthcoming, too cooperative.'

'Perhaps he's just public spirited and wants his girlfriend's killer caught.'

'If he'd have shown some emotion – anger or sorrow – I might have agreed with you, sir, but there was nothing. To him it was as though Feline was just someone he happened to know, and certainly not intimately.'

'That could be his manner. He's not one for parading his emotions.'

'That's possible but I'd have seen something in his eyes,' insisted Ryga. 'He's cool enough to be a killer, and like many men he's learned how to kill during the war. The same goes for Charles Ashmore. Broxham told me Ashmore met his wife, Valerie, in 1947 and they married a year later. Broxham says her wealth helped to fund Ashmore's property empire, but Sergeant Jacobs said Ashmore was doing well after the war, buying up land and selling it on at a profit for development. He could have meant from 1948 onwards but I'd like to know if Ashmore was involved in property deals before he met Valerie and how he got the money. The fact that he was in Lubeck at the end of the war and, according to Broxham, dabbled in the black market, as he says they all did, coupled with the fact that Ashmore has lied about being a major and was a corporal is interesting, what else has he lied about? And where would a corporal get money to kickstart a property empire? Not from *dabbling* in the black market but by *trading* in it in a big way, for example in medicines and other essential supplies.'

'I'll get some officers to check out both men and their alibis for those key dates, Thursday the seventh of December and Wednesday the thirteenth of December, when Feline's body was uncovered.'

'Sergeant Jacobs also said Ashmore owns a motor cruiser, *Liberty*. I'd like to know if it's put into London anywhere over the last couple of months, in particular at Chelsea around the time Phillipe's boat was there on the eleventh and twelfth of November. And another thing – Ashmore could have used his boat to slip into Newhaven Harbour on the day Swinley was killed, the seventh of November, but if he did he must have come from somewhere close by because the fog that afternoon and night would have made it difficult for him to travel at sea from Dover where the boat is registered, or from London around to Newhaven Harbour. And no one claims to have seen any boat enter the harbour then, or on the night Feline was killed, but they might have missed it. I'll ask Sergeant Williams to interview the lighthouse staff.'

'We'll check with Chelsea and with Dover for the *Liberty*'s movements.'

'Either man could have driven to Newhaven and either of them could have killed Feline, but I can't see one of them returning to expose her body unless Ashmore wasn't happy about Broxham taking Feline from him.'

'She was promiscuous then?'

'I don't know. Maybe.' But Ryga got the sense that she wasn't. Perhaps he just wanted it to be that way. 'Or maybe Broxham uncovered Feline's body because he's looking to expose Ashmore for her murder and get him convicted in order to take over his company and contacts, and perhaps also Ashmore's share of wealth acquired illegally and hidden away from his wife. Although I've got no evidence to even suggest the latter, let alone prove it.'

'Could Feline have been blackmailing Ashmore or Broxham or both?'

'Why would she give PC Swinley the information though? As far as I'm aware, she didn't know him. I can't see their backgrounds coinciding unless it was through Feline's aunt, and I'm not sure how we can establish that with the aunt and Feline dead and Phillipe missing, probably dead. Is there anything from the lab yet?'

'I'll chase them up.'

Time seemed to hang heavy with Ryga and grew even heavier as the weather refused to change tack. There came the deep throb of the foghorns out to sea and the occasional angry horn of a car, probably as someone stepped in front of it, or another vehicle pulled out in its path, unable to see because of the weather. It was dark by three thirty.

Ryga studied a map of Newhaven Harbour. If Ashmore's boat had been in the harbour on the night of 7 November perhaps it had moored up at the landing stage close to that alleyway off Fort Road before the fog grew too thick. But how would Ashmore or Broxham have known

Swinley would go down there at that time, on that day? They'd have to know his beat and his shift. And even then he might not have checked that particular alleyway.

Ryga sat back and considered this. There were a number of possibilities. One: Swinley could have told Feline his shift on Saturday 4 November when he had walked along Seaford esplanade and past Ashmore's house. Perhaps Feline *had* been at the house, only Mrs Doulton hadn't seen her. Mrs Doulton could have been out or at the rear of the property. Feline could have been with Broxham in his flat above the garage. Broxham could have lied about being in London. Swinley could have had Feline's London telephone number and told her he had to see her urgently. She arranged to meet him outside the house and they agreed to meet again on the night of 7 November but they had been seen and overheard. Feline had been prevented from meeting Swinley and instead Ashmore or Broxham had done so.

Two: perhaps Feline had included a message in the package on Tuesday 7 November that she urgently needed to see him. She gave him a telephone number to contact her and he had arranged to meet her in the alleyway at nine thirty or thereabouts. She enticed him down the alleyway and either Broxham or Ashmore killed him. The flaw with that was why would Feline do that? Could Ashmore or Broxham have tricked her into depositing the packages? Why would they want Swinley dead? What did he know about them? None of these thoughts got him any closer to the truth. There were too many ifs, buts and whys with both options. Facts was what he needed, and maybe he would find some in the reports that had come in and those he had written, which might jog his memory.

Ryga settled down to patiently and painstakingly go through them. Patience was something some of his colleagues at the Yard lacked, although Sergeant Jacobs wasn't one of them, but it was a skill – or quality, depending on your viewpoint – that he'd acquired over his years at sea and then in the camp. It often resulted in throwing up a small fact that had been missed or a detail that needed further checking. Sometimes it provided inspiration. This time, though, the reports threw up more questions and no answers.

He spread out the photographs Eva had taken since their arrival, wondering how she had got on at the hospital. He hoped her leg wound was healing and she hadn't made things worse by walking so much and driving.

Carefully he went through the photographs, marvelling at how evocative and accomplished they were, and hoping that something might connect with him to help with the case. Williams came in with yet more tea; Ryga was growing a little sick of the taste of it. He pushed aside the photographs to make space for the cup and saucer and gazed down at the raft Tom and Colin had made which they'd been on when they had discovered the body. His hand froze over the picture as something Eva had said struck him. They'd been repairing it when she had come upon them on Saturday and taken the pictures – at first they'd been unaware of her presence. The boys' engrossed, enraptured expressions of pure joy and concentration had tugged at Ryga's heart and had made him think of Sonia's son, Steven. He wanted Steven to have such moments. He had looked at Tom and Colin's faces and felt their joy because Eva's camera, her third eye, had made him see just what this makeshift raft, with its bits of old wood and rope, meant to two little boys who had nothing material in their lives. He hadn't been looking at the raft.

He grabbed his murder case and quickly retrieved his magnifying glass from it with a quickening heartbeat. 'Williams!' he called out.

'Yes, sir.' Williams came hurrying in.

'Take a look at this. What do you see?' Ryga handed over the magnifying glass and swivelled round the photograph.

'It's a wooden raft held together with bits of old rope.'

'And its name. The boys have christened it.'

'Sun.' Williams looked up.

'And the name of Swinley's boat was?'

'*Sunrise*. Well I never. You think it came off his boat?'

'I do.' Ryga rose and reached for his hat, coat and scarf. 'Where will the boys be now?'

'At home having their tea, I shouldn't wonder. School's finished.'

'Then let's go and ask them. Get their addresses.'

Williams left a PC in charge and gathered up his helmet and cape. Ten minutes later they were on Denton Island. The noise of the quays across the harbour was muffled in the fog which was thicker nearer the water. Ryga could taste the salt on his lips and feel the damp clinging to him. The smell of low tide reminded him of ammonia and across the water at North Quay came the grinding sound of the Saw Mill.

'Let's take a quick look around for their raft first.'

It didn't take long to find it. Ryga's torch picked out the piece of wood bearing the word *Sun* the boys had roped up on it. 'Now let's see if we can find the remains of Swinley's boat.'

There were some pieces of wood just past the last of four derelict houses. Even though the boat had been well and truly smashed, the wood was of splendid quality and expertly varnished. There should have been more but Ryga suspected the boys had taken it. Ryga couldn't find the remaining part of the name – *rise.*

As they made for Colin Pleasant's house, Ryga said, 'I shouldn't think there are any prints or evidence left on the remains of the wood, and it's my guess the outboard engine has been ditched in the sea, like Myra's body. I want a thorough search of this shore made tomorrow though for the oars. I couldn't see them and I'd like all the residents questioned.'

'I'll get PC Anmore on to it. This is part of his beat. It won't take long; there aren't many living here now.'

'Ask if anyone saw or heard anything on Thursday seventh of December between eight thirty and midnight.'

'This is the Pleasants' house.' Williams indicated a battered door. From inside came the sound of children shouting. Ryga thought there must be at least ten of them crammed in the tiny terraced house. Williams hammered his fist against the door – there was no knocker or bell. Ryga half expected it to cave in; the occupant thought so too, as Ryga heard a woman shout, 'All right, I'm coming, no need to break the door down.' It was wrenched open by a small, thin woman in a tight-fitting, darned navy-blue jumper and a grey knee-length skirt, over which was a faded floral apron. She was in her mid-thirties with dark curly hair already streaked with grey, and Ryga thought that the last vestiges of her delicacy and prettiness were beginning to fade. On her bony hip was a baby of about six months.

'Oh, it's you, Sergeant Williams. What do you want?' she said warily, her brown, tired eyes flicking to Ryga and registering fear. As though sensing this, the baby began to cry. She jiggled it to no effect. The shouts of the children seemed to grow louder with their mother out of sight. Paper had peeled off the wall in the narrow hallway, leaving bare patches of plaster with darker shades towards the wooden floor that Ryga guessed was damp.

'What's he done now?' Mrs Pleasant said wearily. Ryga

remembered that Eva had told him Colin senior had had a few run-ins with the police.

'There's nothing to worry about, Mrs Pleasant. It's Colin we've come to talk to.'

Her eyes widened and the colour drained from her lined face. 'He's not in trouble, is he?' she asked fearfully.

'No. This is Inspector Ryga from Scotland Yard—'

'Oh, my God!'

'Please, it's all right,' Ryga quickly reassured her as she looked about to faint. The baby started wailing. 'Can we come in?'

Dumbstruck and seemingly terrified of him, she nodded and hurried ahead of them. There was only space for them to walk in single file. The dimly lit passageway smelt musty.

Ryga stepped into a small room with a coal fire, two worn easy chairs in front of it, a wooden table in the middle and around it four children, all girls save for Colin, all with jam around their mouths. Their fighting and talking stopped instantly as they stared at the visitors.

Above the crying of the baby, Ryga said, 'I'm sorry to disturb your tea, Mrs Pleasant, but it is important that I speak to Colin about his raft.'

Colin's eyes widened in his dirty face.

'I told you that raft would get you into the trouble. Shush, for pity's sake,' Mrs Pleasant urged the crying baby. 'Here, Sheila, take her.' She handed the baby over to the oldest girl, who looked to be about ten. She rose and crossed to her mother while her eyes never left Ryga's face. With her mouth still open she took the baby from her mother and balanced it on her hip. Miraculously the baby stopped crying instantly.

Ryga said, 'On the contrary, Mrs Pleasant, Colin's raft has helped me.' To Colin, he said, 'I'm a detective from Scotland Yard.'

Colin blinked, swallowed and seemed to have lost the power of speech, as had all of them. The fire popped as a piece of coal settled lower in the grate. The noise seemed eerily loud.

'I'd like to know how you got the name for your raft, Sun.'

Still Colin didn't speak.

'Answer the gentleman,' his mother rapped.

'We didn't steal it. We found it lying around.'

'I know. When did you find it?' This was the critical question.

Ryga was convinced it was part of Swinley's boat, but he had to make sure that the piece of wood bearing the name hadn't been on the boys' raft for days before the 7 December. If it had then he could rule it out and the smashed remains he and Williams had found were probably those of another boat.

'Saturday morning,' Colin said. 'Just before that lady came with her camera. We thought it would be a good name for the raft. *Sun*.' One of his sisters giggled. He eyed her daggers drawn.

'And it is Colin.'

'You're not taking it back, are you?'

'No. You can keep it.'

Colin looked pleased.

'Did you play on that shore before last Saturday? During the week perhaps, and just didn't see the wood with the name on it?'

'Tom and I check the raft every day after school to make sure no one steals it or messes about with it. We found some new bits of wood on the shore on Friday night but it was dark and mum called me in for my tea, so on Saturday morning Tom and I poked about in it to see if it would be fit for the raft. Then we sees the name *Sun* painted yellow on some wood, like I said, mister.'

'Did you use most of the wood for your raft?' Ryga knew they hadn't because he and Williams had found some but not all of it.

Colin dashed a nervous glance at his mother. She shifted uncomfortably, her face flushed and her fingers pricked at her apron.

'Now . . .' Williams began sternly but Ryga stilled him.

'Please, Colin, this is important. No one is going to get into any trouble for it but I need to know what else you found and what you did with it.'

Again his eyes went to his mother and he licked his lips. One of his sisters sniffed, another plucked at her pigtail.

'Mrs Pleasant?'

'He found some wood and brought it home for the fire. Coal is so expensive. It was only wood washed up on the shore.'

'We shared it between us,' Colin said. 'Me and Tom.'

'I understand. That's all right. What did you do with the oars?'

'Nothing. There weren't none.'

'And the engine?'

'What engine? That wasn't there neither.'

'He only brought the wood back,' Mrs Pleasant said.

Ryga addressed her directly. 'Did you or your husband see anyone along the shore on Thursday seventh of December between about eight thirty and midnight?'

'No.'

'Did you hear anything unusual?'

She shook her head.

Ryga nodded. 'Well, thank you. We won't keep you from your tea any longer. And thank you, Colin.' He handed him a shilling.

The boy stared at it dumbfounded before finding his voice. 'Cor, thanks, mister.'

Sergeant Williams gave Colin a warning look, nodded at Mrs Pleasant and touched his helmet as he left.

As soon as the door closed behind them Ryga could hear excited raised voices from inside the house. 'Quite a household, that.'

'It's a bit of a struggle for Mrs Pleasant with her husband in and out of work but she's a nice party. Pleasant is all right too. It's only when he gets drunk, he thinks he can take on the world in a fight and gets into trouble. I've never known him to take it out on his missus though or the kids. He must have been taken on over the docks as he's not at home.'

For thoroughness, Ryga checked the details with Tom who lived four doors down. The house was quieter than Colin's even though four boys, including Tom, sat around the table eating bread and dripping while a large, formidable-looking Mrs Gileson kept them in check. Tom confirmed what Colin had said and that neither he nor his mother had seen nor heard anything suspicious on the night Myra disappeared and Feline was killed. Ryga also gave Tom a shilling but Mrs Gileson sternly said, 'He don't want paying for telling the truth. It's his duty to help the police.'

'It is, Mrs Gileson,' Ryga answered smoothly. 'It's just at Scotland Yard we like to reward that loyalty.'

Her small eyes, in the folds of flesh on her face, studied him sceptically. Then she nodded. 'I guess London ways is different.'

Tom's beaming face was a delight to behold, Ryga thought as he left. Williams told him that Mr Gileson worked on the railways.

'Ensure that PC Anmore talks to all the occupants, including Mr Pleasant and Mr Gileson.'

Williams said he would. Ryga also requested that an officer interview the lighthouse keepers for any boat movements on both 7

November and 7 December.

As they returned to the station, Ryga said, 'We now know where Swinley's boat ended up and that it was used on the night of Thursday seventh of December because that wood wasn't on the shore before then according to Colin and Tom, and I believe them. The thief, who is probably Feline's killer, ditched the engine and oars. I think that after disposing of Feline and leaving her body under the boat in Sleeper's Hole, he lured Myra to the same spot, knocked her out, bundled her into her husband's boat and took it out.' But Ryga paused as he considered two points. The knowledge that Swinley had a small boat at Sleeper's Hole pointed to the killer being a local man and not Ashmore or Broxham. Not unless Swinley had told Feline and she had told one of them. The second point he expressed to Williams. 'It being low tide at eight o'clock on Thursday night, he'd have had quite a job to lug the boat down to the water, especially with a body in it.' That would take a fit man. Ryga thought of Neil Broxham. Or perhaps two men.

'Maybe he came back when the tide came up.'

'That wasn't until just after two in the morning.'

'But he'd be OK a couple of hours before that, say at midnight, maybe earlier.'

'You're right, Sergeant.' And the killer could have waited on board the Motor Torpedo Boat knowing it belonged to Phillipe Perrier. 'He took Swinley's boat into the harbour using the oars to make sure he wasn't heard. The incoming tide would have helped propel him up the harbour where he travelled under the swing bridge and made for Denton Island shore. He threw the outboard engine overboard along with Myra's body.'

Williams made a clucking noise and shook his head sadly.

'He used the oars to get ashore then smashed up the boat with something he had brought with him to enable him to do that. A large hammer, say, which he used on poor Myra and Feline and which is also probably at the bottom of the harbour.'

'He must have been quite strong to have done that,' William said.

Again, that pointed to Broxham and Ashmore. 'And he must have made a noise.'

'Yes, but at that end of the harbour many of those houses are derelict so there's no one to hear him. And you know that fog, like snow, seems to muffle noise. With the fog, and it being dark, no one would have seen him.'

'A perfect night for murder,' Ryga muttered.

'The oars weren't by the remains of the boat. Colin's father could have taken them after his boy pointed them out and has sold them?'

'I'm inclined to believe Colin and Tom when they say the oars weren't there, and if that is the case the killer pushed them out to sea and let them float away. I want the far shores of Denton Island searched for oars. I'll ask Sergeant Keaton if his officers can search North Quay. I'll also ask Hailsham if he can spread the word and keep a look out for them.' And he'd do both tomorrow.

Twenty-One

The weather matched his mood, or perhaps influenced it, as he set out for the Watch House because it was a bright, though breezy, cold morning. He was greeted with the news that the harbour master, Hailsham, was down with the flu.

Ryga said he was sorry to hear that. 'I wanted to let him know that we've located George Swinley's boat. It's been smashed to pieces, though, on Denton Island shore. The oars and engine are missing. Could you keep a look out for the oars, they might have been cast adrift. The engine could either have been sold or dumped in the harbour.'

'Will do, but if you want to pass the message on to Mr Hailsham yourself, his neighbour Mrs Cray is looking after him,' the young man in his mid-twenties announced. 'She lives at number twenty-four Hill View Road. Mr Hailsham is at number twenty-six. It's not far, just off Fort Road. I only say that because he was deeply concerned about Mr Swinley's boat and about Mrs Swinley being missing. And he was real shook up over that woman's body being found. He took it personally. Says it shouldn't have happened. He's responsible for the harbour and he thinks the terrible things that are happening reflect badly on him. I said no one would think that but he . . . well, he has these black moods, gets maudlin. When he's like that it makes him sick.'

'It's happened before?'

'Yes. He's not in the best of health, not that he'll let you tell him that. Shaking and sweating he was, though that could have been the flu coming on.'

Perhaps he was right. Or could it have been fear of exposure of a crime? But Ryga told himself that he had no evidence or even

165

suspicion that Hailsham was a suspect. But then Hailsham being a local man, would know PC Swinley's beats and shifts. He knew about his boat and he knew the harbour like the back of his hand. He could easily have walked home to Hill View Road from Denton Island after smashing up Swinley's boat, and he could easily have met Swinley at the alleyway entrance off Fort Road and Chapel Street or called him down to the harbour on some pretext. But why would he kill George and Myra Swinley and Feline Perrier? It was the lack of motive that was worrying at Ryga. He supposed that PC Swinley could have discovered that Hailsham was involved in smuggling. But how then did Feline and the mysterious packages fit into it? Was it still drug smuggling, as he and Eva had originally conjectured? Had Swinley been given the drugs in return for his silence? If Hailsham was the killer, why uncover Feline's body? Guilt? Conscience?

'Has Mr Hailsham been harbour master here long?' he asked.

'Two years. He came here from Chichester Harbour where he worked after he was demobbed. He doesn't talk about what he did in the war and no one's allowed to ask him.'

Ryga didn't blame Hailsham for that. 'Why did he leave Chichester?'

'Don't know, and it's not my business to ask.'

But it was Ryga's. He'd try Hailsham's neighbour first.

Mrs Cray answered her door promptly; she seemed a kindly middle-aged soul. And an honest one, if Ryga was any judge, and he'd had enough experience of people to be a fair one. Could Hailsham have fooled her though by making out his symptoms were flu when in reality they were guilt and remorse for murder?

Ryga wondered if there was a Mr Cray, or if Mrs Cray was angling for a match with her neighbour. He said he was sorry to hear that Mr Hailsham was unwell, and to tell him they had found PC Swinley's boat on the shore at Denton Island but had no further news about Mrs Swinley.

'It's a terrible business. I know it's playing on Mr Hailsham's mind and finding that other poor woman's body in the mud. I don't know what things are coming too. It really shook him up.'

'Joseph Moore found the body, Mrs Cray.'

'Yes, I know, but Peter, Mr Hailsham, is more sensitive to these things than old Joseph Moore. He's tormented by the fact that under that boat on *his* shore a poor young woman was lying dead. And he said that the Motor Torpedo Boat belongs to her brother who's also missing. Is there any more news on that?'

'Not at the moment, Mrs Cray. Have you had the doctor to Mr Hailsham?'

'Not much point,' she dismissed, but he caught a glimpse of unease in her hazel eyes. 'It's just one of those things that has to take its course.'

'I hope you don't catch it.'

'Me! Constitution like an Ox.'

'I hope he recovers soon.'

'I expect he does too.'

Ryga made his way to the swing bridge. There was something not quite right there. Yes, Mrs Cray was an honest sort, but she had been uneasy when Ryga had mentioned the doctor. It would need probing further but he postponed it for now. He wanted to speak to Sergeant Keaton. He found the sergeant in his office and asked him to alert his officers to be on the lookout for any abandoned oars and to report to him if any of them had seen or heard anything suspicious on and around Denton Island on Thursday 7 December. He updated him on the investigation, although there was still little he could tell him, but he asked Keaton how well he knew Hailsham.

'As well as I know anyone around the harbour,' came the answer. 'He's a quiet man, keeps himself to himself. Bit on the nervous side sometimes. Smokes like a chimney. Had a tough war, Burma, but doesn't speak about it. Can't say I blame him. He was married. I don't know what happened to his wife.'

Ryga walked back to the police station where he ate Mrs Williams' egg sandwiches, mulling over what he'd learned about Hailsham – his black moods, his bouts of sickness and his deep concern about Myra Swinley. Again, he wondered if it was guilt which was troubling him. Hailsham had been on board Phillipe Perrier's boat twice as far as Ryga was aware. Once when it had been brought in by the coastguard and customs officer, Dakins, and the second time when Ryga had seen him when Dakins had been taking him across the harbour. Had Hailsham been searching for something – a knitting needle, for example? But why? It wasn't the murder weapon.

His telephone rang. It was Jacobs.

'Sorry it's taken so long to get back to you, sir,' Jacobs apologized. 'We're a bit snowed under.'

'Not another fur theft?'

'No, but the smog seems to have brought out every criminal and crime you can think of – it's a wonder the blighters can see or breathe to commit any. The beat officers have been speaking to the wharf and boatmen around Alaska's fur factory though, and a couple of them say they heard the sound of a powerful motorboat just after the time of the robbery. The River Police haven't seen, or picked up anyone, but they can't be everywhere.'

Charles Ashmore's boat sprang to Ryga's mind but he wasn't the only boat owner in the country. And why would Ashmore risk losing his lucrative business and reputation by stealing furs? He wouldn't.

But maybe Jacobs was reading his mind because he said, 'The chief said you wanted us to check out Charles Ashmore's boat, *Liberty*. It was moored up at Chelsea boatyard on the eleventh and twelfth of November. Perrier's Motor Torpedo Boat was also moored there on the eleventh of November. He left in the early hours of the twelfth of November or possibly late on the eleventh of November, no one quite knows, and it did carry a tender.'

'Now that is interesting. Neither Broxham nor Ashmore told me they had been moored at Chelsea, although Broxham did say they had been in London on the twelfth of November but not on board any boat.' And Ryga hadn't asked specifically if they had been. He'd had no reason to. 'They'd have seen Perrier's boat.'

'They might have done but his isn't the only Motor Torpedo Boat moored there. Maybe to them it was just one of many.'

'Is the boat Perrier's main residence?'

'No one seems to know at Chelsea. We're checking records but it's a slow process and the RAF haven't got back to us yet with his last known address.'

The door opened Eva stood on the threshold.

'When did Perrier leave Coastal Command?'

'Hold on. I'll look up my notes,' Jacobs said.

'It was 1943,' Eva said before Jacobs could answer.

'Why then?'

'Pardon?'

'It's Miss Paisley I was addressing, Jacobs. She's just returned from London. Hold on a moment.'

'Because he was wounded,' Eva replied. 'He suffered a head injury,' she said, throwing herself down in the seat opposite Ryga.

Ryga thought of two more men who had suffered head injuries – Sergeant Keaton and PC Swinley. Both had been hospitalized. Keaton had been wounded in 1940, Swinley in 1943 after seeing action at Cassino. He didn't know where Keaton had been admitted or how long he had been in hospital, but he recalled where Swinley had. Myra had told him. Eagerly he said, 'Was Phillipe in Graylingwell Hospital, Chichester?'

'He was. And what's more, I've discovered that not only were he and Swinley there at the same time, but they were in the same ward.'

At last, they had the link between the two men.

Twenty-Two

'It was a ward in the Summersdale block, which was commandeered to serve as an acute battle neurosis unit for front-line casualties,' Eva said after Ryga had told Jacobs he'd ring him back later as Miss Paisley had more news.

'How did you get this?' Ryga asked, taking the paper from her. It was a list of patients.

'I used my charm.'

Ryga raised his eyebrows.

'I drove down to Chichester from London this afternoon after learning that Phillipe had been wounded in 1943 and had been sent to Graylingwell Hospital.'

'How did you learn this?'

'From a friend of his, another boat dweller at Chelsea, who I happen to know.'

'Your circle of contacts is amazing. Is the doctor who gave you this one of them?'

'No, but he is a dreadfully pompous, vain man. I told him I had been asked to take photographs of him for an article a friend of mine was writing about his ground-breaking treatment for mental patients.'

'And he believed you!'

'Of course. I gave him the name of a journalist friend in London and said he could check with him and that I was concerned he hadn't got the message about the photoshoot. But if he didn't want his picture taken then that was fine by me – I'd just take pictures of the other medical experts, perhaps some of his staff. That was enough to guarantee his cooperation. He wanted to wax lyrically about his theories on treating mental illness but I tuned out after the first two words. He didn't notice. All I had to do was interject the occasional "really", "how fascinating", "is that so", "turn this way, please, Dr

Wellbelove", "smashing", "of course", "now pick up that clipboard. Great".'

Ryga smiled as she spoke. 'Was he there when George and Phillipe were patients?'

'Yes. It was easy to get him talking about treatment for those injured during the war. And part of that treatment was knitting.'

Ryga sat back, his mind rapidly working. 'Both Swinley and Perrier learned to knit, hence the knitting needle stuffed down the seat on Perrier's boat. But why no other knitting paraphernalia on board his boat?'

'Perhaps the needle had been there a long time. He'd given up knitting and given away his knitting needles, wool and patterns and had simply mislaid that one.'

'Did Swinley continue with his knitting habit?' Ryga wondered aloud, thinking back to the knitting bag by the fireplace in Myra's house.

'He might have done. It's not the sort of thing you see men doing unless they're fishermen. But there is more I can tell you about Phillipe that might throw some light on why he's disappeared.'

Ryga sat forward, eager to hear it.

'Gus, my friend at Chelsea, is a writer and he's also sociable. The two don't always go together but in Gus's case they do. He and Phillipe would often get drunk together.'

'Is what he told you reliable?'

'Completely. He said that Phillipe often puts into Chelsea but doesn't stay for long.'

'So Sergeant Jacobs told me. He also said that Ashmore's boat was moored there at the same time as Phillipe's on the eleventh of November.'

'That's interesting. Gus said that Phillipe had trouble adjusting after the war. He's prone to dark moods and Gus knows all about those because he also suffers from them, which is probably why he drinks so much. Phillipe's antidote for it was to take off on his boat. Gus also knew Feline. She used to visit Phillipe on board. According to Gus, Feline was – aside from being exceedingly beautiful – modest, quiet and trusting.'

'Not promiscuous then?'

'No. The opposite, she was quite shy.'

Ryga raised his eyebrows. 'I wouldn't have thought she'd like people looking at her then.'

'Modelling was her job. She just had to show off the clothes, look serious, and do as she was told. She didn't have to converse with the clients.'

Ryga thought of what Valerie Ashmore had said. *I don't take any notice of who shows the clothes.*

Eva continued, 'Gus told me that Phillipe was invalided out of Coastal Command in 1943. He had served since 1939 as a pilot and had been involved in several sea-rescue missions in the early days of the war, including the rescue of children in lifeboats who were being taken from here to Canada when the ship they were on board was torpedoed. He clocked up thousands of miles, protecting ships in the Battle of the Atlantic where his Hudson took a hit in 1941 after an exchange with a Kondor while protecting a convoy. He got it back safely. He then flew Liberators in the U-Boat attacks in 1943 and again took a hit, only this time, after managing to get the plane back to base, he crash-landed and ended up with a severe head injury. He was taken to the nearest emergency medical centre but was quickly transferred to a specialist mental hospital after it was diagnosed that he was suffering from battle neurosis. There he learned to knit, as I said, and, according to Gus, was an accomplished knitter. Dr Wellbelove told me that knitting soothes the nerves but at the same time stimulates the brain but not in a negative way. It's something to do with hand-brain coordination. It didn't take long for Phillipe to recover but he couldn't go back to Coastal Command. However, because of his background in art before the war, and his knowledge of paintings and sculptures, he was appointed to work with the Monuments Men.'

There was a tap on Ryga's door, followed by Sergeant Williams with a steaming cup of tea for Eva, which he put down on the desk. Ryga didn't even thank him – his head was spinning with this new information. He knew that during the war the Monuments Men had been tasked with saving works of art and cultural treasures from being stolen by the Nazis and others. Some of them braved the front line to find and recover looted objects; two had been killed in combat.

Eva said, 'As you no doubt know, since the war ended the Monuments Men have been involved in returning stolen works of art and other cultural objects to the countries from which they were stolen.'

'Yes, we've liaised with them at the Yard on a couple of cases. Their correct name is the Monuments, Fine Arts and Archives Section, made up of men *and* women from fourteen nations, a mix of museum directors, curators, art historians, archivists, architects and artists. But Perrier's name has never come up. Is he still working for them?'

Eva shrugged an answer.

'If he was still working with the Monuments Men I'd have thought someone would have reported his disappearance.'

'Not if they believe he is actively on the trail of a stolen work of art. It might be thought too dangerous for him to report in.'

'Or he might have been working off his own bat,' posed Ryga. He began to put the theories that had been running through his mind to Eva.

'Now that we have the connection between Swinley and Perrier it begins to make sense that Feline was asked to deposit the packages for Swinley to collect. Perrier knew that Swinley had returned to his former occupation as a police officer and, whatever crooked activity Phillipe had discovered, he wanted a police officer, and one he trusted, to know about it. He gave this evidence to his sister to give to Swinley. Feline returned from the Continent on the first of December and couldn't get in contact with her brother. And then she heard, or read, that George Swinley had died. She contacted Myra to find out what had happened to the contents of the packages, and maybe even to try and discover what they contained. She might never have known. Her brother told her it was best she didn't.'

'We're assuming that she was just the messenger, but she could have been the instigator. It could have been Feline who gathered evidence about some criminal activity and wanted PC Swinley to have it because she had heard her brother speak of him and she might even have met him if she had visited her brother at the hospital, which she must have done.'

'Yes, you're right. And there shé met Myra visiting her husband, which would explain why the two women seemed to be so comfortable together. They knew one another. Myra trusted Feline and invited her back to the house for tea. But Feline didn't stay. Instead she collected what she needed from Myra, the packages contents, and left.'

'Or found nothing.'

Ryga nodded thoughtfully. His mind raced with this new information, putting it together with what they already knew. And it still didn't quite add up. 'Why was there only one place setting? If Feline had refused tea because she'd discovered the packages, then Myra wouldn't have used her best china.'

'Not unless she fancied treating herself. Yes, I know, unlikely. And if there weren't any packages then Feline would still have stayed for tea.'

'So the likelihood is that Feline was enticed away, with or without the evidence, and Myra either washed up and put away one place setting, which again is improbable, or someone else did.'

'The killer.'

'Yes. To make it look as though Myra had been alone. Myra was then also lured away. She left the house in something of a hurry, and with that person willingly. She wouldn't have known Ashmore or Broxham though.'

'One of them could have used the excuse that he'd just come from Feline and she'd had an accident.'

'But then Myra would have called the police.'

'Not if that person said they'd already done so.'

She was right. He said, 'We've got a connection between Ashmore or Broxham and Phillipe Perrier as well as with Feline. Phillipe could have discovered that Ashmore and Broxham were smuggling or up to some other criminal activity and he wanted to expose them. Or as you said, Phillipe might have nothing whatsoever to do with this and he had an accident on board his boat or indeed has sadly taken his own life, although he left no note for his sister, but suicides don't always. I'd like to find out a bit more about Phillipe. I'll ask Superintendent Street if we can establish if he was still working for the Monuments Men.'

'I'll leave you to it. I'll see you back at the hotel.'

'Thank you, Eva. You've done an amazing job.'

'You're welcome.' She pulled herself up and made a mock salute.

He laughed and telephoned Street. The information wouldn't come through immediately and there seemed little to do on Sunday so Ryga decided to take a break from the case and, armed with sandwiches and a flask of tea provided by the ever-obliging Mrs Williams, he walked to Seaford as George Swinley must have done on the two occasions he hadn't caught the train to collect the packages. He also walked along the esplanade and past the Ashmores' house, noting the absence of cars in the driveway. Then he struck out over the Downs. Walking helped to clear his head and often stimulated new ideas when working on an investigation. This time it failed in the latter but succeeded in the former.

In one way he'd have enjoyed Eva's company, but in another he relished being alone. He liked his own company. Eva's leg injury put paid to her accompanying him and she hadn't suggested they spend Sunday together. Maybe she had sensed he wanted to be alone. She had driven off early that morning and had returned late in the evening. He didn't know where she had been and she didn't say. He wouldn't pry. It wasn't any of his business.

The news that Phillipe Perrier no longer worked for the Monuments Men came through early on Monday morning along with the name of his former head of section, a Miss Leonora Dewsnap who was now the curator of the Towner Gallery in Eastbourne. She'd been Perrier's section head from 1944 to 1949. Ryga telephoned her hoping she would be available to see him. His luck was in. She was in her office and said she'd be delighted to tell him all she could about Phillipe Perrier.

It was eleven thirty when Eva drove the thirteen miles east along the coast to the seaside town. Ryga could see that her leg was still causing her some pain and discomfort and offered to drive her car, but she insisted she was fine and he knew better than to argue. He'd also said he could take the police vehicle, or the train, but Eva wouldn't hear of it. 'If you don't want me in the interview I'll busy myself taking seaside photographs,' she'd said.

'How good are you at taking notes?' he'd asked as they'd set off.

'Not as good as I am at taking pictures, but my shorthand is better than most. I used to be a hundred words per minute but I might be a little slower now. Don't look so shocked, Ryga. Have you forgotten that I started off as a secretary at the Ministry of Information before I persuaded them my talents lay behind the lens?'

He hadn't forgotten – it was just he hadn't expected her to know shorthand.

'And I can type, awfully fast actually, forty words per minutes,' she added. 'My father thought secretarial skills would be an asset in helping me to secure a husband. I think he envisaged me marrying my boss, whoever that might turn out to be – hopefully someone powerful, wealthy and influential, then I could retire gracefully to run an exquisite country house, or a splendid one in the suburbs, while helping to further my husband's career.'

Ryga couldn't help smiling. 'There's time yet.'

She snorted.

'This'll be practice for you.'

'Any more of that and you'll take your own notes, Ryga,' she said with a smile.

He could. He'd developed a method of speed writing, another craft he'd perfected in the camp.

He enjoyed the drive despite the fact that although Eva was a skilful driver, she was a bit too fast on occasions. He made no comment though. The little sports car behaved impeccably. The weather was comparatively mild with rain in the air and few people strolling along the promenade.

They were greeted by Miss Dewsnap, who was much younger than Ryga had expected, about late twenties, although why he should think she would be middle-aged he didn't know. She was also attractive – short, wavy dark hair, intelligent, lively nut-brown eyes behind round-shaped spectacles.

The art gallery was an impressive grand house, donated, she told them, by the owner before the war, during which time the building had been used to house the military while the works of art had been taken away and safely stored in a deep mine. 'Somewhere in Kent,' she added, showing them into her chaotic office at the rear of the building on the ground floor. 'I've only been here a week,' she said by way of apology for the mess.

'I understand that you worked with the Monument's Men, or I should say the Monuments, Fine Arts, and Archives Section, to give you the proper name,' Ryga said.

'Monuments Men is fine. I admit there were only a few women in the section but we always considered ourselves as one of the men, it being a generic term. I worked with them from 1943 until three weeks ago. I returned from Europe on the twenty-fifth of November and took one week off before starting here. Would you like some refreshment?'

They politely declined. Ryga introduced Eva and explained she was assisting him and would be taking notes if that was permissible.

Miss Dewsnap said it was, then she surprised Ryga by addressing Eva directly. 'I've seen your work, Miss Paisley, and I want to say how much I admire it. You capture life in the raw, the feelings and experiences of people that even they are probably unaware of. Your war photography is heart-rending. I hope you are not too badly injured and we'll see more of your photography. I know this is not the right time to mention what I have in mind, because you're here on business about Phillipe, but I'd love to speak to you at some stage about an exhibition of your photographs, particularly those of the Home Front and Women at War. The uncensored ones of what people really experienced.'

Ryga was pulled up with a start. He'd forgotten that Eva was famous. Photographs of her had been in the newspapers, and she was renowned and highly respected in her circle of expertise, which obviously included that of the wider art world. Three books of her photographs had been published. He felt a little shamefaced that he hadn't considered that before, and here he was treating her like an assistant.

'I'd be delighted,' Eva said. 'And let me say that I admire the work you and your colleagues did in the war and are still doing.'

'Thank you. There are only a few of the section left working in Europe now, although still a great deal to do, and many works of art and cultural significance are still missing and in the wrong hands. It will take years, decades even, to rectify that. People other than the government will have to take up the task of locating them, lawyers, curators, archivists and individuals who have been robbed. Phillipe is one of the latter now that he is no longer working for the section.'

'When did he cease working for the Monuments Men?' Ryga asked.

'September 1949.'

'Have you seen him since?'

'No.'

'Did you know he lived on board a converted Motor Torpedo Boat?'

'No, but I'm not surprised. He hated being tied down to one place, and he loathed being shut in. He felt suffocated by it – probably a legacy of feeling confined in the cockpit of the aeroplane when it crashed, although I'm not an expert on these matters. Why the questions about Phillipe? Has something happened to him?' she asked, concerned.

Ryga answered. 'His boat was found drifting in the English

Channel on the twelfth of November. There was no one on board.'

There was a moment's silence while she digested this, her dark-featured face thoughtful and troubled. 'You think he might have killed himself?'

'Do you?'

'No.'

The reply had come almost instantly. 'Why not?' Ryga asked.

'Because there was too much unresolved. Unless . . .'

'Yes?'

She sat back. He could see she was considering her answer, not because she was worried about revealing something, or trying to fabricate a story, but because she was trying to order her thoughts. He let her. So too did Eva.

After a moment, she resumed, 'Phillipe is determined, passionate, brave and painstaking. He also has that leap of imagination that leads to instinct, which was often proved right. He seemed to be able to see into people and their motivations.'

Ryga resisted a glance at Eva as he thought of her third eye.

Miss Dewsnap continued, 'When Phillipe was on the trail of something that excited him or that he totally believed in, he would never give up. The only reason he would kill himself is if he had come to the end of a quest.'

'A personal one?' Eva said sharply, looking up from her notes.

'Yes, and he was on one. He was trying to trace some items that had belonged to his family, which he believed the Nazis had taken from his father before killing him.'

'I thought his father had sold everything to fund their passage to England,' Eva said.

'Not quite everything.' She rose. 'I'll be back in two minutes.'

Eva exchanged a glance with Ryga but neither of them spoke.

Miss Dewsnap was true to her word. Standing next to Ryga, she opened her hand. In it was a tiny portrait in a round case. It was of a young man with fair hair in a red jacket with a high collar and cream cravat.

Eva, looking over Ryga's shoulder, said, 'It's exquisite.'

'Yes. It's an eighteenth-century miniature of the Duke of Wellington painted by Richard Cosway.'

Ryga said, 'It's amazing how anyone can paint something so small.'

She moved round to resume her seat behind the desk and put the miniature in front of them. 'These paintings were often fitted into lockets, watch-covers and even snuff boxes so that people could take them with them. Some would be framed with stands or hung on a wall. They were frequently given as gifts within the family or in courtship. They were popular across Europe from the sixteenth century right up until the mid-nineteenth century. Phillipe was particularly interested in them because his family owned several by an extremely talented artist, and a beautiful woman, called Constance Meyer.'

'The name of Phillipe's boat,' Eva exclaimed.

'Is it? Not surprising, I suppose. Constance Mayer, or to give her full name, Marie-Françoise-Constance Mayer-La Martinière, was born on 9 March 1775 in Chauny, Picardy and died on 26 May 1821 in Paris. She was a painter of portraits and miniatures of women and children, family scenes, self-portraits and miniatures of her father, who was a government official. Following the French Revolution's Reign of Terror, miniature and portrait paintings became very popular. She studied with Pierre-Paul Prud'hon in 1802, a married man with children. During the time when Prud'hon was painting the portrait of Empress Josephine, his wife, in a fit of jealousy, claimed that he was having an affair with the empress. Prud'hon's wife was put into an asylum and Prud'hon was given custody of their children. The Emperor Napoleon also gave him an apartment in the Sorbonne. At about the same time, around 1803, Napoléon, who had purchased two of Constance's paintings, gave her an apartment there too. She became as Prud'hon's assistant and raised his five children. When Prud'hon's wife died, Constance fully expected to marry him, but he refused her even after all the years she'd given him and after having raised his children. Prone to depression throughout her life, she took up a razor and slit her throat.'

Ryga shook his head sadly.

'Prud'hon organized a retrospective of her works the year after her death but, distressed, he died soon after in 1823. They're buried together in Paris's Père Lachaise cemetery.'

'Some artists seem to lead a tragic life,' Ryga said.

'They do, and some have colourful ones. As you said, Phillipe's father sold many of the family's paintings in order to fund his wife and children's escape from France, but Phillipe firmly believed that his father wouldn't have sold the four miniatures painted by Constance Mayer. They would have been easily secreted about his person, but those miniatures disappeared. They were probably taken off his body when he died while being transported to the concentration camp, or when he was captured by the Nazis. Phillipe was determined to track them down, even if it took him the rest of his life.'

'And did he track them down?' Ryga wondered aloud.

'I don't know. But I do know he was getting close in Lubeck.'

'Lubeck!'

'Yes, why? It means something to you? With regards to Phillipe, I mean?' She sat forward, interested. Eva's pen froze over her notebook and she glanced at Ryga. He hadn't told Eva that Broxham had mentioned that he and Ashmore had been stationed in Lubeck. Broxham had only mentioned it in reference to the similarity in the weather of freezing fog and dabbling in the black market.

'When was this?' he asked Miss Dewsnap.

'In the bitterly cold winter of 1946. My team were on the trail of some cultural artefacts taken from various Jewish families in Berlin. You probably know that Lubeck, being in West Germany, was at that time awash with ethnic German refugees expelled from Eastern Germany in the Communist Bloc, and others from there trying to get over to the west. Lubeck is on the inner German border between the two states – the German Democratic Republic, East Germany, and the Federal Republic of Germany, West Germany. It was established in July 1945 as the boundary between the Western and Soviet occupation zones of former Nazi Germany. Some would trade and pay anything to get across to the western sector, knowing that it could be their last chance. Some are still desperately trying despite the high metal fences, barbed wire, booby traps and watch towers. I don't think it will be long before a more physical barrier is erected – a wall perhaps. We were offered some valuable works of art by former German soldiers, and Nazi government officials, in return for safe passage, but they soon learnt we weren't there to bargain with them and pay them for their stolen loot, so they looked elsewhere. I have no proof of that but there was a thriving black market and many British soldiers weren't amiss to dealing in it.'

Ryga rapidly digested this. Broxham had confessed that he and Ashmore had been a couple of those soldiers dealing in cigarettes and alcohol, but as Ryga had already expressed to his chief, he had wondered if it was more than that. He'd considered medicines but not art and artefacts, and judging by the paintings in Ashmore's house, he had an eye for art and a taste for it. Now Ryga had another connection in this case between Swinley and Perrier, and between Perrier, Broxham and Ashmore. Could those miniatures have come into the hands of Charles Ashmore and Neil Broxham in Lubeck and Phillipe had traced them to the two men, who had refused to give them to him? Had Phillipe been amassing evidence for three years while still working with the Monuments Men until 1949, in order to prove they rightfully belonged to his family? Was it this evidence and trail that he had asked Feline to pass on to Swinley, a man he trusted?

Eva's voice broke through his thoughts. 'How valuable would these miniatures be?'

'Incredibly. You're looking at thousands of pounds for each one.'

Eva shot Ryga a look. That was indeed a powerful motive for murder. He didn't think Phillipe Perrier had thrown himself off his boat, or that he had taken off on his tender to do the same. The fact that Ashmore's boat had been moored up at Chelsea the same night as Phillipe's, and the next day Phillipe's boat, along with him, had disappeared meant only one thing as far as Ryga was concerned. Ashmore and Broxham had those miniatures and they were determined to keep them. That had also meant silencing Swinley and recovering the evidence, hence Feline and Myra's deaths. Ryga had found his motive and his killers.

Twenty-Three

'Shall I make for Seaford?' asked Eva.

'Yes.' It was on the way back to Newhaven and to Ryga it made sense to call in there instead of returning to Newhaven, collecting a constable, then driving back to Seaford. But would Ashmore be at home? The last Ryga knew was that he was in London. Broxham might be there though.

The thin, icy drizzle had turned into something much more forceful and looked set to persist for some time. The sky was a heavy grey, making it darker than usual for the early afternoon, and the windscreen wipers had a job to push the rain away as they sped along the coast. But within half an hour Eva was pulling into the drive of Ashmore's Seaford residence.

'Impressive if you like this kind of thing,' she said, eyeing the house.

'And you don't?'

'Vulgar.'

He smiled despite the seriousness of the occasion. He'd have loved her to have met Valerie Ashmore and know what she made of that lady. She might still see her. Although there was no sign of the Rolls-Royce or the sports car, both could be garaged and Broxham could be in his flat above it. Mrs Doulton opened the door to them.

'I thought you'd be back,' she announced before running her cold critical eye over Eva. 'Whose she? One of his mistresses?'

Ryga didn't know if she meant Broxham or Ashmore and he wasn't going to ask. Eva seemed to find it amusing although she covered her mirth with a cough.

'Are either Broxham or Major Ashmore at home?' he asked politely but firmly.

'Major Ashmore is.' She stepped back to allow them entry. 'Wait here,' she abruptly commanded.

Definitely frostier than before, thought Ryga. He wondered what had happened to further chill her already cool reception on his previous visits. Perhaps his persistence in returning. Or perhaps she had overheard or seen something that had given her deeper concern and had increased her hostility.

'There are some valuable paintings here,' Eva said quietly. 'That one, for example, is by Christopher Woods.' She indicated the one that Ryga had studied previously of the men on the quayside viewing the fishing boat in the storm which had reminded him of Eva's late Aunt Pru's paintings. He should have known Eva would recognize the artist. 'He's incredibly sought-after. Another tragic story like Constance Mayer's. Christopher Wood threw himself in front of a London train at the age of thirty.'

The door to the parlour opened and Mrs Doulton jerked her head to indicate they could enter. Charles Ashmore didn't look too pleased to see them, although Ryga thought his expression was one more of wariness than hostility. Ashmore eyed Eva suspiciously, as though she was there to trap him. Perhaps he was trying to remember if he had met her before and if he'd had a relationship with her. Ryga thought Ashmore could hardly forget it if he had. How could anyone? But then maybe Ashmore had so many casual affairs that he had stopped noticing the women with whom he had them.

'What is it now, Inspector? I'm very busy,' he said testily.

'This is Miss Paisley,' Ryga said. 'She's assisting me with the investigation into the death of a woman found in Sleeper's Hole on Wednesday night who you know, Major Ashmore. Feline Perrier.'

His eyes narrowed and flicked between them. 'I read about it. Neil told me you'd been here asking about her.' He turned his back on them and crossed to the fireplace. He was obviously trying to get his thoughts and reactions under control. Ryga said nothing. Turning round, Ashmore tersely said, 'Can we make this snappy? My wife will be home shortly. She's Christmas shopping in Brighton.'

'I understand from Mr Broxham that you and Miss Perrier were having an affair.'

'It was finished a long time ago.' Again, that wary glance at Eva. Ryga suspected that Ashmore was wondering if Eva was a friend of Feline's and one she had confided in. 'When exactly?'

'October.' He thrust his hands in the pockets of his lounge suit jacket.

That confirmed what Broxham had said. 'Your wife told you to end it.'

'Neil told you that, I suppose,' Ashmore snapped, annoyed. 'Well, it's not true. Feline ended it. She said she'd found someone else,' he added with bitterness.

'Yes, your chauffeur. Why didn't you sack him?'

'Why should I? His love affairs have nothing to do with the quality of his driving. You win some, you lose some,' he said in a cavalier tone, daring Eva to react. She didn't, of course.

'Then it's a habit of yours and Broxham's to exchange lovers,' Ryga said smoothly.

Ashmore's face flushed deep red. 'I resent that. And if you are determined to be insulting then I suggest you leave.'

'So you were annoyed and upset at losing Feline to your chauffeur?'

Ashmore's lips tightened. Ryga could see he was making an effort to control himself. 'I couldn't give her the commitment she wanted. She was getting too involved. I wouldn't leave my wife.'

'No, you know a good thing when you see it,' Ryga said evenly without any trace of a sneer, seeing how far it would goad the smooth but worried man in front of them.

'I'll take no more insults from you, Inspector.' He strode towards the door, much as his wife had done in Ryga's previous interview with her, but Ryga's next words drew him up.

'Angry and bitterly jealous over losing Feline, you decided to kill her.'

'Me! My God, are you insane?' He swung round. 'You can't possibly think I would kill anyone.'

'You did in the war.'

'For Christ's sake man, that was different.' He ran a hand over his chin. 'I didn't kill Feline. I couldn't do a thing like that; besides, I was in London.'

'How do you know when she was killed?'

He was stumped for a moment. 'You said her body was found on Wednesday and it was in the papers.'

'She'd been dead for some days, since Thursday the seventh of December. Where were you that night?' Broxham had already told him, but again Ryga wanted to see if both men were singing from the same hymn sheet.

'I don't know. I can't remember.'

'Then I suggest you try or consult your diary.'

Ashmore's eyes flashed fear. 'I was in London, at my apartment.'

'Alone?'

'Yes.'

'All evening and night?'

'Yes.'

'That's not what Broxham told me. He said you were both at The Pelican Club in Mayfair.'

'Well, yes, we were for a while. I'd forgotten. Look, I didn't kill Feline.'

'Then maybe you killed her brother, Phillipe.'

'What! Now I know you're mad.'

'But you do know Phillipe Perrier?'

'No.'

'Please, Major Ashmore, it would save a lot of time if you stopped lying.'

'It's the truth. I don't know him.'

'You met him in 1946 but you've seen him since then.'

Ashmore's troubled eyes flicked between them. He consulted his wristwatch before crossing to the coffee table and opening the cigarette box, where he retrieved a cigarette but didn't light it. He turned back to face them. Ryga could see him weighing up how much to say. He thought it time to increase the pressure. Eva remained silent and watchful beside him.

'You first met Phillipe Perrier when you were stationed in Lubeck with Private Broxham?'

Ashmore's slender hands played with the unlit cigarette.

'When you were a corporal and not a major. You have never been a major,' Ryga continued quietly.

'So Broxham's opened his big mouth. Yes, I was stationed at Lubeck, and yes, I was a corporal. Telling a lie about one's rank is not a criminal offence.'

'But murder and theft are.'

'How many times do I have to tell you I haven't killed anyone and neither have I stolen anything?' But Ashmore was looking increasingly disturbed.

'You traded on the black market in Lubeck.'

'We all did, but I only traded with legitimate items we were given or sent from home – cigarettes, chocolate, food. If you're arresting me for that then you'd have to arrest the whole of my old unit.'

'But you did meet Phillipe Perrier in Lubeck when he was assigned to work with the Monuments Men.'

Ashmore jumped as the mantel clock struck three. He glanced at it nervously. 'All right, I met him, but only briefly. I haven't seen him since.'

'Where were you on the nights of the eleventh and twelfth of November?'

'Why then?'

'Just answer the question, Mr Ashmore.'

The dropping of his rank wasn't lost on Ashmore. He lit his cigarette. 'I was in London. I'm involved in negotiating for a bombsite off Horseferry Road, Westminster for development. I returned here on the evening of the twelfth.'

'By car?'

'Yes.'

'Did Broxham drive you?'

'No, I drove myself.'

'Then your boat wasn't moored up at Chelsea boatyard?'

'No.'

'We have evidence to the contrary. Phillipe Perrier's boat was also moored there. You met him on board his boat on the night of the eleventh of November and took his boat out after killing him.'

Ashmore was staring at him aghast. His face had gone ashen. His smouldering cigarette remained in his hand. 'My boat was in Newhaven where it's usually kept.'

That was a surprise to Ryga. Sergeant Jacobs had said it was registered at Dover and Ryga had assumed it was kept there. Neither Hailsham nor Dakins had mentioned it to him, but then why should they when he had asked if any vessel *unknown* to them had entered and left the harbour on the nights of 7 November and 7 December, not a vessel *known* to them.

Ryga continued, 'You ditched Perrier's body in the sea, then, using the tender on his boat, you returned to the shore somewhere along the south coast and made your way back to London. Perhaps you hired a taxi or caught the train. Or perhaps an accomplice picked you up. Neil Broxham.'

'This is ludicrous. Why would I kill Perrier? I haven't seen him since 1946.'

'You killed him because he knew that you'd stolen, or been given, items of value that had been looted by the Nazis which belonged to him and Feline, some extremely valuable miniatures.'

Ashmore looked baffled. Ryga thought it could be an act but he was afraid his reaction was genuine. He said, 'You refused to give these miniatures back to Perrier. You killed him to silence him, just as you'd already killed PC Swinley, because Feline had told you that her brother had been in touch with Swinley about the stolen miniatures which he was hot on the trail of. You met Swinley on the quayside, where you struck him a violent blow and pushed him in the harbour, leaving him to drown.'

'I know nothing about any of this,' Ashmore pleaded beseechingly.

Relentlessly Ryga pressed on. 'At that stage you didn't know that Swinley had written evidence, which Feline had delivered to him. But you discovered this later from Feline and when you realized that Swinley's widow could have the evidence to convict you, you followed Feline, or had her tailed, and on the seventh of December you saw her with Myra Swinley. You intercepted Feline and killed her and then returned to Mrs Swinley's house, lured her away and also killed her.'

'This is madness,' Ashmore cried. 'I have no idea what you are talking about.'

Sharply Ryga said, 'Then how do you account for your boat being at Chelsea on the same night that Phillipe Perrier disappeared? And the fact his boat was found drifting in the English Channel the next day?'

'I didn't know my boat was there,' Ashmore said despairingly. His face was drawn and grey. His eyes fearful. 'I wasn't on board. I rarely am. I have no idea most of the time where it is and where it isn't.'

Ryga studied him closely. He could see it was the truth. But Ashmore knew who had taken his boat to London and who Phillipe's killer was. And so too did Ryga. 'Where can we find Neil Broxham?'

'I don't know.'

But he did. And Ryga knew too.

Twenty-Four

Ryga sent a constable to the Watch House to ask the assistant harbour master if the *Liberty* was in the harbour. It was. And it was moored up on the west side just across the allotments on a landing stage between the alleyway where Ryga believed Swinley had met his death and the Watch House. Mr Broxham was on board. Ryga gave instructions that if the *Liberty* made any attempt to leave the harbour before he could get there she was to be stopped.

Ryga expected Eva to insist on accompanying him to the boat but she didn't. She said she would type up the notes from their interview with Miss Dewsnap and she'd also put together a report on their interview with Ashmore. Ryga was grateful. Maybe she sensed that for this final interview with Broxham he had to be alone, or with a police officer. It was police business after all. Not that it worried him if Eva was with him, because he respected and trusted her. Even the thought that Broxham might get rough, and someone might get hurt, wouldn't have prevented him from having Eva along – she'd been in far tougher spots. But her agility was hampered by her leg wound, and the fact they would be in cramped space on board a boat would increase the risk. She'd said, 'You don't want to be looking out for me, Ryga, when you should be chasing after a killer.' Ryga had replied that he sincerely hoped there wouldn't be any chasing.

He'd left instructions for the Seaford police to keep a watch on Ashmore's house and to let Newhaven know if he left there. He had also telephoned the Yard and asked for an officer to keep a watch on Ashmore's London apartment and his offices. Ryga didn't think Ashmore would make a bolt for it. He was probably frantically telephoning his solicitor in case charges were brought against him. Ryga lacked evidence though and the same would apply to Broxham, unless he could positively prove the *Liberty* was in Newhaven Harbour on the 7 November and the 7 December, but even if it had been that wasn't proof that Broxham had met and killed George Swinley or Feline Perrier and Myra Swinley. Even if the miniatures were found after searching the *Liberty*, Broxham could say that Phillipe had given them to him. And even if the *Liberty* had left Chelsea at the same time as Perrier's boat, there was again no evidence to say that Broxham had boarded it and killed Phillipe. If he had been seen to go on board he could insist it had been at Phillipe's invitation for a drink and he had left soon afterwards. Ryga needed a confession and he didn't think Broxham was the type to provide it.

Accompanied by Sergeant Williams and a police constable, Ryga made for the *Liberty*. It was still raining heavily, and dark. There was a light on board. He posted the constable on the shore and climbed on board with Williams. The movement of the boat was enough to draw Broxham from the cabin on to the deck. He smiled as though to say, *I thought it might be you.*

'Come inside, Inspector. Make yourself comfortable. I can see by that look on your face, and from the fact you have brought uniformed re-enforcements, that you mean business. And it's raining.'

They stepped into the spacious and elegantly kitted out main cabin. The rain drummed on the deck and the cabin roof, steady and heavy. Broxham waved them into seats. After Ryga took one, Williams eased himself down into another and removed his helmet placing it on the table beside him. Then he withdrew his notebook and pen from the top pocket of his tunic, leaving it undone, much as George Swinley had done on the quayside before being pushed into the water. Had Swinley been on the quay though? Maybe he had come on board this boat and done exactly as Williams had done. Broxham had got behind him, struck him, buttoned up his tunic and manhandled his body over the side of the boat.

Williams' deep brown eyes swept the cabin curiously. Ryga could picture Swinley doing the same. After killing and ditching Swinley in the harbour, Broxham had disposed of the helmet, notebook and pencil elsewhere, possibly out in the English Channel.

Ryga studied Broxham. He was dressed in expensive casual clothes, not looking at all like a chauffeur now, or an employee of any kind, but a leisured gentleman, which in effect was what he was, Ryga thought. And dangerous. Broxham had tried to make him believe that Ashmore was the killer by volunteering information about him, when in reality it was he who was the killer. Here was a clever man who thought on his feet, agile-minded, charismatic, a chameleon, charming, who liked to live dangerously, who missed the adrenalin rush of the war and the wheeling and dealing after it. A man who liked to manipulate people and enjoyed watching what happened. A man who thought he could talk and charm his way out of danger. Well, not this time.

There was a glass of whisky on the table beside him.

'I'd offer you a drink,' Broxham said, noting Ryga's glance, 'except I know you'd say you are on duty.'

'You seem very much at home on your boss's boat.'

'He's a generous man.'

'I suppose he'd have to be, otherwise you'd tell everyone, including his wife, that he is in reality a lowly corporal and not a former army officer. But then that's not all you have on him. He likes his art. Some of it, in the past, acquired dubiously.'

Broxham said nothing and sipped his whisky.

Ryga continued, 'Art that was acquired from Nazis in exchange for a safe passage to West Germany and elsewhere, especially for those wanting to escape war crimes trials or who were afraid of not being declassified as Nazis. Ashmore used this dirty money to kickstart his property empire. You spent and gambled yours away.' It was a guess but a considered one now that he was beginning to understand Broxham's personality.

His eyes flickered minutely but he remained silent.

'You ended up broke and then thought, *What can I do? I know, I'll look up my old army chum.* You discovered Ashmore had been much more frugal with the proceeds of his criminal activities in Lubeck and that he had also lied about his background. He had a rich wife and a lot to lose. So you began blackmailing him three years ago. This isn't Charles Ashmore's boat. It's yours.' Ryga saw Williams' surprise. 'Ashmore also bought you the apartment in London. It just amuses you to play the chauffeur, although it is a good disguise. You are cleverer than Ashmore. He does what he's told. But when he had an affair with Feline you weren't too happy about that. Not only because you had what her brother wanted, which you refused to give up to him, but because you also wanted her. I wouldn't bother to deny it. I know about the miniatures.'

Broxham took another drink but his eyes never left Ryga's face. Ryga wondered if he would continue to deny it. If so, he would have to get proof, and by the time he got it Broxham could be anywhere. Even if he took him in for further questioning, he couldn't hold him in custody forever.

Ryga continued, 'I know that you arranged to meet Feline on the night of the seventh of December on her brother's boat, which, of course, you had seen moored up here. Before she reached it, though, you killed her and hid her body under an upturned boat. I also know that you killed George Swinley, and abducted, and have probably killed, Myra Swinley.' Ryga rose. It was time to bluff it. Williams hastily scrambled up. 'Neil Broxham, I charge you with the murders of—'

'I haven't killed anyone, not illegally anyway, only in the course of duty in the army. And I don't have the miniatures.' Broxham's voice was calm, his expression neutral. He showed no fear or anger.

After a moment Ryga resumed his seat, and so too did Williams. The wind was rocking the boat in an irregular movement, which strained the mooring ropes and caused a creaking sound to the accompaniment of the rain on the deck.

'As you so rightly have guessed, Inspector, I acquired the miniatures from a Nazi in Lubeck who parted with them in exchange for his freedom and passage across to the west. I didn't know at the time where they had originally come from, or who they belonged to. I didn't even know how valuable they were. I was no art expert, but Ashmore was quite knowledgeable despite his humble upbringing. He was, and still is, a competent artist. But the miniatures I kept to myself. Let's say as future insurance.'

'Or until the price is right.'

'It takes time to find the right buyer.'

'Someone who doesn't care where they came from or that they lack provenance. But when did Phillipe trace them to you?'

'In October. He said he had the final proof that they had been the property of his family.'

'And you killed him and his sister, who you discovered had been passing over this proof and more about your thefts, to Phillipe's former friend, Police Constable George Swinley, who you also had to eliminate. And you needed to get that evidence back. So now you have the provenance and the miniatures, and thought you had eradicated all evidence of your thefts and murder.'

'I don't have the miniatures or the provenance,' Broxham said.

'And I didn't kill Phillipe Perrier, Feline or PC Swinley. Neither did I abduct and kill Mrs Swinley.'

Ryga studied Broxham's lined face and hard grey eyes. Here was an experienced liar, so how much store could he set by his statement?

Ignoring his declaration, Ryga continued to espouse the same theory he had already put to Ashmore. 'You met Phillipe Perrier on his boat at Chelsea on the night of the eleventh of November. You killed him and took his boat out into the English Channel where you threw him overboard and left his boat to drift. You returned to the shore using Phillipe's tender. You dumped it somewhere and made your way back to London.'

'Partly correct. I went on board Phillipe's boat in London as you say on the eleventh of November, but that was all. He left his mooring shortly afterwards *with* the miniatures, which I gave back to him.'

'You expect me to believe that!'

'It happens to be true. I thought I would legitimately get them back anyway or at least two of them when they became Feline's. We were going to get married.'

But he spoke coolly, without warmth, love or passion, as though it were merely a business transaction, and Ryga thought that to Broxham that was exactly what it was.

'But you didn't love her.'

Broxham smiled. It made Ryga feel cold and reminded him of some of the callous guards he'd met in the POW camp.

'How could anyone not love Feline, she was stunning,' Broxham declared with a hint of mirth in his eyes.

'Was, yes,' Ryga snapped. 'She wasn't stunning when I saw her body dumped in the mud of Sleeper's Hole, eaten by maggots and sea lice.'

Broxham showed no reaction to the blunt and harsh statement. 'I had no reason to kill her and I'm sorry she's dead and Phillipe too.'

Ryga didn't think Broxham knew the meaning of the word.

'Once I knew the miniatures really did belong to Perrier's family, I saw no need to keep them. And, as I said, Feline would have inherited at least two of them. In fact, Phillipe wanted her to have them all. He thought she should give up modelling and settle down, something he hadn't managed to do and said he would be incapable of doing. He was too restless after the war and his health was poor. I would hardly kill either of them knowing that by marrying Feline I would come into a fortune quite legitimately.'

'Not if you were in prison,' quipped Ryga. 'And that was why you were so desperate to get hold of those packages that Feline deposited with Collier, the newsagent, and which PC George Swinley had collected. Because Phillipe didn't trust you. He knew about your criminal activities with Ashmore and all your dirty dealings in Lubeck.'

Ryga pressed on. 'If your criminal activity was exposed, Feline wouldn't marry you, and you could say goodbye to any rich living. There was a lot at stake, Broxham. But when you killed Swinley you didn't know about the written evidence that he had collected. Feline had simply told you that Phillipe had been in touch with a police officer he had met during the war, who worked and lived in Newhaven. It wasn't until after you had silenced Swinley that you discovered there existed written evidence of yours and Ashmore's criminal activity. You urged her to stay silent, spinning her some story about Ashmore being a crook and you needed all the evidence, otherwise he'd wriggle out of it or put the blame on you.'

Broxham finished his drink before saying, 'I know nothing about any packages. Feline told me she couldn't contact her brother and she was worried about him. Then I read that his boat had been brought into Newhaven harbour, only no one knew who the boat owner was, and that the boat had been deserted. Knowing Phillipe's poor mental health, I thought he had gone out to sea after our meeting and taken his own life.'

'But you didn't come forward with this information.'

'Of course I didn't, because you'd think exactly what you're thinking now, Inspector, especially if the miniatures weren't found on board, which they obviously haven't been, otherwise you wouldn't be here accusing me of stealing them. Someone else has been on board that boat and helped himself to them. Feline didn't have them either. She was abroad. I contacted her in Italy. She was completely ignorant of the fact her brother's boat had been found and said she hadn't spoken to Phillipe for a week. I didn't enlighten her. She said that the last time she had seen and spoken to him had been on Sunday the fifth of November.'

'And when she returned, she told you about the packages George Swinley had collected.'

'Yes. Because I told her that her brother had found the Constance

Mayer Miniatures but that they weren't on his boat, which was in Newhaven Harbour, and that her brother had disappeared.'

'Did you search the boat?'

'Of course. Soon after I read about it being brought in here. I searched it on the night of the fourteenth of November. It was foggy, making it good cover for that kind of activity. It was easy to manipulate the lock. I couldn't find the miniatures.'

'Maybe you didn't look that thoroughly.'

'Like you, Inspector, I know how to search – the army taught me that.'

'How do I know you didn't find them and right now they are in your possession?'

'You don't but it happens to be the truth. You are free to search this boat and my flat above Ashmore's garage.'

'And your London apartment.' Ryga saw Broxham hesitate. He shrugged an answer.

'If you must.'

'Oh, we will.' Ryga left a moment's silence, his gaze fixed on Broxham as he weighed up what he was telling him. If Broxham was telling the truth then someone else had taken the miniatures and there were three people he knew of who had been on board before the fourteenth of November – Dakins the customs officer, his boss Leemings, and Hailsham. Four if he counted the coastguard.

'When did Feline tell you that Myra Swinley was going to Scotland Yard because she believed her husband's death was murder?'

'She didn't.'

'You asked Feline to contact Myra on her return journey home in order to learn from her what the Yard had said and the likelihood they would investigate. Also to find out what Swinley had done with the packages she'd left for him to collect from the Seaford newsagent's. Then you waited for Feline to leave Mrs Swinley's house. You told her about her brother's boat being in the harbour. She met you on board. You took the packages – evidence that the miniatures belonged to her family – and you killed her.'

'No, Inspector.'

Ignoring him, Ryga continued, 'Then you called on Myra and persuaded her to leave the house on some pretext, perhaps saying Feline had met with an accident. You killed her and took her body out in her husband's dinghy and dumped it in the harbour, abandoning the dinghy on the shore of Denton Island where you smashed it up and walked back here to your boat.'

'I didn't know Myra Swinley or her husband, or the fact he had a dinghy. I never met Feline that night and if it's proof you want then I'll give you the name and address of the woman I spent it with, although you would be advised to speak to her when her husband is out.'

Ryga heard Williams suck in his breath. Sadly, Ryga thought Broxham was telling the truth. He asked Broxham to accompany them to the station, which he did without protest, and there Sergeant Williams typed up his statement. Ryga charged him with dealing in stolen and looted property, to which Broxham cheerfully said, 'I think you'll have a hard time proving it, Inspector.'

There was no sign of Eva. The constable didn't know where she was, only that she had left shortly after typing up the interviews with Miss Dewsnap and Charles Ashmore, which Ryga found on his desk. Maybe she was back at the hotel.

He telephoned Superintendent Street at home, as it was now past ten o'clock, and relayed what he had discovered, adding that both men denied murder and they had no evidence to prove it. They might also find it difficult to make the charge of dealing in stolen property stick. Not unless they found something on their premises or they discovered the miniatures.

'So we're back to square one,' Street said, 'if we don't find those miniatures.'

'There's still the four other men who have been on board the *Constance* – Leslie Dakins, Harold Leemings, the coastguard and Peter Hailsham. I'm going to start with the latter because he is allegedly ill with influenza and he was harbour master at Chichester before moving here two years ago. Perhaps he came across Swinley and Perrier in Graylingwell Hospital, Chichester, or visited a patient there and learned about the miniatures from Perrier. He might have kept in touch with Perrier, the latter having a boat. And Perrier could have put in here previously although Hailsham never mentioned it to me. But then he wouldn't if he didn't want to draw attention to the fact he had seen it before and knew the owner. Hailsham also knew George and Myra Swinley, and Myra would have gone willingly with Hailsham if he had knocked on her door last Thursday night. I'd like to confirm that he really is down with influenza, even if it means risking catching his germs,' he added lightly. Then continued more seriously, 'Or perhaps his part in triple murder is making him physically sick.'

Ryga requested search warrants to be issued for the *Liberty*, Broxham's Seaford flat, his London apartment and for Ashmore's Seaford home, London apartment and his offices. Street would see to it. Before leaving for the hotel, Ryga tried one more time to get more information or a confession out of Broxham but didn't succeed. Ryga thanked Sergeant Williams for his help and returned to the Bridge Hotel where he found a message waiting for him from Eva, saying she had returned to London. It didn't say she would be back. And she had checked out of the hotel.

Puzzled, he retired to bed. Had he offended her in some way? He hoped not. Perhaps it was the fact he had asked her to take notes and she didn't want to be treated in such a way. She was a talented photographer, intelligent and fearless. Eva could not sit quietly by while others went about their work. Perhaps her father or stepmother was ill. Perhaps her leg was too painful and she hated to admit it to him. Whatever the reason, he'd have to dismiss it from his mind for the time being. Tomorrow he had work to do, and unless the miniatures were discovered in Broxham's possession, which was looking unlikely, he still had a killer to find.

Twenty-Five

Late Tuesday morning, Ryga gathered up the beat officer in Chapel Street, a puzzled PC Jenkins who said that he couldn't believe for one minute that such an upstanding man as Mr Hailsham could be involved in the murder of that poor woman and Mrs Swinley. He just wasn't the type. Ryga swiftly but kindly told him there was no type. And he thought he should heed his own advice because he had fully expected the killer to be either Ashmore or Broxham and he'd been wrong. Admittedly the properties belonging to Broxham and Ashmore hadn't yet been searched, but earlier that morning Ryga had searched Ashmore's boat. The miniatures weren't on board.

It was just before midday when he knocked on Hailsham's door, which was answered by Mrs Cray in a brightly coloured floral apron. There were dark circles under her bloodshot, tired eyes. She looked anxiously at PC Jenkins.

'I'll not have Mr Hailsham bothered,' she declared.

'I hope not to trouble him too much, Mrs Cray, but I do need to speak to him,' Ryga said, thinking that Hailsham must be genuinely ill because Mrs Cray looked as though she'd been nursing him all night. Had that illness, as he had previously considered, been caused by guilt over a triple murder?

As though reading his mind, or perhaps because Hailsham had been confessing his sins, Mrs Cray quickly said, 'He's got nothing to do with the murder of that woman.'

'We'll only take a moment of his time,' Ryga said firmly and moved to enter.

'You won't get any sense out of him.'

'Because of his influenza, Mrs Cray? Is that what is really ailing him?'

Her fingers plucked nervously at the pocket of her apron.

'Or is there something more?' Ryga quietly persisted. 'Maybe I should see him and find out.'

She blocked the way. 'You can't go up there.'

'I can and I will, Mrs Cray.'

'Can't you just leave him in peace? Hasn't he suffered enough?'

'Guilt?'

She looked taken aback. 'Why should he feel guilty? He's done nothing wrong. All right, so he was in Fort Road the night you say that poor woman was killed and put under the boat, as you have obviously been told, but Mr Hailsham didn't do it.'

No one had told Ryga that Hailsham had been in Fort Road on the night in question, but then why shouldn't he have been, it was his route home. Mrs Cray was a little too defensive.

'Mr Hailsham feels very bad that he wasn't there to stop her from being killed, but how would he know that was going to happen? And he feels dreadful that for all these days the poor woman was there under that rotting boat and everyone was walking around her.'

Not everyone, thought Ryga, just him, Joseph Moore, Hailsham and the person who had uncovered her, her killer, who could be the man upstairs, supposedly ill in bed.

'I'm sorry, Mrs Cray, but I have to speak to him.'

'You can speak but he won't be able to answer you. He'll be all right in a couple of days with the right nursing from me, and peace and quiet, and I'm here to see he gets it.'

'I must insist, Mrs Cray.'

He held her gaze and after a moment she gave a heavy sigh and reluctantly capitulated. 'All right, you can come in, but not him.' She pointed at Jenkins. 'You stay there and don't move an inch. I'll not have your big feet clomping through the house.'

Ryga suppressed a smile and followed Mrs Cray up the stairs to a bedroom at the front of the house, which was in darkness because the curtains were drawn. Ryga could smell sickness as soon as he entered, banishing all his thoughts that the harbour master was faking it. Looking down at the trembling, shivering man with yellowing skin, he felt acute sympathy for him.

'Malaria?'

'You know,' she said, shocked.

'I've seen it many times. Why did you say it was influenza?'

'Because he doesn't like anyone to know.'

'It's nothing to be ashamed of.'

'I keep telling him that. He was in Burma and he's worried if people know he suffers from malaria they'll ask him about it and he doesn't want to talk about the war and what happened. He had a bad time – even I don't know what happened – and to cap it all the poor man's wife and two children were killed in a raid in Portsmouth. After he was demobbed he worked at Chichester Harbour but it was too close to Portsmouth and memories of the terrible loss he suffered. So he came here to start afresh. He says it's time to forget and move on.'

Move on at least, thought Ryga. It was hard to forget even when you tried. But he understood Hailsham's sentiments.

'Do you know if Mr Hailsham was admitted to Graylingwell Hospital in Chichester?' Ryga wondered if the shock of the loss of his wife and children, coming on top of his experiences in Burma, had caused him to have a mental breakdown.

'Not as far as I'm aware.'

Ryga would need to check. 'Have you called the doctor?'

'What can he do that I can't?' she scoffed.

'He can give you a prescription for medication that can ease the symptoms and you don't have to pay for it or the doctor's visit any more. I'll get PC Jenkins to call in at the doctor's house and ask him to pay a visit.'

She was about to refuse but she must have seen he was genuinely concerned. She gave a curt nod.

'I won't trouble him.' Ryga stepped outside on to the landing. In a lowered tone, he said, 'But you might be able to help me further.'

Her light grey eyes narrowed a little. He could see she was enormously fond of Hailsham and perhaps that fondness went deeper.

'You said that Mr Hailsham was in Fort Road on Thursday the seventh of December. What time was this?'

'Oh, I see you're checking I'm telling the truth. You don't believe me,' she declared indignantly, folding her arms across her chest. 'If you must know it was just before six thirty.'

'Where was he going?'

'Home, of course. Here.'

'You saw him arrive?'

She shifted uneasily.

'Please, Mrs Cray, the truth.'

'You're not to breathe a word of this to anyone if I tell you. Not even to the vicar. I'll not have any gossip spread about Peter.'

Ryga guessed what was coming next. 'Of course.'

'He didn't come here but next door, to my house. I'm a widow. My husband died before the war; he was killed in an accident in the docks at Railway Quay. Peter – Mr Hailsham – and I have been friends since he came here.'

Just friends? But Ryga didn't say anything. Besides, it wasn't his business. Perhaps though she was giving Hailsham a false alibi. Was she shielding a murderer? He had urged PC Jenkins to keep an open mind and so should he. But Ryga was convinced that Mrs Cray was not the type to lie and cover up for anyone, even the man she was fond of. He could hear the constable shuffling his feet and breathing heavily and nasally at the foot of the stairs.

'We listened to the wireless until nine thirty. Had a cocoa and Peter left just after eleven.'

'Thank you, Mrs Cray. I won't trouble you further.' Not unless he established a connection with Graylingwell Hospital where Hailsham could have come across Phillipe and Feline. 'I hope Mr Hailsham makes a quick recovery, and I'll see the doctor gets to you.'

He stepped outside, replaced his hat and gave Jenkins instructions to tell the doctor to make a visit as soon as he could. Consulting his watch, he made for the allotments where Sergeant Williams said he would find Lawes, the coastguard officer, who was off duty. Williams knew him well and could vouch for him. They were also neighbours. Williams emphatically declared that Lawes would never steal, and as for murder, well, that was completely out of the question. Ryga trusted Sergeant Williams's judgement but he'd see for himself.

Lawes was a tall man with a hatchet face, dark, deep-set sparkling eyes, a meerschaum pipe in the corner of his wide mouth, a Breton cap on grey hair and a weather-tanned face.

'Not much to do here at this time of the year, but it's restful,' he said after Ryga had introduced himself, although he could see that Lawes had guessed who he was, probably from Williams' description of him. 'If it's about giving you my fingerprints, I did that yesterday.'

'Yes, thank you. Sergeant Williams told me. Did you notice anything unusual about the Motor Torpedo Boat *Constance*, aside from the fact there was no one on board?'

Lawes pushed back his Breton cap. 'No. It was all neat and

shipshape. Lovely craft, well looked after. Nice to see it being put to good use instead of being used to kill people or prevent us from being killed.'

Ryga agreed. 'Was there any paperwork or packages lying around?'

'Not that I saw. Mr Dakins might be able to help you there. He'd checked all the cabins before I came on board. I never went over her. I was on the bridge the whole time. He didn't say he had found anything.'

'I thought you were first there?' Ryga had got that impression. He tried to recall what Dakins had said. He'd searched her and hadn't found any contraband, and there was nothing to say who the owner was. Ryga had assumed that search had been conducted after the coastguard had moored the *Constance* up on the customs berth before she'd been moved across the harbour to the landing stage close to the Watch House. His assumption had been wrong.

Lawes was saying, 'As it happened, we were delayed leaving here, and when we reached her Mr Dakins was already tied up alongside and on board. It was a calm day. He came out on deck, said the vessel had been abandoned and asked if I could take it back to Newhaven where it could be more thoroughly searched for details of the owner. I moored it up on the landing stage just behind the customs launch and left Mr Dakins to it.'

This sounded like the truth. Ryga didn't think Lawes was his killer, but just to be thorough he asked him where he had been on 7 December. 'Singing,' came his somewhat surprising answer. 'I was practising with the Sea Cadets, for Christmas wassailing to raise money for more equipment for them.'

'And that was where?'

'In St Margaret's Church hall, here in Newhaven, of course.'

And several people could vouch for that. 'Did any of your colleagues go on board the *Constance*?'

'No. There was only young Jacob with me, and he brought the coastguard vessel back here while I piloted the *Constance*.'

'How long was Mr Dakins on board before you arrived?'

'About ten minutes, I guess.'

Plenty of time to find the miniatures. He could have stolen them, but had he known about them beforehand? Ryga asked Lawes if the salon porthole had been open. Lawes said it had been. He'd noticed when he had alighted from the vessel.

As Ryga hurried towards the Watch House his mind raced with the possibility that Perrier had arranged a meeting with Dakins on board his boat. Dakins had gone out in the customs launch, tied up alongside the *Constance*, climbed on board and killed Perrier and dumped his body overboard, then, secreting the miniatures, he'd called up the coastguard to report a drifting boat and had been on board when the coastguard had arrived.

How had he known about the miniatures though? Had PC Swinley told him about them? Or had Phillipe? It was feasible that Dakins had come into contact with Perrier in the past in this harbour or previously when Dakins had worked in London. The conversation Ryga had had with Dakins and his boss Leemings ran through his mind along with the antipathy between the two men and the fact that Leemings had also searched the *Constance*, which had startled Dakins. Yes, certain things were falling into place.

At the Watch House, Ryga asked Hailsham's deputy if he could take him across to the Customs House mooring. A few minutes later Chief Preventive Officer Leemings greeted Ryga with the news that Dakins wasn't on duty until six p.m. That suited Ryga because it gave him the opportunity to find out more about Dakins to put with what he already knew and what was running through his mind about the man.

Leemings showed him up the stairs to a small office on the first floor where he offered him a seat across a tidy desk with clipboards stacked on it and in and out basket trays neatly displaying paperwork. There were sea charts on the wall and a variety of shipping timetables and tide times. From the window Ryga could see across the harbour, and the sounds of boats being loaded and unloaded came through the ill-fitting windows along with a cold draft. Leemings looked like a man who had for a long time been struggling to achieve something but had given up.

Ryga didn't mince words but launched straight in. 'I got the impression from our last interview, Mr Leemings, that there is some rivalry between you and Preventative Officer Dakins. Why is that?'

He didn't answer.

'Is it because you dislike him?'

Leemings shifted uneasily but still said nothing.

'Or is it because you don't trust him?' That got a reaction. A flicker of surprise. Leemings studied him suspiciously as though he were setting a trap. Ryga recalled that Dakins had said Leemings wasn't in the best of health, that he had suffered a breakdown and was struggling with his job. But that might be far from the truth.

'Why don't you like him, Mr Leemings?' Ryga asked quietly.

'Because he's too keen,' Leemings sharply replied, as though he had been waiting a long time to say it.

'I'd have thought that was a bonus. A hardworking man is an asset.'

'And he's sly.'

'What do you mean?' Ryga asked, although he knew full well what Leemings meant. Perhaps that was what he himself had sensed to begin with about Dakins.

Leemings straightened up one of his trays even though it didn't need it. When his eyes came up they were sorrowful rather than angry. 'Every time I query something he's always got an answer.'

'You mean he's smart,' Ryga provoked.

'*Too* smart. He's always rushing to go out on the launch and alone if he can. He has a ready answer if I tell him he shouldn't have done so. He says it's his job and not his fault that I can't go and we're short-staffed. He shouldn't have even gone out to the *Constance*. His job isn't rescuing boats or people. He should have left it to the lifeboat and the coastguard. He said the lifeboat was engaged elsewhere. I checked. It was. The coastguard was delayed. The *Constance* wasn't in any danger of floundering on rocks or drifting into the shipping channel. I know that the owner could have been seriously ill on board, and urgency was required, but he doesn't have to dash off like that when there's a risk to his safety and possible loss of the customs launch.' Leemings tone wasn't bitter but resigned.

'And Dakins said he wasn't afraid to risk his life unlike some. Meaning you.'

Leemings winced and nodded.

'Why did you really go on board the *Constance* to search it?'

Leemings ran a hand over his round pale face. His eyes searched Ryga's, beseeching him to understand. 'I knew it would be pointless but I wanted to see what it looked like inside. Whether its interior and contents could tell me what . . . if . . .'

'Anything of value had been on board,' Ryga finished for him, when he dried up. 'You think Dakins is corrupt, that he's on the take.'

'I can't prove anything,' Leemings said wretchedly. 'And my boss thinks the sun shines out of Dakins' rear end. He says I'm sour and old fashioned. I say I'm honest, thorough and a stickler for routine and procedures, but that doesn't seem to count for much these days.'

Ryga could see the man had almost given up trying to prove that he thought one of his officers was on the take. Ryga was his last chance. And Ryga's intuition trusted Leemings. Yes, he could be bitter enough to throw the scent on to Dakins but Ryga knew enough about men to know when they were genuinely wretched. And Leemings was. Ryga also sensed Leemings was honest. There was too much about Dakins that he, himself, distrusted, especially now he knew Dakins had been on board the *Constance* alone for ten minutes and in all likelihood Broxham didn't have the miniatures.

'I'd like to know Dakins' rota for some dates. Can you help me with that?'

Leemings looked taken aback. He had obviously expected Ryga to be of the same opinion as his boss. He pulled himself up and Ryga saw a glimmer of light in the tired eyes.

'It's Thursday the seventh of December I want to know about first.'

Leemings rose and pulled open a drawer in a wooden filing cabin. After consulting some paperwork in a file, he said, 'He started at two p.m. and signed off at ten thirty.'

'Were you on duty?'

'No. It was my day off.'

'And how did you spend it?'

'Fishing off the pier and then had a couple of pints in The Hope Inn.'

'Until what time?'

'Why are you asking me all these questions?' he said, looking downcast again.

'Because I'm trying to establish where a number of people were on the night Mrs Swinley disappeared, and if anyone saw her or the woman she was with, the same woman whose body was found in Sleeper's Hole on Wednesday night.'

'Well, I didn't see anyone except those in the pub, including Joseph Moore and the landlord, who will tell you I was in there until closing time, ten thirty, and walked home.'

Ryga could easily check that. But knew he didn't have to.

'And where was Dakins last Wednesday night?'

'The same shift as now – two p.m. to ten p.m. He was duty officer, working alone.'

That meant no one would have noticed him slipping across the harbour on the customs launch to uncover the body. But why do so? If he was guilty of theft and murder, why not leave Feline there until someone else found her possibly weeks or months later in a horrendous state? He asked what rota Dakins had been working on Tuesday 7 November when Swinley had ended up in the harbour. The answer was again two p.m. to ten p.m.

Ryga made a decision. 'Mr Leemings, I need you to do something for me.' Ryga explained what he wanted. 'I'd appreciate your cooperation.'

'You have it.' Leemings look thoroughly cheered. As they shook hands he appeared to be a different man than the earlier one. It was as though a weight had been lifted from his stooping shoulders. Ryga thought it was the fact that someone at last believed in what he was saying about Leslie Dakins. Ryga hurried back to Newhaven police station to make his arrangements.

Twenty-Six

Later that evening, Ryga, once again with Sergeant Williams and a police constable, made his way to the harbour but this time to the Motor Torpedo Boat, *Constance.* It was almost déjà-vu, thought Ryga, of his previous day's interview with Broxham. Had he got it right this time? There was still a lot he didn't know and much that didn't tie up, but he was hoping Dakins would provide the missing information. From his analysis of Dakins' personality, he thought he would be more likely to confess than someone of Broxham's mentality, and that was what he was banking on, he had told Superintendent Street.

As before, he posted the constable outside, but this time asked him to take cover in Joseph Moore's hut, much to the old man's delight. Moore volunteered his services if needed but Ryga told him it wouldn't be necessary. He didn't say who they were meeting or why. He told the constable that he would use his whistle to signal when he was ready for his assistance but urged him to keep a sharp lookout and if Dakins left the *Constance* without him and Sergeant Williams then he was to go after him.

Sergeant Williams took up cover in the cabin just off the salon where Ryga said he was to remain until he was summoned. He wanted Dakins to think he was alone on board. Soon the sound of a small boat's engine caught the air. Ryga, on deck, crossed to port. Leemings had done as he'd requested and Dakins was in the tender from the customs launch.

'Hello, Inspector,' Dakins called out. 'Mr Leemings said you wanted me on board to verify that the *Constance* was how I found her and nothing's been disturbed. Although I must say it's very late for such an escapade.'

'Yes, I'm sorry, but Mr Leemings told me you were on the late shift and time is important. I've almost narrowed it down to who murdered PC Swinley and how. The owner of this boat is connected with it. I think you can help me.'

'I don't see how,' Dakins said, as he brought the small craft round to the stern. Ryga caught the line and tied it off on the *Constance*. There was a ladder at the stern, and Dakins climbed nimbly up it and boarded the boat. He had with him a strong flashlight. Ryga didn't fancy that being brought down on the back of his head.

'Let's go down to the salon,' Ryga said, showing his own torch light into the bridge, now the galley. He waited until Dakins descended to the salon before following him. It was gloomy, but Ryga had also bought an extra battery-powered light, which he had already put on the table. He switched it on, throwing shadows around the cabin, and switched off his own torch.

Dakins did the same, saying, 'I went over this vessel thoroughly after the coastguard, Lawes, brought her into Newhaven. There was nothing on it to provide the identity of the owner, who we now know, and no contraband on board.'

'Not contraband, no, but there was something.'

Dakins looked puzzled, but behind his confused expression was unease. 'You believe there was something which I missed.'

'You didn't miss it.'

For a moment Dakins looked stunned and then wary. He moved slightly to Ryga's left. As he did the boat rocked a little. Ryga didn't think the movement was solely to do with Dakins, but Williams drawing closer.

'Are you accusing me of taking something?' Dakins hotly declared, but his voice echoed with fear.

Dakins might be able to bully Leemings and others but he wouldn't get away with it with him.

'Yes. You were the first person to board this boat, and you found something that you helped yourself to.'

Dakins mouth fell open at the bluntness of Ryga's reply. The hand carrying the torch twitched. He moved slightly forward. Ryga steeled himself. 'I wouldn't do that, Dakins. I am not George Swinley, and neither am I vulnerable, like Feline Perrier and Myra Swinley.'

Dakins' body jerked. His hand twitched again, his tongue came out and slaked his lips. 'I don't know what you mean.'

'Leslie Dakins, I'm arresting you for the murders of—'

'No!' he shouted. 'I haven't killed anyone.'

'You have the motive for killing Mr and Mrs Swinley and Feline Perrier – the items you stole from this boat. You have the opportunity – you were on shift and able to leave unchallenged because of your position in the Waterguard. You have the means – the customs launch, or its tender, to moor up alongside the harbour. And you have the weapon – that torch or another like it.' Ryga held his gaze. 'And don't think you can bluff it out with me. I have enough to charge you and will see you in court.'

Dakins' skin blanched; his body started shaking. 'Please, you must believe me, I haven't killed anyone. I only took what was on this table. Can I sit down? I don't feel well.'

'Over there with your back to the helm. Sergeant Williams?'

Williams emerged from the cabin. 'Relieve him of his torch, Sergeant. Then take this down.'

Dakins now looked completely beaten. Ryga had thought he would try and bluster for a while but the fact he would be charged with murder – a capital offence – was enough to make him cave in much quicker than Ryga had expected. Ryga remained standing opposite Dakins across the table, while Williams' bulky figure blocked the door to the galley.

'It was on this table, a box, along with a letter,' Dakins said miserably.

'And the logbook.'

Dakins nodded. 'I swear, I haven't killed anyone.'

'You'll need to convince me of that. You followed George Swinley on Saturday the fourth of November when he caught the Seaford train and you saw him rendezvous with Feline Perrier. You overheard part, or maybe all, of their conversation and began to see a way that you could make some money.'

'No. Why would I follow him?' Dakins said wretchedly.

It was a valid point and one that Ryga had struggled with until his earlier interview with Leemings. 'Because you were afraid that Swinley was on to you. Maybe he even hinted to you as such. Or perhaps Mr Leemings, who knows you are crooked, had passed on his concerns to PC Swinley, who he occasionally met in The Hope Inn.'

Dakins swallowed hard and rubbed his eyes. 'I'll lose my job.'

'You should have thought about that before you started stealing.'

'I don't . . .' But Dakins realized it was pointless bluffing.

Ryga said, 'When you saw Swinley turn towards Ashmore's house you had confirmation that he was on to you because the miniatures are not the only things you have stolen – you've been turning a blind eye to Broxham's smuggling operations for some time, in return for a share of the goods, or perhaps payment.'

Dakins swallowed hard.

'I'm right, aren't I?'

'Yes.'

So Ryga's suspicions were confirmed. Broxham had resumed his black-market operation and Dakins was corrupt. He felt the thrill of victory. 'You told me you had seen Swinley walk in the direction of the Downs knowing that if I asked at Ashmore's house neither Ashmore nor Broxham would admit to seeing Swinley. You'd hope I would think Swinley was just going for a breath of fresh air. What you didn't know was that he was collecting information in Seaford about the miniatures.'

Dakins clasped his shaking hands tight together on the table.

'Perhaps Broxham told you not to worry about Swinley, or ordered you to deal with him, and you did. You decided to kill him.'

'Please, you must believe me. I haven't killed anyone,' Dakins pleaded.

Ryga thought he looked close to crying. Ignoring his denial, Ryga pressed on. 'You took the customs tender to the landing stage off the alleyway, which you knew was part of Swinley's beat. There, after tying it off, you intercepted Swinley at the top of the alleyway and told him you suspected some illegal smuggling was going on that night. He took out his notebook and pencil to write it down, but you urged him down the alleyway on some pretext of hearing a noise. On the quayside he dropped his pencil, or you nudged him and dislodged it. He bent down to retrieve it. You struck him on the back of the head with your heavy torch and pushed him into the harbour.' But Ryga paused as he remembered the police constable's helmet. It wasn't found on him and it would have resisted a blow to the head if the constable had been wearing it. Dakins could have struck Swinley a blow on the back of the neck and then pushed him in the harbour and the helmet had become dislodged. It would take some doing with the strap under the chin, but it was possible.

Fear and misery shone in Dakins' eyes and on his countenance. 'All I did was take the box and the letter, which were on this table. I didn't think anyone would miss the miniatures.'

'No, because you killed their rightful owner, Feline Perrier, and you hoped to get away with it.'

'I keep telling you, I'm not a killer,' Dakins said wretchedly.

'On the night of the seventh of December you had ample opportunity to bring the customs tender across the harbour, meet Feline Perrier, here in Sleeper's Hole, kill her and put her body under an upturned boat. You lured her here, telling her that her brother's boat was moored up and there was something on it that was addressed to her, which of course there had been – the letter and the box of miniatures. After disposing of Feline, you called on Myra Swinley because the letter you had stolen from this boat explained that Phillipe Perrier had given the evidence of how he had traced the miniatures to PC Swinley. You were afraid she would tell all.'

Dakins wrung his hands continuously. Williams sniffed and scratched at his notebook.

'You called on Myra Swinley and, of course, you were in uniform and she trusted you. You spun her some yarn about uncovering a smuggling operation and that in doing so you believed you had found something belonging to her husband – his notebook – and could she come with you to identify it.'

'I didn't do any of this. I was at work,' he bleated.

'You took Myra's body up the harbour in her husband's boat, ditched her overboard and then smashed the boat up on the shore of Denton Island and walked back to the customs tender, which you took back to the customs landing stage.'

Dakins' terrified eyes darted around the shadowy cabin as though seeking refuge. He rubbed a shaking hand across them. 'I swear to you, Inspector Ryga, I only took the miniatures. My God, this is the end for me. I'll go to prison.'

'You'll go to the gallows for three murders unless you can convince me otherwise.' Ryga said tersely. Dakins was a thief, but was he a killer?

Dakins licked his lips. 'I didn't kill PC Swinley. I have an alibi.' Taking a deep breath, he said rapidly, 'That night, seventh of November, I was at Railway Quays with Neil Broxham, on board his boat.'

'And?'

'I transferred some goods to it.'

'So, not only were you turning a blind eye to Broxham bringing in contraband, you were also stealing from your bonded warehouse, fiddling the figures so that no one would miss the goods, or if they did then you would claim that it was all that had been delivered.' And Leemings had suspected as much, but couldn't get proof, and Dakins had made out that Leemings was getting muddled and forgetful. Dakins had been so convincing that his bosses and colleagues believed that Leemings had lost his grip.

'Yes.'

Had Swinley discovered this? Had Perrier known that Broxham was smuggling and selling stolen goods and had given Swinley the evidence? Or had Feline found out what her lover was doing and had told her brother? Did this in fact have anything to do with the miniatures?

'Does Charles Ashmore know about this illegal operation?'

'I don't know. Maybe.'

'How many times have you done this?'

'I forget. A few.'

'And does Broxham know you stole the miniatures?'

'No. The letter said he had taken them from a former SS officer in Lubeck in payment for getting him out of Germany. I thought if I told Broxham I had them he'd say they were his and wouldn't give me anything for them.'

'What else did Phillipe's letter say?' Ryga asked sharply, feeling saddened by the sordid affair, yet more repercussions from the war that had cost another three lives, possibly four if he included Phillipe Perrier.

'That he would be dead by the time his sister received it. He had achieved what he set out to do – locate and restore the miniatures to his family. He left them to her as a legacy and asked her not to marry Broxham.'

'He exposed Broxham as a crook.'

Dakins nodded miserably.

'And you thought you might also use that as blackmail. He also mentioned Frederick Charles Ashmore in the letter, his fraudulent rank and their black-market dealings in Lubeck.'

Again Dakins nodded, his eyes downcast.

'Where are the miniatures now?'

'In a drawer in my lodgings at Seaford. I'm not well,' Dakins bleated. 'I thought that I'd be able to give up work and retire to a warmer, drier climate.'

The only climate Dakins was going to get was either hot as hell, if he had committed the murders, or cold and bleak with the smell of disinfectant and a view of prison walls. 'Sergeant Williams, let's escort Mr Dakins to the police station.'

'With pleasure, sir.'

Twenty-Seven

D akins, had the motive, means and the opportunity. But as the minutes ticked on Ryga sat at his desk in his tiny temporary office and picked at it. Broxham and Ashmore, if they felt so inclined, could confirm Dakins' illegal activities on the night of the 7 November. But it wasn't so much the alibi that was disturbing Ryga it was the small facts of the case that gnawed away at him.

There was PC Swinley's missing helmet. There was that one place setting at Myra's table. There was the use of her best china. And there was the knitting bag without any knitting projects or patterns.

The door opened, letting in a cold draft of air from the corridor, interrupting his thoughts. Ryga expected to see Williams bearing yet another cup of tea but he was pleased to see Eva. She looked tired but was flushed with excitement.

'I've just heard that you've arrested Dakins and not Broxham.'

'Who told you?'

'Joseph Moore. He seems to have taken on the role of town crier. I met him as I was about to enter the Bridge Hotel thinking you would be there. He says it's not for murder.'

'How does he know that?'

'If you didn't tell him then either he's especially astute, he's been eavesdropping, or someone's got a loose tongue.'

Ryga would go with the latter. He knew it couldn't be Sergeant Williams. The young PC who had accompanied them would be in for a roasting.

'It could be for murder if his alibi doesn't hold up, but it will,' Ryga said, 'because I think he's telling the truth. He's crooked and a thief but he's not the killer.' Ryga relayed what had happened at his interviews with Neil Broxham and Leslie Dakins.

Eva listened attentively. When Ryga had finished, she said, 'I returned to London because something Miss Dewsnap said made me

213

reflect.'

'That you're a talented photographer and not a shorthand typist.'

She pushed a hand through her blonde hair. 'That and the fact that neither am I a police officer. It's not your fault, Ryga – I asked to tag along and no doubt will do so again. I listened and watched you interviewing Ashmore. You were doing your job. I wasn't doing mine. And as I drove back here with you I kept thinking about what she had said. I felt that I had lost my edge, much as I had done with that picture of Colin and Tom. I didn't see into the picture. You saw the name on their raft, which had come off Swinley's boat. I didn't. I've been going through the motions – no, don't say I'm being hard on myself, I'm not. Just realistic. I returned to my apartment and developed the remaining negatives of that film, and those of another roll of film I shot on that morning, and I looked, really looked, as you did with the boys' raft.'

Williams came in and put a tea in front of her. 'The best china, eh?' She smiled up at Williams who beamed back before slipping out. 'You're an observant man, Ryga, but then you need to be in your job and so do I, but I also need to see with my heart when I photograph people, particularly with my type of photography – the uncensored versions, life in the raw as Miss Dewsnap said, the feelings and experiences of people that even they are probably not fully aware of. These are the pictures I took on Denton Island on Saturday morning.' She spread them out on Ryga's desk. 'They're not up to my usual standard – no, they're not, Ryga,' she insisted when he made to protest. 'But I'll soon be back on form.'

They were excellent. Ryga saw a woman shaking out her mat, and another talking on her doorstep to a neighbour. He saw in their countenance a hard life, a struggle to make ends meet, much as he'd seen in Mrs Gileson and Mrs Pleasant. He saw children playing further along the shore with old bits of wood, a couple of boys in rolled-down socks and baggy hand- me-down short trousers kicking a ball, a small girl, not much more than four, sitting on the stones with a dirty face, crying, with a rag doll in her lap. He saw the vicar walking past the children, deep in thought, confusion etched on his hatchet face.

'He must have been visiting a parishioner.'

'But look at his face, Ryga. Really look. What do you see?'

Ryga looked and saw immediately what Eva meant. 'A man

tormented and deeply troubled, but then he has a nagging, embittered wife whose brother is serving time in Wormwood Scrubs . . . Williams!' Ryga suddenly called out and the sergeant materialized.

'Has PC Anmore interviewed the occupants of the cottages on Denton Island as I requested?'

'Yes, but none of them remember seeing the boat being smashed up or hearing anything on the night of the seventh of December. Mrs Pearce in the last of the cottages said the vicar had been to see her but she couldn't remember when it was. She's old and a bit soft in the head. She doesn't really know what day it is and sometimes if it's day or night, poor thing. We, and the neighbours, do our best to keep an eye on her.'

Then it probably wouldn't make any difference, Ryga thought, if he despatched an officer there now to ask her if and why the vicar had called on her on Saturday morning. Williams was called away by a constable. Ryga addressed Eva. 'Before you came in I was going over the elements of the case that have been nagging at me. Those that haven't been satisfactorily answered. There's the fact that PC Swinley's helmet was missing; that Myra used her best china; that there was only one place setting. There is also the knitting bag in Myra's house. It was beside the wrong chair – by that I mean the one opposite to where Myra's slippers were – and it was devoid of knitting patterns.'

'I don't follow.'

'In the POW camp we devised a code that carried news from one prisoner to another on the progress of the war as new prisoners were brought in or we picked up intelligence from some of the German guards. We had men who spoke and understood German who managed to keep that fact a secret. Occasionally we had to pass on information amongst ourselves on escape plans. The code was written in pencil in the margins of the limited number of books we had, or on sheet music, if we were fortunate enough to be sent some, on letters we occasionally received from home from the Red Cross, even on packaging on parcels received from the Red Cross. Our captors never interpreted the code, or realized it was a code, even though they saw it. I think that in the hospital Swinley and Perrier did the same, so as not to alert the nurses, doctors and other patients about how they were feeling. Or maybe they were just having a bit of fun, trying to stimulate their brains and while away the time. Boredom is dreadfully grinding.' He paused. Eva made no comment and for that he was grateful.

'I think that Perrier wrote on knitting patterns, in code, how he had traced the miniatures to Broxham, and he might also have told him about Broxham's criminal activity in the hope he could prevent his sister from marrying him. It was knitting patterns that Swinley was collecting from the newsagent. Myra would have thought nothing of them if she saw them in the knitting bag.'

'Didn't she knit?'

Ryga already had a view on that but he again called Williams who arrived promptly. 'Does Mrs Williams know if Myra Swinley knits? Has she ever actually seen her knitting?'

'I don't know, sir.'

'It's late, I know, but it is important. Could you ask her?'

'I'll just pop along the road now, sir. Won't be a tick.'

Once he'd gone, Ryga said to Eva, 'I don't think Myra knitted. If she did then there would have been another knitting bag by her slippers and I think a knitting project on the go. There would also have been patterns at least somewhere in the house, in the sideboard or a shopping bag in the understairs cupboard. Either Feline took the knitting patterns or she left them with Myra to bring to us and the killer took them. But to get back to the vicar. He was the last person to speak to Swinley. Then there's the fact that Joan Isaacs was on the same homeward-bound train as Myra and Feline; and she had been in London, according to the vicar, visiting her brother in prison. Was she? And who would Myra have confided in if anyone?'

Triumphantly, Eva said, 'The vicar. And now we have Isaacs on Denton shore on Saturday morning, checking that he'd left nothing incriminating behind after smashing up Swinley's boat. Just look at his expression and body language. I haven't met him, Ryga, but he is a deeply disturbed man with something on his conscience. That's what I captured and it's what I failed to see.'

'Well, you've seen it now.' Ryga rose and as he reached for his hat and coat, Williams came in breathless.

'Mrs Williams says that Mrs Swinley brought knitted garments in for the merchant seaman – scarves, mittens, woolly hats – but she's never actually seen her knit.'

Ryga addressed Eva. 'Myra wouldn't have even looked at the knitting patterns.' To Williams, he said, 'I want you to accompany me to the vicarage.'

'They'll be in bed!' Williams exclaimed, probably thinking he should be too. His shift had officially ended an hour ago.

'Then we'll wake them up.'

'Why are we going there, sir?' Williams asked puzzled.

'Because of something you said.'

'Me!'

'Jonathan Grimley. A bad lot.'

'Yes, but he's in prison. Don't say he's escaped?'

'Not that I'm aware of, but you said he came here in 1946 after serving a stretch for four years for dealing in black-market goods. The same year PC Swinley resumed his duty as a police officer. You told me that Grimley was up to his old tricks almost the moment he was released and was caught stealing petrol. Who caught him at it? Or do I need to ask?' Ryga threw a glance at Eva who answered.

'PC Swinley.'

Williams said, 'Well, yes, it was him. But you can't think—'

'I can, which is why we must talk to the vicar.' He turned to Eva. 'Do you want to come along?'

'Wouldn't miss it for the world.'

Twenty-Eight

There was no answer. No one stirred and no lights came on. Worried, Ryga said, 'Let's try the church.'

It too was in darkness, but the door was unlocked. Ryga pushed it open. For a moment he stayed Williams' hand in the process of switching on the lights. As Ryga's eyes grew accustomed to the dark he picked out a figure sitting slumped on the corner of the pew before the altar. He glanced at Eva and then nodded at Williams. The church was suddenly bathed in a dim light but the figure didn't move. Ryga walked down the aisle with Eva beside him and Williams behind them, his boots squeaking in the quietude. As they drew level, Isaacs looked up, a haunted expression on his grey, gaunt features, his eyes sunk deep in their hollows, empty, staring, devoid of emotion.

'Where's Mrs Isaacs?' Ryga asked gently. Here was a man on the verge of a breakdown.

'She called me weak and spineless.' He buried his head in his bony hands. Ryga slipped in beside him on the hard church pew, while Eva eased herself down on the pew in front of them, her face solemn and sorrowful. Williams, who had already removed his helmet, placed it on the hard pew and slipped in next to Eva. He withdrew his notebook and pencil.

Ryga said, 'I should caution you, Vicar.'

'I know what I'm saying, as God is my witness. I'll not go back on my word, take it down Sergeant Williams. I tried to help her. God knows how I tried but it was impossible in the end. I should have done something sooner. It's my fault. All those pointless deaths.'

'Mrs Isaacs was responsible?' Ryga asked.

The vicar nodded. Williams looked aghast.

'I knew that she was beyond help. It wouldn't have stopped.'

In the silence that followed Ryga caught the sound of a boat in the harbour. 'Why did she push PC Swinley into the harbour?'

218

'I thought at first he had slipped. That it was an accident. The coroner said it was. Joan was out that night. She said she was going to visit Mrs Feathering. She knew PC Swinley's beat. She'd seen him talking to me outside the church hall. And she knew where he would go from there. PC Swinley was always punctual, and a man of routine. I didn't even suspect she had anything to do with Swinley's disappearance. Then on the Wednesday before last, after the coffee morning with the elderly in the church hall, Myra told me she was going to London to the Yard the next morning because she was convinced that George hadn't died accidentally. I didn't think anything of it when Joan said she was going to London to visit Jonathan on the same day as Myra was visiting Scotland Yard. I called on Myra that evening, as Mr Hailsham has probably told you. He saw me in Fort Road.'

He hadn't because he was ill but Ryga recalled what Mrs Cray had said, that Hailsham had been in Fort Road on Thursday 7 December *when that poor woman was killed and put under the boat, as you have obviously been told.* She'd also said *you're not to breathe a word of this to anyone, not even to the vicar.*

'I wanted to find out what the Yard had said but Myra wasn't in. I thought the train was delayed or she'd caught a later train. Then Joan didn't come home. At first, I thought that maybe she too had been delayed in London or decided to catch a later train. It was only when she finally got in that I knew what she'd done.'

He took a breath. Ryga could see by his pained expression that he was visually recalling it.

After a moment, Isaacs resumed. 'Joan had seen Myra and Feline Perrier on the train together. She overheard part of their conversation. Feline was talking about information she'd passed on to George at her brother's request and asked if Myra had it. Myra denied all knowledge of it but admitted that it could still be in the house. Feline said that her brother was missing and she thought the information might help to find him and could be connected with George's death. Of course, what Joan heard she immediately translated it into being connected with her.'

'But why?' Eva asked.

He stared at her with sorrowful eyes. His bony hands were clasped tightly in his lap. 'Joan was fearful of her secret being exposed. I don't know the medical term for it but she had some kind of paranoia, a persecution complex, they said at the hospital.'

'Graylingwell?' Ryga interjected, recalling that Sergeant Williams had told him the Isaacs had lived in Bognor Regis, which wasn't far from Chichester where Graylingwell Hospital was situated.

'Yes. I had to have Joan committed there in 1943.'

At the same time as Perrier and Swinley.

'I was an army chaplain in the war. I didn't know how bad things had got with Joan until I arrived home on leave in 1943. I applied for compassionate leave and was granted it. I got Joan into Graylingwell where she was looked after. I served another year while Joan was being taken care of there and then the army let me go. The war was almost over anyway. Eventually I was able to have her home again. Before she came out of hospital I applied to the bishop to move us to another parish to give Joan the chance of a fresh start. There was a vacancy here and I accepted it. I wish to God I hadn't.'

'Because of PC Swinley.'

Isaacs sighed heavily. 'Usually Joan was fine but she could become obsessed. She'd think the whole town was against her, and many were, or they became that way, because she made them feel like that towards her. Her hostility drove people away and that gave her more reason to think she was being persecuted. I thought being near Jonathan might help her. I knew Jonathan was wild and had been in trouble with the police and that he'd already served one prison sentence, but there was always the chance of reforming him.

'It was 1946. It seemed to be going well. Joan didn't recognize Myra or George Swinley, probably because she'd only seen them a few times in the hospital grounds on visiting days and, of course, Joan was not only in a different ward to George Swinley but she was also on medication that made things, well, shall we say, hazy. But I recognized them both after we arrived here and they recognized me and Joan. Nothing was ever said though. It was the past.

'Then PC Swinley arrested Jonathan for petrol theft. Joan just wouldn't believe he was guilty – she saw it as part of a conspiracy against him and her. Jonathan was convicted and sent to prison. And Joan's feelings of hatred and persecution intensified, especially as Jonathan refused to have anything to do with her. She worshipped and adored him and she came to believe that George Swinley had turned him against her. But it wasn't that. Jonathan had discovered that Joan wasn't his sister. She's his mother.'

Ryga did a double take. Eva looked surprised and Williams' mouth fell open.

'You should have sought help for her,' Eva said.

Isaacs looked wretched. 'But that would mean everyone knowing about her mental health and even possibly that she'd borne an illegitimate child. She'd have been sent back to a mental institution. I couldn't allow that. Joan told him she was his mother shortly before he was sent to prison. He couldn't forgive her for hiding it from him all those years. He was raised as her brother to hide the shame of her pregnancy. I never knew of it. Not until after I discovered Joan had killed PC Swinley. And I didn't know that until after she had killed Myra and Feline.'

'You should have turned her in. You aided and abetted her in a crime,' Ryga said.

'I had to.'

Out of love or fear? 'How did she kill PC Swinley?' Ryga asked.

'I don't know exactly. He'd dropped something, his pencil maybe, or his notebook, he bent over to retrieve it, she came up behind him and pushed him into the harbour.'

'Why would he have been writing in his notebook?'

'He might have seen or heard something and wanted to make a note of it. I don't know.'

Ryga nodded thoughtfully. He caught Eva's eyes and cautioned her to keep silent, seeing that she was making leaps of deductions, as was he.

'And Myra and Feline Perrier? How did Joan kill them?'

Isaacs swallowed, and ran a hand over his thin greying hair. 'She heard on the train, or as they alighted, I'm not sure which, that Feline was going back to Mrs Swinley's house and she followed them at a distance. Joan waited outside Myra's house and saw Feline leave carrying something. She followed her along Fort Road then accidentally on purpose bumped into her and introduced herself as the woman she had met in the hospital when her brother was there. She managed to get Feline to turn her back and struck her across the back of her head with a heavy stick she'd found lying about. She dragged her body further down into Sleeper's Hole, pushed her face into the mud until she suffocated then put the old boat over her body so nobody would find her. Then she returned to Myra. She said that she had found something in Sleeper's Hole that she believed belonged to

George. It was in his small boat but she didn't like to take it or touch it. She said she thought it was his notebook. Myra went out with her and when she bent down to look into the boat, Joan hit her. She fell into the dinghy which Joan then took up the harbour towards Denton Island. She managed to manhandle Myra's body into the water not really caring if anyone saw her. She left the boat on Denton shore, came home and told me what she'd done.'

'And you returned to Denton that night and smashed it up.'

'Yes. If it wasn't found people would think that Myra, upset at her husband's death, had decided to end her life.'

Williams gave a heavy sigh. Ryga dashed a glance at Eva and saw that she too was sceptical. Before she could speak though, Ryga said, 'Some of what you say is true, Vicar, but not all of it, and I'll tell you why. If Joan had seen Feline leaving the house, killed her then returned to Myra's, Myra would have had plenty of time to clear away *all* the tea things, and she would have gone upstairs to change and drawn her bedroom curtains.'

The vicar shifted and his skin grew even paler, almost transparent. He wrung his bony hands in his lap.

'And if Joan *had* pushed PC Swinley into the harbour he'd have been wearing his helmet and the likelihood is it would still have been lodged on his head or around his neck when his body was found and it wasn't. Swinley removed his helmet not because he needed to mop his brow or because he had a headache – he did so out of respect for you, Vicar. He wasn't a churchgoing man because your wife had made that impossible for him, but he was quietly religious in his own way and men always remove their hats in church, just as I have done and Sergeant Williams here has removed his helmet. And seeing you, George would automatically have done the same. So here is what really happened.'

Twenty-Nine

'Y ou didn't speak to PC Swinley outside the church that night but at the entrance to the alleyway that leads down to the harbour at the junction of Fort Road and Chapel Street. You knew exactly what time he would be there. As you so rightly said, PC Swinley was generally punctual, and a man of routine. Because of the weather there was no one about. As you saw him approach you called out. Not his name but an exclamation or some such and went further down the alleyway. He approached, keeping his torch low, and came across you on the harbour side. What did you do, Vicar? Did you make out you were distraught and that you might kill yourself?'

Isaacs remained silent.

'Swinley needed to reassure you and make you feel comfortable, and because of that, and out of respect for you, he removed his helmet and tried to settle you. You calmed down, apologized and said you were deeply worried, because although Grimley was in prison he was involved in more serious crimes than petrol theft and you and Mrs Isaacs were being threatened to keep silent about it. Am I on the right lines?'

Isaacs hesitated for a moment, his eyes flicked to Eva and Williams, and then back to Ryga. He could see it was over. He had no choice but to tell the truth, and Ryga sensed he was relieved to do so.

'I told him that I had been made to agree to meet a man who was blackmailing us over evidence he had that Jonathan was deeply involved with smuggling. I couldn't pay him. I have no money. The rendezvous was not until later that evening and I thought he might not come because of the fog, but I had to be there just in case. As I waited, I began to think there was only one way out.'

As he faltered, Ryga took up the sorry tale. 'Swinley said not to worry, he would report it, and that you and Mrs Isaacs would be safe.

He unbuttoned his tunic pocket and took out his notebook and pencil. Why?'

'To make a note of the time of the rendezvous and the name of the blackmailer, which I made up.'

'He could have done that later.'

'He could but PC Swinley was a stickler for recording everything and wouldn't wait until later in case his memory failed him.'

Something Swinley had told young PC Jenkins, Ryga recalled. 'You took his torch and shone it on the notebook so that he could write in it.'

'Yes.'

'Then you pretended to see or hear something in the harbour and urged him to look and listen. He turned. You pointed down the harbour towards the sea. Then you struck him a forceful blow on the back of the head with his torch. He fell to the ground.' Ryga vividly recalled the location. 'You took the notebook to remove the evidence he'd written down of your meeting, kicked the pencil into the sea, buttoned up his tunic, which was a mistake – it alerted Myra Swinley that something was wrong with her husband's death. She knew her husband's habit of always leaving the buttons undone until he had replaced his notebook and pencil. You put his torch back in his pocket. Again, another mistake. If he'd been writing in his notebook he'd have found somewhere to prop the torch – a post, the harbour wall. If he had heard or seen something in the harbour he'd have picked up the torch and shone it out into the harbour and it would have fallen into the water with him. You manhandled his body into the sea, hoping the tide would carry him out. But the tide was coming in and eventually it took his body up the harbour until it sank and on rising got wedged under the grid iron at Railway Quay.'

The vicar's body seemed to curl up on itself. He hugged his bony chest with his thin arms. His nose was running and he made no attempt to reach for a handkerchief. Williams opened his mouth to say something then closed it again, frowning. Ryga knew the question that was on the sergeant's lips. He voiced it. Gently he said, 'Why did you kill PC Swinley, Vicar?'

He sniffed but the snot still stayed on his upper lip. 'You wouldn't understand.' He shifted and wiped the sleeve of his coat across his nose.

'Was it out of love for your wife?'

Isaacs's tortured eyes held Ryga's for a moment.

'Did she goad and torment you into doing it? Did she say that if you really loved her you would see that Swinley was punished for persecuting her son and locking him up? There was the constable strutting around the town, everyone respecting him while they sniggered behind her back at her brother's fate. She deserved better. She was after all the vicar's wife, and as such should be held in high regard. But you had failed her. You had never given her what she wanted and what she was entitled to.'

Isaacs flinched and nodded miserably.

Ryga left a small pause. Williams cleared his throat then flushed because it sounded so loud in the vast echoing silent cavern of a church.

'What did you do with his police helmet?' Ryga asked quietly and conversationally.

'I didn't think it would sink and I didn't want it to be found quickly. I thought the greater the delay the less chance of his death being considered suspicious. I threw it over the gates into the old works. No one ever goes in there. It's been shut for years.'

Where no doubt they would find it. Ryga continued, 'Then the Wednesday before last, after the coffee morning, Myra confided her concerns to you and said she was going to the Yard as she believed her husband had been killed. You and Joan got very worried. When I asked Mrs Isaacs when she had last seen Mrs Swinley she said Wednesday, at the coffee morning, and I saw a fearful look cross your face, but I dismissed it as your fear of your wife's vicious tongue and hen-pecking manner. But you were terrified that the Yard would investigate and discover the truth. You had to know if that was going to be the case. Pretending to act out of solicitude for Myra, you asked her to telephone you from London to tell you what the Yard said. Which she did. Was she optimistic that we'd investigate?'

'She said that although you were sympathetic she didn't think you would, but she might have evidence that could change that.'

Feline Perrier. Perhaps Myra had found Feline's name and London telephone number in one of her husband's pockets along with the Seaford newsagent's number. She wouldn't have known that the latter was a newsagent until the Wednesday before her visit to the Yard when she had called him. She had put the thought aside but after her meeting at the Yard, and as she was in London, she had telephoned

Feline, wondering why her husband had noted down her London number and had learned about the packages.

Ryga continued, 'After leaving the Yard Mrs Swinley first telephoned Miss Perrier, whose brother had been in hospital with her husband. Miss Perrier told her she'd left some packages at a Seaford newsagent's for George to collect, the contents of which might give Myra more information about her husband's death and help to find Miss Perrier's brother who was missing. Myra was to meet Miss Perrier on the train home from Victoria and they were going to look for them in the house.'

Isaacs said, 'Myra told me what time train they were catching.'

'And you told your wife this. Did Joan really visit London and the prison on that Thursday?' Ryga knew he could check that.

'Yes, we thought it would be her alibi, if she needed one, for being in London at the same time as Myra, but Jonathan wouldn't see her.'

'And that made matters worse with her paranoia.'

Isaacs nodded.

'She wanted Myra punished.'

Again, Isaacs nodded.

'And when Joan also telephoned you from London you told her about Feline and the packages.'

'She thought the contents contained details of her committal at the asylum and she was convinced that Myra would use this evidence to prove that she had killed PC Swinley. I had to protect her.'

'And she threatened that if she was accused of killing PC Swinley she would tell the police it was you.'

Isaacs wiped his running nose with his back of his hand which he then pushed through his thinning hair. He'd begun to tremble, not from fear, Ryga thought, maybe from cold but probably from shock.

'I tried to persuade her that whatever was in the packages wasn't anything to do with us but she wouldn't believe me. I met Joan outside Myra's house. We waited a short while, then I knocked on Myra's door and was invited in. I saw that Miss Perrier had a bundle of knitting patterns in her hand. Myra told me that she could now tell Scotland Yard when they phoned that she had evidence her husband was killed and by whom.'

Perhaps Feline had known it was knitting patterns she'd been depositing and had told Myra this on the train. Maybe Feline could read the code and she read the name Broxham and that was who she and Myra believed was the killer.

Ryga said, 'The evidence didn't point to you, or to the fact that Joan had been committed to the asylum. It was about someone else, completely unconnected with you or your wife. Phillipe Perrier had traced the theft of valuable works of art stolen from his family by the Nazis.'

'But that can't be true.' He pushed his fists in his eyes.

Outside a clock struck the hour. Only one muffled gong sounded. Ryga continued. 'What did you do with them?'

'I took them off Feline after . . . after I killed her. I didn't want Joan to see them. I pushed them in the furnace at the vicarage as soon as I reached home, without looking at them.'

'Tell me, how did you get Feline to leave Myra's house? Did you use the fact that her brother's boat was moored up at Sleeper's Hole?' Ryga could see he was correct.

'PC Swinley had told me that Perrier had found a Motor Torpedo Boat abandoned in France and converted it into a home. We'd been talking about boats in general one day and he knew that I had met Perrier in the hospital while visiting Joan.'

'But you said nothing about its owner when it was brought in after being found drifting in the English Channel, because by then you had killed Swinley and you didn't want any attention drawn to you and your connection with Perrier. Feline went with you willingly, eagerly, but before she could reach her brother's boat you struck her, suffocated her and then hid her body. And while you were killing Feline, Joan was already inside Myra's house. She had to prevent her from answering the telephone and taking the call from Scotland Yard.'

The church was freezing cold. Williams was looking on open-mouthed. Eva watched solemnly.

Ryga continued, 'There was only a short time gap between Feline leaving and Joan knocking on Myra's door. Joan kept Myra talking until you could return, which didn't take long. You told Myra that you and Miss Perrier had found something on her brother's boat, which belonged to PC Swinley, his notebook probably, and Miss Perrier had asked if you could go there immediately to identify it. Of course, Myra agreed. She trusted you implicitly. You're the vicar. She even trusted Joan, and felt sorry for her. But before she got to the Motor Torpedo Boat you struck her and put her body in her husband's small

227

boat.'

Isaacs pressed his hands together in front of his chest as though to pray. His eyes had taken on a faraway look as though everything that had happened, and was happening, didn't concern him but had taken place elsewhere with someone else. For a moment Ryga wondered what his war experiences had been. Perhaps seeing so much death and suffering had made him disturbed and neurotic. Joan's paranoia couldn't have helped settle his nerves but instead had, year after year, served to make them worse until he could no longer distinguish between right and wrong, real and fantasy. The first time Ryga had seen him in this pulpit he'd been muttering, perhaps praying for deliverance and forgiveness.

Ryga, his voice even-toned and gentle, said, 'While you killed Myra and took her body out into the harbour on her husband's boat, Joan cleared away one place setting. But she made a mistake. Myra had used her best china to impress her visitor. Myra wouldn't have used that if she hadn't invited Feline into her house – she'd have used her everyday crockery. And if she had intended killing herself she would hardly have made tea before doing so or used her best china. In addition, she didn't go upstairs and draw the curtains and change before having her tea, and she would have done if alone.

'Joan took the sleeping pills and nerve tonic from the house because, if Myra's body was found, at the inquest the doctor would mention he had prescribed both and it would be assumed that Myra had taken them with her to swallow before throwing herself off her husband's boat. Joan returned to the vicarage to wait for you. After disposing of the body, you rowed up to Denton Island where you smashed up the boat before ditching the engine and letting the oars go adrift. Why did you return on Saturday morning?'

'It was all like a bad dream. I couldn't believe I had done it. I still can't. Joan said we had to keep quiet. But I . . . I wanted to check that the boat was there, or what remained of it. Seeing it made me physically sick. Had I really killed that beautiful young woman and Mrs Swinley? I couldn't have done. It wasn't possible. I had to check.' He gulped and closed his eyes as though trying to shut out the vision.

'Yes, Vicar, she was no longer beautiful. And having uncovered Feline's body, you couldn't cover it up again.'

'No.'

Gently Ryga said, 'Joan didn't take her own life, did she?'

'When I heard from Joseph Moore that the man you had arrested hadn't committed the murders, I knew you would come to us. The killing had to stop. Joan's suffering had to stop.'

And yours, Ryga added to himself. 'How did you kill her?'

Isaacs bowed his head. Tears rolled down his face, mingling with the snot but no sobs came from him. His voice didn't even shake when he said, 'She's in the bedroom. She's at peace now. There'll be no more killing. No more tormenting and suffering. It is over now, isn't it, Inspector?' He looked up beseechingly.

'Yes, it's over.' Ryga nodded at Williams, who put away his notebook and pencil, buttoned his tunic pocket, donned his helmet and rose, 'Come along, sir.'

Ryga slipped out of the seat. Isaacs rose somewhat shakily and let himself be led outside, where Ryga blew his police whistle and another constable quickly emerged from the dark. Ryga gave instructions for both him and Williams to take the vicar to the police station, give him a cup of tea and see he was safely locked up. Tomorrow, or rather today, Isaacs and Dakins would be taken up to the Yard for further questioning and formal statements to be made. Then remanded in custody until trial.

He, along with Eva, entered the vicarage with the key that the vicar had handed to him. They found Joan in the ice-cold bedroom as Isaacs had said. There were no strangulation marks, but to Ryga's experienced eye she had been suffocated by the pillow that now lay on the floor beside the bed. There was an empty glass beside her which Ryga guessed would contain traces of a drug, a sleeping draft most probably, prescribed to either Isaacs or his wife. Even in death she looked haggard and tormented.

'It's a sorry tale,' Eva said.

Ryga sadly agreed.

It was just before five a.m. when they finished there. The body had been taken to the hospital mortuary. Eva had taken photographs and Ryga had despatched the glass and its residue to the Yard lab. He locked up the vicarage and, turning up the collar of his Macintosh, said to Eva, 'Let's walk down to the sea.'

'Good idea.'

He needed to clear his head. The streets were deserted. The early morning air was crisply cold. They walked in silence past Sleeper's

Hole and the entrance to the old fort until they came to promenade of West Pier. There they halted by the railings. The sound of the waves washing on to the shingle was comforting. Across the harbour entrance Ryga could see the white light of the lighthouse and on the other side, at the end of the breakwater, the intermittent lights of the other lighthouse. The sound of a boat's engine starting up pierced the night and in the distance came the shunting of a train.

He felt tired and saddened. There was little elation in his soul, although he felt satisfied he'd got justice for the Swinleys and for Feline and her brother.

Eva broke the silence. 'So many deaths for nothing. Sadly it seems all too common, such a waste.'

Ryga knew she was referring not only to the case but also to war.

'Did Phillipe commit suicide?' she asked.

'Yes. The Seaford police have found the letter Phillipe wrote which Dakins took. It was at Dakins' lodgings. In it, Perrier says that he'd completed his final mission, restoring – he thought – the miniatures to his sister while exposing who had traded in them. He had urged his sister not to marry Broxham, who was a crook.' Ryga hoped the miniatures would end up with Miss Dewsnap in her art gallery. After a moment, he said, 'What will you do now?'

'Well, I can't face the prospect of Christmas with my father and stepmother, the neighbours, aunts and uncles all telling me it's time I gave up this ludicrous business with the camera and settled down, *if* I could find myself a nice man, which they think exceedingly unlikely given that I'm not one to tow the domestic line. I think I might go to Scotland.'

'Don't they have Christmas in Scotland?' he joked.

'Yes, and Hogmanay which is even worse – all that Happy New Year stuff and how things will be better. I seem to have heard that too many times. You're right, Scotland is not the best idea, unless I can find a remote island.'

'You'd be bored.'

'I would. So I'll take Miss Dewsnap's advice and do what I do well – take photographs of life in the raw. OK, yes, it was your previous advice and, as you said, there is plenty of hardship and poverty in this country to chronicle.'

'And plenty of life, not all of it hard and sordid.'

'No.' She paused then added, 'What about you?'

'I'll probably do what I do well – work.'

'Very sensible.' There was silence between them. Eva broke it. 'I drove to Portland on Sunday to my aunt's cottage – well, mine now. I called in at The Quarryman's Arms. You know that Sonia's left. The landlord said a man called Ryga had telephoned. He said there was no forwarding address and the brewery don't have one for her. I checked. As have you. But I asked around. Sonia didn't tell anyone what she intended doing. I don't think she's gone off with that bully of a husband but she might have gone where she hopes he won't be able to find her and where she can start afresh. Don't worry, Ryga, you'll find her.'

'We haven't managed to find her husband.'

'You will. I know you – you're dogged to the point of obstinacy but with instinct, intelligence, a quiet thoughtfulness and the ability to reason, which prevents that obstinacy from becoming stupidity and truculence.'

'Well, thank you for the testimonial.' He smiled.

She returned it. 'You won't give up. Someone will know something or have heard something. Or the highly capable Sergeant Jack Daniels will get a lead. Now, we need something to warm us up – I'm freezing and you look chilled to the bone despite that awful Macintosh.'

'I don't know what you've got against it,' he joked. 'I like it.'

She raised her eyebrows. 'I've told you before – it makes you look a hundred and four.'

'I feel it sometimes.'

'Breakfast will cure that.'

'It's far too early. Nowhere will be open.'

'That's where you're wrong. I know a splendid all-night transport café on the A26 just outside Lewes.'

'And you probably know all the lorry drivers.'

'I do. They're a friendly crowd. I might even get some good photographs. And the café serves wonderful bacon and eggs.'

'Then breakfast it is, Eva,' Ryga said, smiling.

Books by Pauline Rowson

The Inspector Andy Horton Series
Tide of Death
Deadly Waters
The Suffocating Sea
Dead Man's Wharf
Blood on the Sand
Footsteps on the Shore
A Killing Coast
Death Lies Beneath
Undercurrent
Death Surge
Shroud of Evil
Fatal Catch
Lethal Waves
Deadly Passage
A Deadly Wake

Art Marvik Mystery/Thrillers
Silent Running
Dangerous Cargo
Lost Voyage

Inspector Ryga 1950 set mysteries
Death in the Cove
Death in the Harbour

Mystery/Thrillers
In Cold Daylight
In For the Kill

For more information on Pauline Rowson and her books visit
www.rowmark.co.uk

Printed in Great Britain
by Amazon